More praise for 8 Seconds

"Jim Moore's writing gift was a considerable one: He could take his remarkable professional accomplishments and the experiences of a well-lived Montana life and blend them with his wonderful imagination, bringing to life stories that were unfailingly relatable and yet unlike anything else on the market. Never has this gift been more generously shared than in his final novel, 8 SECONDS. To those well-versed in the fictitious Bruce family, saddle up for one last adventure. To those who've not yet made the family's acquaintance, I have some good news: You're about to get some fresh fuel for your reading habit." — Craig Lancaster, author of *And It Will Be a Beautiful Life* and *600 Hours of Edward*.

"Jim Moore sets his latest murder mystery in 1950 in the Bozeman area; the story centers upon a group of friends, all participants in college rodeo events. After an outing to the local hot springs one evening, no one notices that Summer Hetherington has been left behind. When her dead body is discovered in a pool at the hot springs the next morning, a lengthy murder investigation begins, and the prime suspect is one of Summer's closest friends, Cass Bruce.

"Drawing from a lifetime of experience as a rancher and attorney, Jim Moore writes legal thrillers in a distinctly Montanan way. In his compelling page-turner, 8 Seconds, he gives us keen details of rodeo, ranching, and the law, coupled with a clear understanding that life goes on even under the most dire circumstances. His characters are direct and forthright. All except for the murderers, of course. The stakes here reflect this directness — these are not far-fetched tales of grand conspiracies and melodrama, riddled with plot holes. Here, realistic folks struggle with feelings of loss, guilt, and concern for their reputation, while the quest for the truth plays out in trial. Fortunes change and even lives end, in fewer than 8 seconds." — Keith Suta, Writer and Broadcaster

"Typical of Jim Moore's mystery novels, 8 Seconds is a fast paced thrill ride of suspenseful curves and angles that keep the reader continually guessing. Set in the author's native Montana, it is filled with place names and descriptions familiar to many Montana readers. In addition, this novel is loaded with details about rodeoing and criminal law that readers will find fascinating."
— Bob Brown, former Montana Senator and Secretary of State

"Jim has crafted a well-told story with characters and settings which truly have the flavor of what could be a genuine Montana incident, and which offers a surprising twist at the end." — Gary Forney, author of several articles and five books on early Montana history

"You can just about taste the dust from the rodeo grounds in Jim Moore's final novel - 8 Seconds. Set in central and southwest Montana in the 1950's, this classical who-dun-it combines courtroom drama with an authentic glimpse into the ranching life many still live today," —Stephen Ore, author of *Round Trip*

Jim Moore's books about the Bruce family:

Ride the Jawbone, set in 1902, features a young rancher/lawyer, T. C. Bruce, who must defend an odious hobo accused of murdering a young woman and tossing her body off the train, the famous Jawbone Railroad. Craig Johnson, author of the Longmire series, called it "One heck of a read."

Jim Moore

The Jenny, set in 1920, tells of T. C. Bruce's daughter, Merci, bringing a WWI aircraft, a Curtis JN4, to Two Dot, in central Montana. When her mechanic is murdered, her brother, Spencer, with the help of T. C., defends the accused murderer, the son of a neighboring rancher.

In *8 Seconds*, fast forward to 1950, and Spencer's son, Cass is the accused. His aunt, Merci, a lawyer in Billings, asks an associate to defend him, and he agrees if she promises to help. She agrees, determined to find the real killer.

Other books by Jim Moore:

Election Day: Conceived to answer a "what if" question by using the US Constitution and its amendments, Jim weaves a story of intrigue that is also a civics lesson. Craig Lancaster, author of 600 Hours of Edward and its sequels, calls it a "crackerjack of a read."

The Body on the Floor of the Rotunda, set in modern times, finds another Bruce family descendant defending a lady senator accused of murder in the Montana capitol. Neil Lynch, former state senator, says, "This novel deserves to be read by everyone who loves our great state."

The Whole Nine Yarns, Tales of the West showcases Jim's storytelling prowess in nine eclectic short stories.

8 SECONDS

JIM MOORE

RAVEN PUBLISHING, INC
NORRIS, MT

8 Seconds

Copyright © 2017 Jim Moore
Cover art © 2017 Don Greytak
Second edition © 2021, Jim Moore
ISBN: 978-1-937849-25-2
Raven Publishing, Inc.
PO Box 2866, Norris, MT 59745
www.ravenpublishing.net

Printed in the United States

Library of Congress Cataloging-in-Publication Data

Names: Moore, Jim, 1927- author.
Title: 8 seconds / Jim Moore.
Other titles: Eight seconds
Description: Second edition. | Norris, MT : Raven Publishing, [2021] | Summary: "Cassius Bruce, a senior at Montana State College in 1950
performs in both bareback and saddle bronc competitions with the college rodeo. He enjoys every aspect of rodeo until the news of the murder of a lovely coed who was his friend and fellow rodeoer reaches him"-- Provided by publisher.
Identifiers: LCCN 2021010070 | ISBN 9781937849252 (paperback)
Subjects: LCSH: Rodeo--Fiction. | Murder--Investigation--Fiction. | Montana--Fiction.
Classification: LCC PS3613.O5626 A615 2021 | DDC 813/.6--dc23
LC record available at https://lccn.loc.gov/2021010070

For my lady, Kay,

The one who ran the barrels.

Introduction
My Dad
by Aurie Moore

When I rode in the car with my dad, he was usually silent. A question would elicit a one or two-sentence reply, and then again, silence. I wondered what he was thinking.

My dad was an only son with four sisters. He joined the Navy at 17. When the war ended, he returned to Two Dot and enrolled at the University of Montana. He dreamed of studying Law. Instead, my grandfather made it clear that my dad was needed on the ranch. Without much choice, he transferred to Montana State College and studied Agriculture. During Spring and Summer quarters, he went back to the ranch to help calve and cut hay.

He joined the college rodeo team. Rodeoing became his way of proving himself and his rebellion. He was a champion bareback and saddle bronc rider. My grandfather was not thrilled about his rodeoing, so my dad did his best to keep it quiet. He won a bareback competition and was given a large silver belt buckle. The next Saturday night, he headed to town with his shirt untucked to hide his belt. His dad stopped him at the bottom of the stairs and said, "So, pull up your shirt and let me see that buckle." He wore the buckle for the rest of his life.

In a national championship at the Cow Palace in San Francisco, he entered the bull riding contest. It was only his second time on a bull. The bull won, putting his horn through my dad's lip and taking out his front teeth forever.

On the rodeo team, he met my mother, who had grown up on a farm and loved horses. He became, as he put it, one of her many suitors, until she finally agreed to marry him.

After my grandfather died, my dad signed up for a remote-study law school program. The school sent shelves of thick, brown legal books. He studied by himself during the winters, sending his carefully hand-written assignments to Chicago for grading. At the end of three years, he took the Bar Exam and failed.

A year later, he took the Bar Exam again. This time, certain that he had failed again, he drove home to the ranch. The next morning, he was astonished by a call from the Montana Supreme Court asking him why he wasn't in Helena in the Court chambers. They were swearing in the new attorneys, and he was the only one missing.

He started his law practice first with Gordon Hickman, and then with Barry O'Connell and Mark Refling. Money was tight, but his fledgling practice gave him the ability to leave the ranch and to pursue his dreams. He loved the law.

My dad was first and foremost a storyteller. He reveled in stories about our history of our family. At any summer gathering, he and his cousin Buck Moore would stand for hours and tell hilarious stories about the past for the rest of us to laugh at and learn from.

My dad's happiest years came when he retired, met Janet Muirhead Hill and became one of the Raven Publishing authors. He spent mornings typing his stories in a freezing upstairs room. He read and edited the manuscripts that the other Raven authors were writing with enthusiasm. He lived for book signings and the social outlet that they brought. He was as excited to have his first book, *Ride the Jawbone,* published as he was to have married my mother. Writing, he said, gave him a reason to live.

I think I finally know now what he was pondering on those silent car rides. He was reminiscing about rodeoing, life on the ranch, and the mysteries of the law. In his mind, he was quietly weaving the stories that became his books.

CHAPTER ONE

Nine thirty PM
Saturday
May 13, 1950
Hunter's Hot Springs

Summer straightened her clothes and stood for a moment. She wiped away a tear, dropped the swimsuit into the bucket along with those worn by Hannah and April and pushed through the dressing room door into the gloom of the pool area. As she turned to close the door behind her, a hand grasped the thick braid of her hair, jerking her backward and leaving her chin and throat exposed. She only had an instant to resist before something sharp pierced the skin beneath her chin. Pain such as she didn't know existed radiated upward into her brain until everything went black. Her lifeless remains collapsed onto the wet pavement.

Jim Moore

Summer never felt her body being dragged to the edge of the pool where it slid quietly into the water. In an instant her assailant disappeared into the darkness behind the building.

CHAPTER TWO

A t first glance that Sunday morning, the water of the pool seemed absolutely still. Only the movement of loosened tendrils of caramel-colored hair revealed the quiet flow of water from the inlet to the outlet. The tendrils fluttered and waved around the long, thick braid that held the remainder of the mane in place.

Face down on the hard concrete of the pool bottom, its arms outstretched as though reaching for a warm embrace, the body was visible through the clear water. The western-style shirt, patterned a dark red, had pearl snap buttons at the cuffs. A belt, with the name *"Summer"* hand carved deeply into the leather, encircled the waist of Wrangler denims. Riding boots, also hand carved and colorfully inlaid, covered the feet. A silken white neckerchief mimicked the tendrils of hair by waving in the flow of the water. Such was the scene in the quiet of the morning when Park County Sheriff, Joshua Waddell, responded to a frantic call. Mrs. Stensrud,

Jim Moore

who operated Hunter's Hot Spring, had found a dead body.

When Doc Winters arrived, the body lay face up on the concrete next to the pool. Kneeling beside it, Doc pointed at the handle of the icepick protruding from beneath the young woman's chin. "She might have drowned, but it's more likely the icepick got her," he said, looking up at the sheriff. "At least it happened quick." His voice echoed faintly around the cavernous room.

The sheriff, thirty-two years of age, dark-eyed and craggy-faced with short, straight hair, held his tall, slender body erect as he squared his broad shoulders. He didn't wear a uniform or a side arm. A star pinned to the pocket of his western shirt was partially visible beneath an unbuttoned denim vest. The pocket that held the star also held a small bag of Bull Durham tobacco, its tag hanging out. A weathered and soiled western hat rested low on his forehead. His tongue worried a stiff stem of brome grass in the corner of his mouth. He nodded his head at the doctor's remark.

"I hope it was quick." He threw the grass stem to one side. "I guess to determine the cause of death, the body has to be autopsied, and I understand the pathologist is in Butte. Can you arrange that?" He paused. "I've never dealt with this kind of thing."

The old physician pushed himself to his feet and stretched his back. "Don't worry. I'll handle it. This kind of thing's no fun for any of us."

"Mrs. Stensrud said a bunch of college kids were here last night, apparently competitors in the college rodeo in Bozeman, yesterday." He gestured toward the lifeless body. "That girl was one of the college crowd. The bastard who did her in may be one of the same bunch." The sheriff took a deep breath. "Might as well begin the investigation right now. I'll get all the information I can from Mrs. Stensrud and then head to Bozeman. Try to find the other ones who were here last night."

Doctor Winters shook his head. "What a waste of a young life." Heaving a sigh, he added, "I'll have the boys load the body into the county ambulance and get it on the way to Butte."

Waddell nodded. "I'll stop at the county attorney's office on my way through Livingston. Better tell Merrill Hodder first thing. It's not something he'll want to hear."

"No, he won't. But when you find out who did this, he'll be the one who has to prosecute the rascal." Winters stood with his hands on his hips. "So they were rodeo people." He glanced at the sheriff. "How long does a rodeo bareback bronc ride last, Josh?"

"This is ranch country, Doc, everybody knows it's eight seconds if the rider makes it to the whistle." He squinted at the doctor. "Why do you ask?'

"It didn't take eight seconds for that poor girl to die."

CHAPTER THREE

Sheriff Waddell's drive along the winding highway over the Bozeman Pass took forty minutes. Courtesy required that he let the Gallatin County sheriff know the reason he was in town. The sheriff's office in Bozeman was located in the jail, an old brick structure next to the courthouse on Main Street. The sheriff's private office was a cubbyhole off the front entrance. Abel Parsons, Gallatin County Sheriff, bald but for a white fringe above his ears, looked up from a desk covered with paper. He heaved his five-feet nine-inch rotund body from his swivel chair to offer his hand to the Park County sheriff.

After a brief exchange of pleasantries, the Park County Sheriff pulled a chair away from the wall, turned it around and sat with his arms resting on the back.

"What can I do for you?" Parsons asked.

Waddell heaved a sigh and said, "This morning Mrs.

Stensrud found a dead woman, apparently a college coed from Bozeman, in the pool at Hunter's Hot Springs. Mrs. Stensrud runs the place. She said some college rodeo contestants came over to the hot springs after yesterday's performance in Bozeman. She said no one else was there, so the dead woman must have been one of them."

Parsons nodded for him to continue.

"I need to find the others who were at the Springs with the dead girl. They should be at the arena in Belgrade this afternoon for today's rodeo. Thought I'd get myself out there and ask around. See what I can learn."

"Yup, you'll need to do that. But it seems to me the first thing you should do is get yourself up to the college, see if you can find out that girl's name and if she lives on the campus. Next thing is to make sure that nobody disturbs her belongings until you've had a chance to learn what they might tell you."

"How can I find out her name? I don't know my way around that campus."

"I suggest we start with the Dean of Women." Parsons stood and reached for his hat. "See if she can help us with the name. If not she can probably send us to someone who can."

Waddell's eyebrows shot up. "You'll go with me?"

"Yes. I've met the dean. She's always been helpful. It seems that much of your investigation will take place in my county, so I'll do what I can to make it easier for you. We law officers should cooperate."

The younger sheriff put out his hand. "I'm glad you're willing to help. I never went to college, and I've only held this job for two years. I'd be lost up there in all those buildings without knowing where to go or what to do."

Parsons slapped his worn fedora onto his head. "Well let's get on our way. We'll learn all we can from the dean. Then we can get to the rodeo arena at Belgrade. The show starts at one thirty."

The dean was helpful. Her assistant found only one student named Summer, a junior from Roundup. She was living in the Chi Omega Sorority house. Her last name was Hetherington.

At the sorority house, Sheriff Parsons told Mrs. Newman, the housemother, of the death of Summer Hetherington in as gentle a way as possible. The poor woman was completely bewildered by the news. For a bit she seemed unable comprehend their request for access to the student's belongings. She soon recovered enough to explain the living arrangements at the house and give them a short tour. None of the girls had a private room; they shared space. Summer's clothing and other belongings were in a room with the belongings of three others.

Sheriff Parsons asked in his gentle voice, "Could you gather all of her stuff together, pack it up and keep it safe until Sheriff Waddell can collect it? It will all become part of the investigation into her death."

"Yes. I can do that." She looked around. "I may ask one of the other girls to help me."

"It would be better if you did it alone ma'am. There may come a time when questions are asked of those who handled her belongings." He paused. "We'll need a written statement from you saying that no one but you was involved in the task."

The housemother's face crumbled, as understanding dawned that this was an investigation of a crime, and one of her beloved charges was the victim. "Yes, officer, I'll pack it all up and have it ready when you return."

Both sheriffs, hats in hand, offered their thanks as they exited the doorway. At the parking lot, Sheriff Parsons glanced at his watch. It was almost noon. "The rodeo arena's newly built, just east of Belgrade. It's only about eight miles out there. How about we stop at Bill's Grill? Quick service there. We can eat a bite and get to the rodeo arena shortly before the performance begins. The ones we're looking for are bound to be there."

CHAPTER FOUR

The day was pleasantly warm. Dust, stirred up by the rodeo animals in and around the newly built arena, clouded the air. People in western wear were everywhere. Their chatter blended with the sounds of bawling cattle and the shouts and curses of men working with the livestock. The two sheriffs surveyed the scene. The arena oval was about two hundred fifty feet long and half that wide, surrounded by a woven wire fence. At one end were the corrals to hold the bucking stock. At the other end, corrals held calves for roping and steers for bull dogging.

The rough stock contestants, those who rode the bareback horses, saddle broncs, and bulls, were gathered at the western end of the arena near the bucking chutes. The peace officers ambled along until Parsons spotted a young man down on his knee buckling a spur onto his boot. A bareback rig, an association saddle, a buck rein, and a pair of chaps lay nearby. Parsons asked, "How about him?"

"He'll do." Waddell stepped across the open space toward the kneeling cowboy.

The young man pulled a spur strap tight before looking up at the two men wearing badges who stopped before him. The rodeo rider stood to face them. The younger officer was first to speak. "A bunch of college cowboys were at Hunter's Hot Springs last night. Were you one of them?"

The young man stood silent for a moment, a quizzical look on his face. "Yes, I was there. Why do you ask?"

Waddell ignored the question. "Was a girl named Summer Hetherington with you?"

"Yes, Summer was there." He picked up his bareback rig. "What's wrong? Did we leave a mess that the proprietor's complaining about? We thought we cleaned everything up before we left."

The tall law officer spoke again. "I'm Josh Waddell, Sheriff of Park County." He gestured with his thumb. "And this is Abel Parsons, Sheriff of Gallatin County. We need to talk with you about that. And we need to get the names of the others who were at the hot springs last night. We'll want to visit with each of them."

The young cowboy glanced over his shoulder toward the arena. "Look, I don't know what this is about, but I'm up in the first section of bareback riding, and I have a saddle bronc later on. I have to get ready." He turned his head to scan the length of the arena. "Summer Hetherington runs the barrels. She's probably at the other end of the arena."

Sheriff Abel Parsons, kind of face and soft of speech, joined the conversation. "What's your name, son?"

"It's Bruce. Cass Bruce."

Parsons nodded. "We understand that you're busy right now. But it's important to get the names of those who were at the hot springs last night. I'm guessing you know them."

A look of impatience crossed the young man's face as he nodded.

"We won't bother you anymore right now," Parsons said, "How about you come to my office at the county jail on Main Street after the rodeo?"

Cass frowned "Sheriff, why don't you tell me what's going on?"

Sheriff Waddell answered, his voice sharp in contrast to that of the older officer's. "It's important. That's all you need to know right now."

Cass frowned. "Well, if you say it's important, it must be. I'll let the others know. I'll see if some of them can come to the jail with me."

Parsons spoke. "One at a time would be better. There isn't much room in my office."

Josh Waddell added, "But we'll want to talk to every one of them—individually—sometime soon."

Cass hoisted the bareback rig and gathered the cinch and latigo in his grasp so they wouldn't drag. "All right, I'll stop by when I get my gear put away after the show. Now I need to get this rig on a horse before the announcer calls my name."

Waddell spoke again, this time with a fierce piercing stare. "See that you get there right after the show. We'll be waiting."

Cass Bruce, equally as tall and muscular as the sheriff, growled, "It'll be around six or six-thirty." He started toward the fence and turned. "It would help if I knew what's bothering you two. It must be something worse than a messy swimming pool."

Waddell muttered, "It's bad." Then he asked, "What's your name again? I want to be sure I've got it right."

"Cass Bruce, Cassius Thaddeus Bruce, if you need to know my full name."

The two officers watched him climb the fence and drop into the alley behind the bucking chutes. Parsons turned to his younger colleague. "That one doesn't appear to know anything about the murder."

"Could be an act," Waddell snarled.

CHAPTER FIVE

Cass entered the arena through a narrow contestants' entry gate. He stopped for a moment to take in the scene. The configuration of the rodeo ground was the same as most of the others he'd seen. Eight chutes for the bucking stock lined one side of the arena. Each chute was just long enough and wide enough to hold a large horse. A solid sliding gate in the ally separated each chute from the one in front of it.

Cass watched as the first of the bareback horses were herded down the alleyway and into the chutes. When the lead horse was in the farthest chute, a worker pushed the gate closed behind him. The process continued until there was a bareback bucking horse standing in each chute. One of them would be his to ride.

He turned his attention to the east end of the arena where more small pens were located. One held the roping calves and the horned steers used for bulldogging. As with the bucking horse chutes, an alleyway led from the corrals to the small chute from which the calves were released. Each calf roper pursued the calf, lassoed it about the neck, threw it to the ground and tied its legs together. The roper who did it all in the fastest time was the winner. The same chute allowed the release of the steers to be wrestled to the ground by the bulldoggers.

There was a large gate in the fence next to the calf chute that provided entry to the arena for those on horseback. The barrel racers, riding their fastest horses, came through that gate on the run to begin their figure eight scramble around the three barrels. Thoughts of Summer Hetherington crowded Cass's mind. She must be down there somewhere, probably currying her horse before she saddled him for the day's race.

Cass walked along the front of the bucking chutes looking for the horse he'd drawn for the day's bareback event. Harry Croswell, fellow rough stock rider, grabbed his arm to stop him. "Have you seen Summer? Hannah said she wasn't at the fairgrounds to load her horse." Cass raised his eyebrows as Harry continued. "Hannah loaded Summer's barrel horse, along with her own, and hauled them out here. But she still can't find Summer."

Cass shook his head. "I haven't seen her. But I haven't looked for her either." He looked toward the arena fence where he left the law officers. "Two sheriffs caught me just a moment ago. They asked if Summer was with us at Hunter's Hot Springs last night."

"You told them she was, of course?"

"They seemed to know that. But something serious must have happened, because they want me to come to the jail after the show. They want the names all of us who was there."

Harry looked puzzled. "What could've happened?"

"I haven't any idea. But I'd better go to the jail when we're done and find out."

Croswell jerked his head in the direction of the chute boss. "Charlie Hussey's getting impatient. We better get our horses ready."

The bareback horse Cass had drawn was in chute number six. He draped his bareback rig over the top plank of the chute gate and climbed the gate to look down on the back of the animal. The horse was bay, tall and muscular. Straddling the rails, one foot on the second rail from the top on each side, he grasped the bareback rig by its handle, dropped the cinch down one side of the horse and then allowed the latigo to slide down the other. One of the chute hands, working from the outside, shoved a wire hook through the slats on the chute gate, snagged the cinch with the hook and pulled it up under the belly of the horse. Cass moved his feet down one slat and grasped the D rings of the bareback rig, one ring in each hand. He held the rigging in place on the horse's withers as the chute hand tightened the cinch to Cass's satisfaction. Last, he ran his fingers through the horse's mane to assure himself that there were no twisted clusters of hair that might snag a spur. With a nod of thanks to the helper, the young rider clambered down the backside of the chute to the ground.

He pulled a small flat piece of sheepskin from his back pocket, unbuttoned his Wranglers and shoved the sheepskin into the back of his pants. If the cowboy spurred the bareback horse in a manner that scored points, his tail bone banged hard against the horse's backbone. The sheepskin provided the needed padding.

The rodeo performance began, as always, with the playing of the national anthem. The rodeo contestants, as well as everyone in the audience, stood with hat in hand until its end. Then the announcer began the customary patter, welcoming the crowd, introducing the stock contractor and directing the crowd's attention to the bucking chutes for the first section of bareback riding.

Contestants from Western Montana College, the University of Montana, Utah State University, Eastern Montana College and Dickinson State College were in attendance. Cass climbed up two planks on the chute to look over the back of the bareback horse as the announcer introduced a young man from Eastern Montana College as the first rider of the day. The horse ran the two jumps out of the chute but then leapt high in the air with a twist to the side. The rider was quickly deposited in the dirt. Three more followed in quick succession. Two made successful rides, one was bucked down.

Tall, heavyset, good looking and easygoing, Justin Madden of Montana State, was next. His bareback horse bucked straight away and smooth. The judges score both horse and rider. Justin's boots kicked high and wide. His spurring action would have scored enough to get him in the money. Unfortunately, the horse's action lacked the necessary appeal, and the judge's decision would reflect it. Cass figured Justin was out of luck this day.

When just one more bareback rider remained before

Jim Moore

Cass's turn, he climbed the backside of the chute to straddle it once again. For an instant a familiar feeling flashed through his senses. It was neither fear nor even apprehension, but only a slight sense of anxiety. What he was about to do could be dangerous. The feeling disappeared as quickly as it came. He reached down to grasp the handle of the bareback rig with his left hand, then slowly walked his way down the rails until he could settle his backside on the horse, each foot resting on a chute rail, his right hand gripping the top rail of the chute. He scooted himself forward until his crotch was pressed firmly against the hand that grasped the handle of the bareback rig. Satisfied, he turned his head slightly toward the gate man and nodded.

The instant the chute gate swung open, the horse turned on his hind legs, front hooves high off the ground, to leap high out into the open arena. With the turn, Cass dug his spurs into the depression between the horse's neck and the horse's shoulders, the action needed to "start" the horse as required by the rules. Cass's spurs raked upward at the beginning of each of the horse's upward leaps and flew skyward as the leap reached its peak. The animal bucked in a large circle, all the while kicking high behind. The action of horse and rider made for a showy ride. When the eight-second whistle blew, Cass grasped the horse's mane with his right hand and looked around for a pickup man. One was soon at his side. Cass put an arm around the pickup man's waist and skidded across the pickup horse's rump to drop to the ground. The usual feeling of exhilaration after a successful ride brought a grin to his face. The chatter of the announcer penetrated his consciousness. "A classy ride, folks. Give that cowboy a big hand." Cass waved a hand in response to the smattering of applause, but his focus was on the two judges, each of whom was marking something on a card. He was sure his ride would score points for the team as well as for himself.

Cass was still grinning as he reached the holding pens at the far end of the arena where they removed the bareback rigs from the horses. One of the stock contractor's hired hands called, "Nice ride kid. You done good."

Cass grinned. "Horse bucked high and kicked."

"Good kind to draw."

The young cowboy gathered his bareback rig and stepped through a gate to the outside of the arena. He looked for Summer among the timed event people gathered nearby. He saw Hannah Dodson, all five feet three inches of her, running up to him with a stricken look on her face. She grabbed his arm. "Summer never got back to the Chi Omega house last night! Nobody knows where she is or what happened to her."

Cass stopped stock still. "Didn't Justin drop her off at the sorority house door?"

Hannah's eyes widened. "She wasn't with Justin, Cass."

"When we left, I assumed she was in his car."

Hannah's face twisted. "Oh my God, Cass, did we just leave her there?"

"If we did, she surely would've called for someone to come back and get her."

"One of her sorority sisters told me the house mother is beside herself with worry."

Cass groaned. "That must be what those two sheriffs want to ask us about. Something bad must have happened to Summer."

Jim Moore

"Sheriffs? What sheriffs?"

Cass repeated what he had told Harry Croswell about the sheriffs' request for names.

Hannah wrapped her arms around her midriff and moaned, "Oh God, Cass, I don't like this."

He shifted his bareback rig from one hand to the other. "As soon as the show's over we better get everyone together at the Fairgrounds and try to figure out what happened." He turned to begin the trek back to the bucking chutes but said over his shoulder, "Spread the word. I'll do the same."

Back at the bucking chute, Cass Bruce stood by the fence as others of the Montana State rodeo team worked their way through the events, his mind half on the action and half wondering about Summer. When Wayne Foley's name was announced as the next up, Cass turned his attention to the calf chutes. He enjoyed watching the tall calf roper. The man was slender and sinewy, broad of shoulder and graceful in his every movement—the handling of the rope, the dismount and the throwing of the calf to the ground. The twirl of the pigging string around the calf's legs was smooth and so fast as to be a blur. Wayne always scored well. Today his run was as swift and fluid as always. His would be the winning time.

Foley had honed his skills at a calf roping school conducted by a national calf-roping champion. His parents' wealth allowed him to purchase one of the best calf-roping horses in the business, already trained and proven. Despite their different backgrounds, Cass thought of him as a friend.

Zeke Howard, another Montana State contestant, also did well in the calf roping events. Howard was five feet nine, and big bodied. What Wayne Foley did with grace, Howard did through pure muscle. Today his time was two tenths of a second slower than Foley's.

The last of the calf ropers made their runs. The bucking chutes would be filling with saddle broncs. Cass dragged his association saddle into the arena. Time to get ready for his next event. Things didn't go well right from the start. The horse chose to fight the chute, rearing and pawing in an attempt to escape its confines. When the saddle was at last in place, the horse leaned against the chute side making it impossible for Cass to slide a foot into the stirrup. He and three chute hands pushed and shoved to move the animal all to no avail. Noting the stock contractor's impatience, Cass said to the gate man, "Jab him with something sharp." A chute hand used a pitchfork to jab the horse once. The animal moved just enough for Cass to poke a boot into the stirrup.

The gate opened just as Cass managed to get both feet forward and dug into the horse's shoulders. The animal, however, must have spent his energy in the chute. He offered only three high, crooked leaps before the bucking became little more than a smooth lope to the other end of the arena. The ride over, Cass walked back to the bucking chutes to try to convince the judges he should get a re-ride. They just shook their heads.

The barrel race was next. In the middle of the arena three thirty-gallon barrels were placed in a triangle with about fifty feet between them. The racer entered the arena with her horse on the run. When she crossed a certain line, the timer clicked a stopwatch. The object was to bend the horse, running at top speed, around each barrel and back across the finish line without knocking a barrel over. When she crossed

Jim Moore

the finish line the timer registered her time. The one with the fastest run was the winner.

Without Summer Hetherington, Hannah Dodson was the only barrel racer for the Montana State team. Cass watched her race the horse around the barrels, short legs pounding his sides and determination on her face. Her run was fast enough to place second for the day. Through it all, however, his mind was on Summer. What could have happened to her?

CHAPTER SIX

By five thirty that evening, the calf ropers, the bulldoggers and the barrel racers had brushed, fed and watered their horses and put them in stalls at the Gallatin County Fairgrounds. The college rodeo participants who had gone to Hunter's Hot Springs the night before clustered near the large front door of the horse barn. Others who just liked the company of those who participated were there as well. One such fellow had explained it by saying, "I don't want to be a saddle bronc rider. I just want to stand around where the saddle bronc riders stand around." The late afternoon had turned chilly and the warmth of the sun angling through the opening felt good.

Cass Bruce hurried the length of the alley from where he'd helped Hannah unsaddle, water and feed Summer's horse, Hannah at his side. The gabble of the gathered throng was muted and solemn. Their conversations ended abruptly when he stopped and took a deep breath.

Jim Moore

"As you all know, a few of us went to Hunter's Hot Springs after yesterday's performance. And you know by now that Summer didn't make it back to her sorority house last night. That's what two sheriffs asked me about. They want the names of everyone who was at the hot springs. They didn't tell me anything more than that." Cass blew out a long breath. "Something terrible must have happened to Summer, but they wouldn't tell me what it was."

Zeke asked, "That's all? They just want our names?"

"Yup. The sheriffs told me to bring the names to the jail. The younger one of the two told me I'd better do it as soon as we're finished here, so that's what I'll do." He looked around. "What could have happened to Summer?"

Justin Madden said, "I don't know. We thought she was in your car when we left the hot springs."

Cass's puzzled look remained. "She wasn't with us. You were already moving when I started my car. There was no one there when I drove away, so we all assumed Summer was with you."

Hannah Dodson said in a small voice, "We must have just left her there. That's what happened. Somehow we just left her there." She was all crunched together, arms wrapped around her torso. "Now something awful has happened. Why else would those sheriffs be asking questions?"

April Menard, the tall and attractive young woman standing next to Justin Madden, spoke with authority. "My grandfather was a police officer. I've heard him talk about crime investigations. You'd better be prepared to explain why Summer was left behind. And you'd better be prepared to fill in all of the details. The questions will keep coming.

They won't be satisfied until they've learned all there is to know about everything that happened last night."

Zeke spoke up. "Not much to tell. We were all just soaking in the warm water, a couple of us had a beer in hand, when someone hollered, "It's almost ten. We've got to get going or the girls will miss curfew.'"

Harry added, "That was me. We all rushed to get out of the pool and into our clothes. Then we ran out to the cars. I didn't see who got in which car. It was all just a scramble."

Cass asked, "Anybody remember any other details? The kind of thing April mentioned."

Hannah raised tear-filled eyes to scan the crowd. "What could have happened to her?"

Cass straightened and looked from one to another of the group. "Well, it's time to find out."

As he turned to leave, Hannah Dodson hurried to grab his arm. "Can I go with you? Summer's been my friend since we were children. I need to know what went wrong."

"I asked the sheriffs if some of you should be with me. They didn't seem to want anyone else."

"Will you let me know what you find out? As soon as you can?"

"I'll do that, Hannah. Catch you at the Student Union?" At her nod, Cass strode toward his automobile.

CHAPTER SEVEN

The old brick jail presented a forbidding appearance as Cass parked his car and walked slowly up the sidewalk. As he reached the front door, Sheriff Abel Parsons pushed it open and waved the young man inside. He led Cass to a small room where Sheriff Josh Waddell waited at a table, surrounded by four wooden chairs. Parsons gestured for Cass to take one of the chairs. When they were all seated, Waddell leaned toward the college student with his forearms on the table. His voice registered impatience. "Did you bring the names of everyone who was with you last night at Hunter's Hot Springs?"

The piece of paper Cass Bruce pulled from his hip pocket had been folded twice. He passed it across the table to Waddell. "There were nine of us. Their names are on that list." He sat with the palms against the table edge as he spoke. "Now, please tell me what's happened to Summer."

Waddell ignored the question as he scanned the list.

Sheriff Parsons shifted his heavy body and heaved a sigh. "Here's the thing. Mrs. Stensrud found the dead body of a young woman at the bottom of Hunter's Hot Springs swimming pool this morning. We're pretty sure it's Miss Hetherington."

Shocked, Cass instinctively pushed back from the table. "Dead! Good God! What happened to her?"

Waddell answered. "When we got her out of the water we found an icepick jammed up under her chin." Cass, stunned, sat wide-eyed and motionless, as the sheriff continued. "Do you know how that icepick might've gotten there?"

Cass sat speechless as he tried to process the news. A picture of his beautiful friend played in his mind. The idea of an icepick in her lovely throat turned his stomach.

Waddell barked, "Well?"

Cass gave his head a tiny shake and blinked his eyes. "No, sheriff, I have no idea. Why would anyone do such a thing to Summer? She never offended anyone. She could never make anyone that mad. She was just too nice." He looked from one Sheriff to the other. "Who could've done it?"

Waddell extended his forearms farther along the tabletop. His gray eyes were focused on Cass as he pointed at him. "How about you?"

The young man pushed back from the table, away from the accusatory finger. "Wait a minute. Are you accusing me of killing Summer?"

"I just asked a simple question. What's your answer?"

His grief turned to anger. "No, Sheriff, I didn't kill Summer." He turned to Sheriff Parsons, seeking someone to understand. "She was a good friend."

Jim Moore

The Gallatin County Sheriff reached for the paper with the names. He ran his eyes over it from top to bottom, then dropped it on the table and quietly changed the subject. "How did all of you get from here to there last night?"

"We traveled in two cars, Justin Madden's Pontiac and my four door Chevy sedan."

"Which car was Summer Hetherington in?"

Cass, his frown deepening, said, "She was with me on the way to the Springs. There were five of us in my car."

"So, she traveled to the hot springs with you. But she didn't come back with you."

Cass slowly shook his head. "No sir. She didn't."

Parsons waited a second to let Cass ponder. "I'm sure you can understand why that might raise a question in our minds?" When Cass sat, unmoving, without response, he added, "You must have wondered why she didn't get in the car with you for the return to Bozeman?"

Cass's brow wrinkled as he worked his mind to recall the night's events. "We left in a hurry to get the girls back to the dorms before the curfew. There was a rush to get in the cars. I asked about her, and one of the guys said the girls got in the car with Justin. He was driving out—so I followed."

Sheriff Parsons continued to speak softly. "Here's how it seems, son. You and the other people on that list were the only ones at Hunter's Hot Springs last night. The dead woman went out there with you. She didn't come back with you. She's dead. Who could have killed her other than someone whose name is on this list?"

Cass's shook his head. "Sheriff, I didn't kill Summer. And I can't believe any of the others would do such a thing."

He looked from Parsons to Waddell. "If what you tell me is true, there had to be someone else around that place."

Waddell's harsh voice sounded again. "Then tell us who it was and how that person could have murdered that girl while she was in the company of all the rest of you."

Cass slumped in the chair. "I can't." His hands dropped from the table edge to his lap. "But I can tell you I didn't do anything to Summer. And neither did any of the others on that list."

Waddell slapped the table hard as he thrust himself forward. "Enough of this. We need the truth. One of you did it. That's for certain. Maybe it was you. Did you do it?"

Cass was on his feet in an instant. "You've had enough? I'm the one who's had enough. I've lost a good friend. I came here like you asked, and I've answered your questions. Now you're accusing me of killing her. Well, to hell with you." He gave the chair a shove as he turned for the door. He stepped out and yanked it closed with a bang.

Abel Parsons heaved a sigh and looked across at his fellow law officer. "The youngster is understandably distressed." He sighed. "Josh, one thing I've learned in my twenty-two years in this office is patience. When questioning a suspect, go slow. Don't try to push too fast. Give him time."

"You think I shouldn't have implied he was the killer?"

"I just think making him angry didn't help."

Waddell's face colored. "I messed up? Is that it?"

Parsons raised a calming hand. "Probably won't make any difference." He smiled. "Just wanted to share a thought about the job we both have."

Waddell shrugged. "You're probably right. I need to slow

Jim Moore

down. There's nothing that tells us that sport committed the crime—yet." He sighed. "But a murder in my county. Good God, the responsibility to solve it scares the hell out of me."

"It should." Parsons struggled to his feet. "Now comes the hard part. Someone has to tell her parents."

Josh dropped his head and moaned. "God, I hate the thought of just calling them cold. But to drive there is near to a full day's trip. Can't take that time if I'm to try to find out what happened down there at that swimming pool."

"I know the sheriff in Musselshell County. I'll ask him to go personally to the girl's family. He won't want to do it, of course. Who would? But he'll understand it'll be better that they hear from someone they know rather than in a cold telephone call from a stranger."

Waddell's face showed relief. "You'll do that?"

Parsons smiled. "As soon as you're out of here. You have to get back to Livingston." He stood. "That housemother should have the girl's belongings packed by now. I'm sure you'll want to take them with you to your evidence locker. There may be something that'll provide evidence in the future."

Waddell stood. "Yes, of course. The county attorney isn't going to be happy when I dump all of this on him so late in the day." He paused. "I'll need to talk to the others who were at the pool. I hope I can do it without too many trips to Bozeman."

Sheriff Parsons leaned on the back of his chair. "I'll help. We know their names. They should be easy to contact. In the morning one of my deputies will start to find them. We'll ask each one to come here to answer questions. I'll take notes and share them with you. That should cut down on the time you have to spend in Bozeman. You can follow up later with any that might have more to offer."

"That sure will help!" Waddell put out a hand. "Thanks, Abel, for everything you've done so far. I hope I can continue to call on you as this thing goes forward."

"You can. We'll work together." Parsons squeezed the hand. "And we'll get the one who did it."

Chapter Eight

At a quarter after seven in the evening, all of the rodeo crew but Justin and April were seated at tables or standing close by in the lounge of the Student Union on the campus. Wayne Foley stood off to the side. His fiancée, Doris Hamilton, dark haired, five feet ten, muscular and with the figure and the facial features of a movie star, stood next to him, one arm wrapped into his.

When Cass came through the door, Hannah rose from her chair and grasped his shirtsleeve. "What did you find out?"

Cass, sober faced, peered down at her and then looked around at the others. "Summer's dead." He allowed a moment for that to register. "What's worse, if anything can be, both sheriffs seem to believe that one of us killed her."

"Dead?" Zeke Howard's face showed disbelief. "They think one of us killed her? That's ridiculous!"

Cass, exhausted from his confrontation with the law

officers, looked around for a place to sit. Harry saw the look and climbed from his chair. Cass slumped into it. "Here's the thing they kept saying, 'Summer went out there with us, but she didn't come back with us.' Her body was found in the pool. They believe we must have known she was still there when we left." He paused for a moment. "The younger sheriff seems absolutely certain that one of us killed her and the rest of us know who it is and will try to cover it up."

Hannah, arms crossed, eyes on the floor, muttered, "It just doesn't seem real. I can't believe Summer's dead."

Cass turned to her. "Those lawmen convinced me she is." He dropped an elbow on the table. "It seems they can't wait to pin it on someone. The young one, Sheriff Waddell, even accused me of killing her."

Croswell asked, "What are you going to do?"

Cass straightened. "As long as I'm here I'm going to get a hamburger. Then I'm going to my room and try to digest this. I still can't get it through my head that anyone could kill Summer. In the morning I'll call my dad. He's a lawyer and he'll know what to do."

Justin sat in his parked Pontiac on the street in front of the Alpha Omicron Pi sorority house. April leaned against the passenger door at the other end of the seat. "Don't you understand? I'm not saying he did it. I'm just saying he had the chance."

Justin shook his head without looking at her. "Never could've happened. It just isn't in Cass Bruce to kill anyone."

Her impatience was evident. "Listen to what I'm saying. Just as you were starting the car, I heard Cass holler that he'd

Jim Moore

dropped his wallet. He ran back into the dressing room to get it." She waited for his reaction. When he didn't speak, she leaned toward him for emphasis. "He didn't come running back out until we were driving away. He had time to do it."

He turned to face her squarely. "Ah, c'mon, April. You know Cass. Why would he do such a thing?"

She straightened and shifted in the seat. "They've been going steady. Maybe she dumped him."

"Going steady? Cass and Summer? No way. She was too popular to be going steady with Cass or anyone else."

"Maybe not going steady, but they spent a lot of time together."

"Even if that's true, it's not a reason for murder."

"Maybe not, but who knows. I just think we should go to the sheriff tomorrow and tell him. If we don't, they might accuse us of withholding evidence."

The young man grinned. "Now you're talking like a cop. I guess some of your grandfather did come through to you."

"Will you go with me or do I have to go alone?"

Justin reached for her hand. "No, April. I won't let you go alone. What time should I pick you up?"

CHAPTER NINE

At ten o'clock that night Josh Waddell was tired to the bone after the return drive over the Bozeman Pass to Livingston. He still needed to break the news to Merrill Hodder, the Park County Attorney. Hodder lived in a brick house in the older part of town and just kitty-corner across the street from the Catholic Church. At sixty years of age, he had held the office for the last twenty-five years. He was an erect five feet nine inches tall, had thick gray hair. He opened the door at Waddell's knock and spoke before Waddell could say a word. "Doc Winters called me. It seems we have a murder on our hands."

The sheriff nodded and followed Hodder along a dark hallway to a small office in the back of his house. He took the chair behind the desk. When Waddell was seated in a facing chair, he said, "Tell me what you've learned so far."

The sheriff leaned back to stretch his legs. "Not much. The girl's name is Summer Hetherington. Her home is near

Jim Moore

Roundup in Musselshell County. An icepick was driven up under her chin and left there. That's probably what killed her, but we'll know for sure when we get the autopsy report." When Hodder didn't comment, he continued, "A bunch of college rodeo contestants were at Hunter's Hot Springs last night. Sheriff Parsons and I talked to one of them, a fellow named Cass Bruce. He gave us the names of the whole bunch, nine in number, and told us that they traveled to the Springs in two cars. The Hetherington girl was in his. He claims no one noticed that she wasn't in either car for the trip back."

"How did he explain that?"

"He couldn't."

"What else did he have to offer?"

Waddell frowned. "Not a lot. It seemed to me that he's trying to avoid telling us too much." He paused. "I kind of lost my patience and asked him if he was the killer. Parsons gave me a scolding for that."

"Well, what's done is done." The county attorney leaned forward with his elbows on the desk. "There are some things that must be done right away. You need to interview all those who were at the pool and talk to the dead girl's friends and acquaintances to find out what was going on in her life. We must go through her belongings to see if there's anything that will help us. We have to find out if anyone else could have been around the pool area last night, someone that those kids and Mrs. Stensrud don't know about. We don't want to make the assumption it had to be one of them only to learn someone else had the means, motive, and opportunity."

Waddell seemed bewildered. "That's a lot to do. Sheriff Parsons has offered to contact the rest of that rodeo group and find out what each of them has to say. That'll really help."

"He better get it done in a hurry. Spring quarter ends at the college in couple of weeks and they'll be scattered to the four winds for the summer."

"I didn't think of that."

Hodder pushed his chair back and stood. "It's late. Take the girl's belongings to your evidence locker. We'll go through her stuff soon to see what we can learn from it." He walked Waddell to the door. "In the morning, drive back to the hot springs and take a good look around. Maybe someone else was there and left tracks." He offered a kindly smile. "But enough of that for now. Go home, kiss your pretty wife and get some rest. You'll need it as this thing moves along."

CHAPTER TEN

Monday morning, Spencer Bruce had just settled into his office in Harlowton when his secretary buzzed that he had a telephone call. He pushed some legal papers aside as he lifted the phone to his ear. He was surprised to hear his son's voice. Cass spoke quickly. "Dad, something really bad has happened. One of the college barrel racers was found dead at Hunter's Hot Springs yesterday morning."

"It was on the front page of the Billings Gazette this morning. Did you know the girl?"

"Yes, she was with a bunch of us who went to Hunter's after the rodeo. Somehow we didn't realize she wasn't with us when we left." Cass's voice shook. "Two sheriffs caught me at the Sunday show and asked a lot of questions. In the end the sheriff from Park County accused me of killing Summer."

Spencer frowned as he straightened in his chair. "He

accused you of killing her?" He asked, his voice heavy with disbelief. "What did you do to make him think such a thing?"

"Nothing. That's the problem." Cass paused. "Well, he didn't come right out and accuse me, but he kept asking if I did it." Cass added, "We left in a hurry and each thought she was in the other car. They found her dead in the pool yesterday morning. Those sheriffs think one of us must have killed her and that the rest of us may be covering it up."

Spencer asked, "Is that possible that one of your group killed her without you or any of the others knowing it?"

"I don't see how, Dad." Cass blew out a long breath before recounting the events of that evening. "Dad, that sheriff seems like he could go off half cocked. I don't know what to do."

Spencer's voice was quiet. "If what you tell me is correct, you needn't worry about any accusations the Park County Sheriff made. The law enforcement people will continue their investigation. In the process they'll find out it wasn't you." He shifted the phone to his other ear to make notes on a yellow pad. "Give me the names of both sheriffs again."

"The older one, the one from Gallatin County, is Parsons. I don't remember his first name. The young one from Park County is Waddell. I believe he said his first name was Josh."

Spencer began to speak, stopped, and then continued, "I was about to say I'd call the county attorney in Livingston to ask what they've got. But it seems better to wait and let the investigation go forward. If the law officers talk to you again and if they still seem to think you had something to do with the girl's death, we'll decide how to respond."

"All right, Dad." Cass heaved a sigh. "It helped a lot just

Jim Moore

to talk to you. "Now I have to study for my finals. It's just over a week till graduation."

"Yes, your whole family will be in Bozeman to help you celebrate. We're all proud of you, son.

CHAPTER ELEVEN

Meanwhile, Justin Madden drove April Menard to the sheriff's office. Abel Parsons led them into the same small room where he and Waddell had questioned Cass Bruce the night before. After introductions were finished and they were settled in chairs across from him, he asked, "Are you part of the rodeo crowd that was at Hunter's Hot Springs Saturday night?"

They nodded.

"Then you must be here to tell me something about Summer Hetherington's death." He waited, hands clasped across his belly.

Justin and April exchanged a glance before she turned to Parsons. "Yes, there's something that happened that night that we think you should know."

"And what might that be?"

"We were all just soaking in the warm water and didn't pay too much attention to the time. Someone noticed how

41

Jim Moore

late it was so we all kind of scrambled to get dressed and into the cars to leave. Right before I closed the door to Justin's car, I heard Cass Bruce call out that he'd left his wallet in the dressing room. And he ran back to get it."

"So?"

April seemed nonplussed. "So he had the opportunity to do that to Summer, you know, stick her with the icepick after all the rest of us were out of there."

Parsons' eyebrows went up. "How long was he in the pool area alone?"

"I don't know," She crinkled her brow. "Not too long."

Sheriff Parsons shifted in the chair. "What you've just told me certainly is helpful. Sheriff Waddell and I will follow up on it." He leaned forward and rested his forearms on the desktop. "What else can you tell me about the doings at the hot springs? Had Cass Bruce and Summer Hetherington been arguing?"

"No, not that I heard, anyway."

"Well, what reason would he have to murder her?"

April looked surprised. "I don't know of any."

Justin had listened without comment but now he came to his friend's defense. "Sheriff, I don't think April is trying to accuse Cass of killing Summer. We both know him well. Frankly, I don't believe he could kill anybody. He's too kind hearted."

The young lady seemed relieved by Justin's comment. "That's right, sir. I'm not accusing Cass of anything. It just seemed important to tell you about the business with the wallet."

Parson's smiled. "You're right about that." He stood. "It

is important , and I appreciate your willingness to come here voluntarily to talk to me. I'll share it with Sheriff Waddell, today." He moved around the corner of the desk. "I need to talk to the others who were out there with you." He led them to the door. "Will you ask any of them that you see to drop by my office—today if possible? Perhaps one of them will have something to offer, something that's as important as your report about the wallet."

Justin put a hand on April's back to move her along. "I'll be seeing most of them. I'm sure they'll want to help. We all just want to find out what happened to Summer."

CHAPTER TWELVE

A bel Parsons looked up from paperwork to see a tiny but nicely built young woman standing in his doorway. Her hair was a bright copper colored mass of curls. At his inquiring look, she said, "April and Justin said you wanted to visit with those of us who were at the hot springs, night before last."

Parsons stood, smiling. "Of course, I need to visit with all of you. It's helpful that you came here so soon." He gestured to a chair and then settled back into his own. "Why don't you start by telling me your name?"

"I'm Hannah Dodson. I'm a junior at Montana State." She was quiet for a moment. "Summer Hetherington is—was—a really good friend. It's hard to think she isn't here anymore."

The sheriff nodded and leaned back in his chair. "What can you tell me about her?"

"We're both from Roundup. Her parents have a place

on the river west of town. My folks have a ranch northeast of town. Summer and I've been in school together since the sixth grade."

"What kind of person was she?"

"She was warm and friendly. It seemed there was always a smile on her face. Everyone liked her."

"She was a barrel racer, right?"

"Yes, sir. I am too. Summer has—I guess I should say had—a horse that could really scoot." Hannah stopped. The sheriff seemed to be waiting for more so she went on. "She had the horse but didn't have a way to haul him. I have a two-horse trailer and the vehicle to pull it. So we'd load both horses and travel to rodeos together." She managed a wry smile. "She and her horse usually beat me and mine."

"Did she have any enemies? Anyone you know of who might want to do her harm?

Hannah was shaking her head before he finished. "No! I don't know of a single person who didn't like her." She wiped at her eyes. "She was just too nice to have enemies."

The sheriff shifted in his chair and leaned forward. "Has there been any change in her behavior lately? Anything to make you think something in her life had changed?"

Hannah thought for a second or two and nodded. "Now that you mention it, the last little while she's seemed kind of preoccupied at times. I asked her once if anything was wrong. She just said, 'no' in a way that told me I shouldn't ask anything more."

Parsons made a note on a pad on his desk. "What else can you tell me?"

The young woman shook her head. "I can't think of

anything else that might be helpful."

"I guess Summer Hetherington and Cass Bruce were attractive people with a mutual interest in rodeo. Were they going together?"

A puzzled look appeared on Hannah's face. "You mean going steady?" She shook her head. "I don't think they were 'going steady.'" She made quotation marks with her fingers. "They were friends. Summer struggled some with a statistics course. Cass helped her with it. He's really smart."

"Is that all there was to it? Just time studying together?"

"Look, Sheriff Parsons, those of us on the rodeo team all spend time together. The ones who work the timed events—the barrel racers, the ropers and the bulldoggers—have horses and keep them at the fairgrounds. We must care for them. Many days there'd be several of us down there at the same time. It wasn't uncommon for the rough stock riders to be in the bunch. And we'd often stop someplace for a Coke or a burger afterward." The sheriff inhaled to speak but she cut him off. "And sometimes only two or three of us would go off to do something together. Cass and I drove to Pony one day to look at a horse that a guy had for sale." She grinned. "Wasn't much of a horse."

"Anything else?"

Hannah looked toward the corner of the room as she thought. "I know Cass took Summer to a movie once at the Rialto Theatre. It was an old show, a classic, that Summer wanted to see." She turned back to the sheriff. "They laughed about it afterward. Said it was really bad and boring." Hannah thought some more. "Summer told me that she went for an airplane ride with Cass one time."

"Do you know if either Summer or Cass thought their relationship was more than casual? Like going together?"

"I really don't think so. But how am I to know?"

"What about the rush to leave the Springs that night?"

"Yes, we were in a hurry. When someone mentioned how late it was, we all scrambled to get dressed and out to the cars." She paused, remembering. "April and I just changed out of our suits into our clothes. Summer rinsed off in the shower first. She was just putting on her underwear as I ran out the door. April wasn't too far behind me."

"Did you see Miss Hetherington after that?"

Hannah shook her head. "No, I didn't. I hurried out and jumped into Justin's car. I thought Summer would be coming soon and get in Cass's car." Hannah wiped away a tear.

"I've been told that Cass Bruce got to his car and then remembered he'd left his wallet in the dressing room. I guess he went back to get it." The sheriff paused while offering an inquiring look. "What can tell me about that?"

Hannah's eyes widened in surprise. "I don't know anything about that. When we were loaded up, the guys started the cars and we drove off."

Parsons gave her a sympathetic smile. "Is there anything else that happened out there that you can recall, anything at all that might help us find out what happened to her and why?"

She shook her head. "No sir. But if anything else comes to mind, I'll let you know." She stood. "If you're finished with me, I'll be on my way. Next week is finals week and I need to study."

Sheriff Parsons rose slowly and moved around the corner

Jim Moore

of his desk. "Thank you again for the information. I'm sure it will all be helpful to Sheriff Waddell and the Park County Attorney over in Livingston. "He gestured for her to precede him to the door. "Please remind the others in your group that I'd like to visit with them too."

Outside the jail, Hannah heaved a big sigh before starting the long walk back along Willson Avenue and up the hill to the campus.

CHAPTER THIRTEEN

The county attorney's offices in the Livingston courthouse consisted of a small waiting room at the front, a larger conference room through a doorway to the right and Merrill Hodder's private office directly ahead. At mid-afternoon Hodder looked up from his paperwork when Josh Waddell appeared at the office door. He shoved papers to the side and waved the younger man to a seat.

Josh dropped his western hat on the floor and sank into a wooden chair. "I just got back from Hunter's Hot Springs. Talked some more with Mrs. Stensrud. She is certain nobody but those college kids was at her place on Saturday night. She did a walk through the whole place and found nothing out of order but didn't check the pool itself after the rodeoers left. That's the reason she missed the body until Sunday morning. She's certain the girl was killed by one of the college bunch."

Hodder swiveled his chair and rested his arm on the desk top. "Well, eliminating possibilities is progress." He leaned forward. "I have the pathology report. The icepick penetrated the lower part of the brain—killed her instantly."

"That's what Doc Winters thought at the scene," Waddell said. "That's all they found?"

"All for now. They'll get around to doing a full autopsy soon and let us know if there's anything else."

"I still think that kid, Cass Bruce, is holding back on us. I wish I had more on him, because I think he's guilty."

"Your instincts may be right," Hodder agreed. "Sheriff Parsons called a few minutes ago. He's talked to some of the others who were at the Springs. One girl told him that after they all hurried to the cars, that Bruce fellow hollered that he'd forgot his wallet and went back to the dressing room to get it. Another one of the group, a girl, said Summer Hetherington was slow getting dressed and was alone in the dressing room after the others left." He watched Waddell's face change as the information sunk in. "That's right. Bruce went back for his wallet. She was there. No one else was around. It seems he alone had opportunity to do the deed."

Waddell smiled. "Now all we have to do is find out his motive. What was his relationship to that girl?"

The county attorney relaxed back into his chair. "Already got that. The same girl who told about the wallet indicated that Miss Hetherington and Cass Bruce were going steady. Another one said she couldn't say they weren't." He smiled a wide smile. "Sheriff Parsons has been a big help. He may learn more as others who were there talk to him."

Waddell joined in the smile. "I don't suppose you've got any other helpful information for me."

"Not yet." The smile disappeared. "Parsons said the dead

girl's parents will arrive in Bozeman this evening. Her mother will want to pick up her daughter's belongings right away. We can't let her have them, of course, until we've thoroughly gone through them looking for evidence." Hodder heaved a sigh. "God, I hate these after-the-crime conversations with the relatives. They're hurt and unreasonable." He looked across at the younger man. "They'll probably be back here tomorrow. You'd better be ready for snarling and crying." After a pause, he added, "It might be a good idea to call Sheriff Parsons again. Find out if another one of the rodeo group may have been to his office by now." He squinted his eyes in thought. "And ask him to get Cass Bruce to his office again. You two sheriffs need to ask more questions of that fellow."

CHAPTER FOURTEEN

Cass arrived at a quarter to eleven in the morning to find both sheriffs waiting, Parsons in his chair behind the desk, Waddell seated in one of the wooden chairs off to the side. The Gallatin County Sheriff half stood and gestured for Cass to take the other chair facing the desk. Waddell didn't move.

When Cass was settled, he said, "All right, I'm here. What now?"

Waddell answered in a voice even more brusque than in the past. "We've learned some things about the happenings out at Hunter's Hot Springs since we saw you last."

The college student turned to him. "Like what?"

"Like you forgot your wallet and went back to get it. At a time when there was no one else in the pool but you and the girl who was murdered."

Cass cocked his head to the side as a quizzical look passed over his face. Then he nodded. "Now that you mention it, I remember. The wallet fell out of my jean's pocket as I was dressing. I laid it on a shelf in the men's dressing room and then forgot it when I finished putting on my Wranglers. I remembered when I didn't feel it against my hip when I sat in the car, so I went back to get it." He faced the Park County Sheriff. "But I was in the men's dressing room. I didn't see Summer. She could have been in the girl's room, I suppose. I sure as hell didn't kill her, if that's what you're implying."

Abel Parsons spoke in his soft voice. "We're not implying anything, son. We're just trying to learn what happened out there last Saturday night. I'm sure you can understand."

Cass swiveled to face Parsons. "Yes, Sheriff, I understand. But every question I've been asked makes me believe you've focused your investigation on me."

Waddell leaned forward. "Well, there's a reason. You seem to be the only one who was alone with the girl before her death. What we want to know is why?"

"I wasn't with her. I never saw her."

Parsons peered at Cass and spoke softly again. "Just tell us more about your relationship with her. Did you two have a fight? Did she want to break up with you?"

"What do you mean? We were never going together, so how could we break up?"

Waddell said, "You can say you weren't going steady but we've heard from others that you were. It seems to be common knowledge among your friends."

"What friends?"

"More than one has told us so." Parsons puffed out a small sigh. "Look, son, it appears that you had the means, an icepick. You had the opportunity, you were the only one in the pool area when she was killed."

Cass was on his feet. "Listen, I didn't kill her. And I'm done here." He turned for the door.

Parsons stopped him. "Do you know how to fly an airplane?"

Cass turned back to face him. "Yes, why?"

"Did you take that girl for airplane rides?"

The young man's frown deepened. "I took Summer flying once. So what?"

Parsons cocked his head. "Just asking, that's all."

Cass cast his angry glance from one sheriff to the other before turning again. "You two've made up your minds. Don't call me again. If you want anything else from me, call my Dad. His name is Spencer Bruce. He's a lawyer in Harlo." He stomped out of the office and onto the street.

Inside, Waddell looked at Parsons with a wry smile. "He's guilty as hell!"

An hour later Cass called his father. "Dad, they've made up their minds. They're convinced I killed Summer. What shall I do?"

Spencer didn't hesitate. "Come home."

"I have finals all week. Will after that be soon enough?"

"It will do. They won't do anything right away." Spencer's tone softened. "There has to be a solution to all of this, son, a way to convince the sheriffs that you had nothing to do with that girl's death. We'll figure it out."

"Thanks, Dad. I've been scared to death."

"Don't worry, Cassius. Come home as soon as you can and we'll figure this out." After a pause, Spencer added,

"They must be bluffing unless they have something on you that they aren't telling. Even if they think you were dating, that's not a motive. They won't proceed without that."

CHAPTER FIFTEEN

Sheriff Waddell eased into a chair before the county attorney's desk. "Cass Bruce admitted that he returned to the dressing room for his wallet when the Hetherington girl was still there. He denies that they were going steady, but admitted he escorted her to movies and took her flying." Waddell added, "He said his father's a lawyer—kind of like he was challenging us to charge him."

"Father's a lawyer?" The county attorney squinted an eye as he ran faces through his mind. "Yes! Of course. Spencer Bruce. I've met him at bar meetings. Has a good reputation."

The sheriff cocked his head. "A reputation too good for you to want to take him on in a trial?"

Hodder grinned and shook his head. "No, of course not. It's unlikely that his father would defend him anyway. No reputable lawyer would do it." Hodder straightened. "You've told me Mrs. Stensrud is certain there was no one else in the building that night. Couldn't someone have sneaked in?"

"She swears that no one could or did."

"All right, let's see what we've got." Hodder pulled down a finger. "We have the means —the icepick." Another finger. "We can only speculate at the motive—a lover's quarrel of some kind." A third finger. "We have the opportunity; he was in the dressing room alone with her." He pursed his lips in thought. "The last is the most important. It would be difficult, for any defense attorney to overcome that fact. It seems all the others will say she was alive when they left the dressing room. Only Cassius Bruce was in the building after that. She was dead the next time anyone looked."

He nodded his head once as though reaching a conclusion. "There seems to be no way around it. He has to be the murderer"

Waddell smiled a smug smile. "Then charge him. And do it soon so I can arrest him before he leaves Bozeman. I'd rather not have to travel all the way to Wheatland County to do it."

Hodder shook his head. "There's no big hurry, Josh. It's more important to do this right than it is to do it fast. Keep asking questions. Someone is bound to slip and give us the motive, if he did it. We need to compile a list of witnesses and prepare a summary of the testimony we expect from each of them." After another brief pause, he looked sharply at the sheriff. "The icepick. Where'd the icepick come from?"

"Mrs. Stensrud said the kids asked for ice to cool their beer. She gave them a chunk in a bucket with an icepick."

"Where's the icepick now?"

"It was still stuck in the girl's throat when Doc Winters had the boys load her in the ambulance. It must be with the clothes she was wearing, maybe still in Butte"

"See if Doc's gotten that stuff from the pathologist. If so, get it into your evidence locker. If he doesn't have it, get in touch with the pathologist in Butte, and get all of the girl's clothing and things. Get that icepick. Remember Josh, chain of custody, always the chain of custody. Get a receipt. We need to find out if there are finger prints on the pick. Probably not but we need to know." After a pause, he asked. "Have you gone through her belongings.

"Not yet, I haven't had a chance," Waddell sounded defensive when he added. "I don't know how I'm expected to get everything done."

"Bring them here, and I'll help you. We might find a motive in her notebooks. Maybe she kept a diary."

CHAPTER SIXTEEN

Later that afternoon Abel Parsons quietly escorted Summer Hetherington's parents to his office. After holding a chair for a red-eyed Mrs. Hetherington, who settled slowly into it, he moved around the desk to his accustomed place. Leaning toward the two, he began. "I want you both to know how sorry I am about your daughter. I understand that she was a very fine person. I'm certain you were proud of her."

Ephram Hetherington, tall and skeletal, answered. "Summer is our only child. She's everything to us." He made a choking sound. "Or *was* everything to us." Mrs. Hetherington began to whimper and Ephram patted her knee.

Parsons drew a breath and began. "Well, it's my duty to tell you the things we've learned so far." He looked from one to the other. "Your daughter was found lifeless in the pool at Hunter's Hot Springs near Springdale after coming there with eight other members of the college rodeo team."

The mother dabbed her eyes with a handkerchief, head down. The father, stoic and sober, said nothing.

"This is difficult for me to tell you but I must," the sheriff said. "An icepick had been thrust up under her chin. It appears she died instantly."

Small sobs shook Sue Hetherington's body. Her husband dropped to one knee and pulled her as close as the chair allowed. Parsons watched in silence until the sobs became a whimper and finally came to an end. Ephram Hetherington squeezed his wife's shoulders before returning to his chair and asking the question that Parsons knew would come and hated to answer. "When can we see her and take her home?"

"Because this appears to be a homicide, it was necessary to have an autopsy performed. The pathologist is in Butte so your daughter was sent there. I don't know when the pathologist will complete his work and release the body."

Mrs. Hetherington seemed to crumple and began crying again. Hetherington rested his hand on his wife's knee. Facing the sheriff, he asked, "What about her belongings? Can we pick them up at the sorority house?"

"I hate to have to tell you these things, but with a criminal investigation going on, her belongings are now being held as possible evidence. I believe the sheriff and county attorney of Park County will release them just as soon as they can."

"Why are those people involved? I thought you were handling this?"

"Hunter's Hot Springs is in Park County. I've just been helping with the investigation."

Ephram Hetherington pushed forward in the chair. "So

there's nothing we can do but wait? Good God, man, it's our daughter you're talking about. I can understand the need for an autopsy, although the thought of it makes me sick. But we should have a right to her belongings."

"Your feelings are understandable." Parsons stood. "I'll call Sheriff Waddell, tell him you're here and make arrangements for you to meet with him and the county attorney tomorrow. Where will you spend the night?"

"At a motel, I guess. Can you recommend one?"

"The one at the corner of Main Street and Eighth Avenue is clean and respectable."

"We'll go there. We'll stop here in the morning so you can tell us how to find the Park County Sheriff." He stood and put out a hand. "Thank you for asking the sheriff in our county to tell us about our daughter. Hard as it was for us, it was better than hearing it from a stranger."

In Livingston the following morning, Sheriff Waddell walked with the Hetheringtons to the county attorney's office. When they were seated, Merrill Hodder began with the words Summer's parents would hear all too often. "I'm terribly sorry about your daughter. I know she was precious to you."

Ephram Hetherington, grim faced, responded. "She was. More than any words can tell." He stopped and squinted at Hodder. "We're here to find out when we can take her home."

"The pathologist will release the body as soon as the autopsy is completed. I can help make arrangements to have it sent to Roundup, if you want."

Sue Hetherington began to weep. Her husband stroked her arm before turning back to the county attorney. "I hope

Jim Moore

you will. We've had no experience with this kind of thing."

"I'll call Butte after we're finished here. What else can I help you with?"

Hetherington barked, "You can tell us who did this thing and how soon he can be tried and convicted."

Hodder, startled by the vehemence in the man's voice, pulled back slightly, but spoke calmly. "We have a suspect. He's one of the college rodeo team, but the information we have right now isn't adequate to justify the filing of charges."

"Well, when will you be able to do it?"

"I can't tell you that." He leaned forward for emphasis. "I'm as anxious as you are to find the one who did it, but before we charge anyone, we must be certain we have the evidence needed to convict him and send him away for life."

Hetherington scowled. "I want the bastard hung, and I want to watch when they do it."

CHAPTER SEVENTEEN

On the following Monday, there was much chatter about the death of Summer Hetherington. Some acquaintances knew that Cass was a member of the rodeo team. A few of them posed questions to him. His reluctance to speak of it soon brought the questions to an end. The same was true on Tuesday.

The Bozeman Daily Chronicle briefly reported the death of a student coed in its Monday edition. The Tuesday edition added little to it. On Wednesday, a front-page headline blared *Student Suspect in Killing.* The accompanying article described in detail the events that led up to the death of the Summer Hetherington. It named the nine rodeo contestants who were at Hunter's Hot Springs and hinted that one of them had to be the murderer. By midmorning the word on the campus was that Cass Bruce may have had something to do with the girl's death, and soon it seemed to be the consensus that he was the killer. The effect of the gossip was immediate. Talk ceased whenever Cass approached a group. People were polite but didn't seem anxious to spend time in his presence.

Cass blamed the newspaper for printing what must only be a rumor.

By Thursday things were even worse.

Cass wandered from the Ag Building up the hill to the Student Union to spend the hour before his next test studying in the lounge. The first three students he met along the walkway were remote acquaintances who shifted their eyes as he approached.

There were several students, men and women, in the lounge when he walked in. Most had their heads down while scanning books and making notes on tablets. None of them acknowledged his entry. He found an empty easy chair, settled into it and began his own study routine. Once he looked up from his work to see a short chubby fellow and an even shorter girl approach. Their eyes suddenly focused on him. The man pointed a finger at Cass as he whispered something to her. Her eyes widened. When they realized Cass was watching them, they scurried on by.

On the walk back to the Ag building, another acquaintance crossed the lawn to avoid speaking to him. Something was different. He learned the reason when he met Harry Croswell at the doorway.

Harry grabbed his shirtsleeve to stop him. "April Menard told the sheriff that you went back into the Hunter's Hot Springs dressing room after everyone else but Summer was out of there. Made it sound like you had the opportunity to kill her."

"So that's how they found out."

"Who?"

"Those two sheriffs. They called me in again, and I talked to them some more. They asked me if that's what happened. I agreed that I went back to the dressing room to get my wallet, because I did. But Summer wasn't in the pool area. I never saw her."

"So you already know. Anyway, it's the word around the campus that the sheriffs have decided you're the one who did Summer in."

Cass scowled at his friend. "You believe that? That I'd kill Summer? That I could kill anyone?"

Harry let go of the shirtsleeve. "No, I don't. I know you couldn't kill anyone, much less Summer. But the word's out."

"I can't believe it." Cass looked off into the distance for an instant. "Now I understand the strange looks I've been getting. Everyone thinks I'm a murderer."

Harry shook his head. "Not everyone. Not me. But there are plenty who're quick to believe every rumor."

Cass grabbed Harry's hand. "Thanks for telling me what April did. And for believing me. I'm glad you feel that way."

It was difficult to focus. He arrived in the classroom early and took his usual seat near the front. Others straggled in, noted where he was and chose seats in another row. Two graduating seniors with whom he'd shared classrooms through most of his time in college passed down the aisle without acknowledging him. When the bell signaled the end of the hour, he handed in his test and headed for the door. Three who had finished before the rest, were visiting in the hallway. As he came through the door, they moved a few feet

Jim Moore

away so that he didn't pass too closely.

Cass Bruce had become a pariah on the Montana State College campus. He stood in deep thought for a long minute near the corner of the administration building. At last he inhaled deeply and blew out a long sigh. Time to get home as his father suggested. But first, do something about his college education.

Jefferson Little, Dean of Agriculture, was well liked and approachable. His attention was fully focused on Cass as the young man spoke. "You must know by now that many on the campus believe I murdered Summer Hetherington at Hunter's Hot Springs" The Dean nodded and Cass continued, "Sir, I don't want to stay here and face the kind of looks I'm getting wherever I go. And I don't want to watch people whispering and pointing fingers at me."

The dean had a soft voice. "What are you suggesting?"

"I'm to graduate Saturday, but I still have one final exam. I want to skip both the final and the graduation ceremony. Get my degree in absentia."

Little leaned back in his chair. "Have you talked to your professor about skipping the final? Will he give you passing grades anyway?"

"He should. My grades have been good all quarter." Cass paused to frame the words. "But, sir, it's Professor Jamison from range management. He's not easy to talk with. Has a tendency to brush off his students' concerns."

"He does have that reputation." Dean Little turned in the chair to stretch his legs. "What do you want from me?"

Cass leaned forward. "I hope you'll encourage him to give me a passing grade without the final exam. That's all I need from him." He stopped, inhaled, and then continued. "And I need your agreement to let me get my degree in absentia."

A small smile appeared on the dean's lips. "Why would I do those things?"

"With all due respect, sir, you should do them because handing a degree to an accused murderer isn't the kind of image the Montana State College wants to project."

Now the smile became a chuckle. "You've thought it through, haven't you?" He wiped a hand across the desktop. "And you're right about the image. I've been wondering how to handle the situation. Now you've solved the problem for me." He rose from his chair. "Forget the final. I'll take care of Jamison. And you needn't appear at the graduation ceremony."

Chapter Eighteen

L ate on that pleasant warm day. Cass, having carried the last of his belongings from his basement room, was stuffing them in the back seat of his auto when Hannah Dodson—all five feet three inches of her—appeared by its door. Surprise at her appearance caused him back up a step. A frown crossed his face. "You shouldn't be here."

She cocked her head to ask, "Why shouldn't I be here?"

"Everyone thinks I'm a murderer. You should stay as far away from me as you can."

Hannah shook her head. "I don't think you're a murderer, Cass. And neither does anyone who knows you." She thrust her hands in her skirt pockets and shrugged. "Don't let all the idle gossip bother you. Those who gossip don't count." Hannah nodded toward the trunk full of bags, boxes, loose shoes and boots and the canvas bag. "You can't be packing to leave. You have graduation Saturday."

"That's exactly what I'm doing—leaving. As soon as I

finish cleaning out my room I'm going home."

Looking up at him, she asked, "What about graduation? Will you be back for your degree?"

Cass shook his head. "No. I've already made arrangements with the dean to get the degree in absentia." He looked at Hannah's upturned face. "Everyone on campus seems certain I killed Summer. I can't stand the looks, the whispers, the kind of treatment I've been getting. It just doesn't make sense to stay here. Dean Little agreed. I think he was relieved that I won't be around to create a problem. He and the president won't have to worry about some scene they might have on their hands if a murderer crossed the stage."

Hannah dropped her gaze and then looked up again at Cass. "You may be right." She turned to stare off into the distance for a second. "I need to haul Summer's barrel horse back to her parents' place. I'm not looking forward to a conversation with them, but the horse can't stay here."

"Yeah, I don't envy you. Summer's parents must be going through hell."

"You know about the rodeo at Bridger this weekend?" Hanna asked. "It's an RCA show. Some of the champions will probably be there, the Lindermans, Bud and Bill, if no others. You've said you like to compete with the best. Since you're not staying for graduation, will you go?"

"I think I will. I don't care about the champions. They don't know who I am and wouldn't care if they did. There shouldn't be anyone there who's heard about Summer. No one to look at me like I'm a murderer."

Hannah smiled. "Good. I'll be there too." She turned

Jim Moore

away and took a couple of steps back toward the campus. Over her shoulder she added, "It'll all work out, Cass. Those sheriffs will find the real killer. Then you can laugh in the faces of the people who didn't believe in you."

Of all his friends on the campus, Cass felt the most comfortable with Hannah. Their conversations were easy, probably because they enjoyed many of the same things. They had rodeo in common, of course. But there were other things: the top ten tunes on The Hit Parade, the latest corny jokes, and even the creative arts. They'd gone together to a couple of exhibits at the campus art school and had fun critiquing the various students' offerings.

Cass watched as Hannah, who wore a light blouse and a dark colored skirt, strode southward and around a corner. She was tiny of stature. Her hair was the color of polished copper and curly beyond control. When she smiled the freckles that covered her face seemed to grow in size. And she smiled often, a smile that reflected her radiant personality. She wasn't beautiful in the classic sense, but she was nice to look at. Cass had long ago decided that "cute" was the best word to describe her.

As he finished cramming his belongings into the trunk, he thought about not being here at Montana State next year. But he should see Hannah at rodeos from time to time. He hoped so.

Chapter Nineteen

Friday morning, the residue from the morning meal was stacked on a counter next to the sink. Cass and his parents sat around the kitchen table, each with a coffee cup. His father smiled as he said, "All right, Cass, tell us all about it."

The young man pursed his lips "All right. Here it is. The two sheriffs, one from Park County and the other from Gallatin County, seem to believe I murdered Summer." He went over the details of the fateful night at Hunter's Hot Springs. When he got to the part about leaving Summer behind, he stopped, swallowed hard, and blinked back a tear before continuing his monologue.

When he finished, Spencer asked. "What evidence do they have to implicate you?"

"They have me going back to get my wallet. That seems to put me alone with Summer. There were three guys in my car. When I came back from getting my wallet, I asked if

Summer was coming. One of them said the girls all got in Justin's car, which was pulling out, so I started the car and drove away."

"And you explained that to the Sheriffs?

"Yes, but apparently they don't believe anything I say." Cass thought for a moment. "Oh, yes. Sheriff Parsons asked if I know how to fly. I told him I do and that I took Summer for an airplane ride once. He seemed to think that meant something."

Spencer straightened his back. "Is that all?"

"That's all they told me."

"Doesn't seem to be enough to bring charges." He paused for a moment. "But they may have information they didn't share with you." He faced Cass directly. "If that's the case, son, they may charge you with the killing."

The young man's face showed the anguish he'd been suffering. "Good God, Dad." He quickly asked, "You'll defend me, won't you?"

Before Spencer could respond, Eunice spoke in a voice that boded no argument. "That wouldn't be a good idea." She raised a hand, palm out. "Before this goes any further, we need to involve Merci." She gestured toward the kitchen where the telephone was located. "Spencer, you and your sister have always discussed difficult family matters. Call right now. Tell her what's happened." She turned to her son. "Your aunt has good judgment. She'll help us make the right decisions."

Spencer hurried to make the call. The others heard him in a brief conversation before he placed the phone on the counter and called to Cass, "Merc wants to hear it from you."

Cass hurried to the phone. "Hi Auntie. It looks like I'm in big trouble this time."

"Indeed, it does." He heard the rustling of paper. "I'm really busy all day today. Could you come to my office in Billings tomorrow? I'd like to discuss this with you in person. And, if you don't mind, I may ask another lawyer from this office to join us."

"Of course, I can be there." He paused "There's an RCA rodeo at Bridger this weekend. I'd planned on going to it."

"Tomorrow's Saturday. We'll visit early and then you can be on your way to Bridger. You'll be better off at the rodeo than brooding there in Harlo."

"You're probably right. What time shall I be at your office?"

"Say nine o'clock. Then we can get you on your way." Merci paused. "Now let me talk to your dad again. I'll explain my thinking to him."

Cass handed the phone to his father and returned to sit with his mother. For the first time since the earliest conversation with the sheriffs he felt some relief. Merci's voice let him believe that someone would know how to get him out from under the threat of an arrest so his life could return to normal.

Spencer placed the phone in its cradle and joined the others. He smiled as he spoke of his sister. "Merci's giving orders as usual." To Eunice he added, "You're not to fret if Cass goes to a rodeo in Bridger. A rodeo will do him good, according to Merc." The smile widened. "And I'm not to occupy my mind trying to plan a defense to a charge that hasn't been—and may never be—filed."

Chapter Twenty

Merci replaced the phone and leaned back in her chair, hands folded together and resting on her midriff. It had, by habit, become her posture while contemplating difficult questions. From the things she was told, there seemed little actual evidence that her nephew had committed a crime. The things Cass said, even if it could even be called evidence, were too scanty to create a genuine concern. However more compelling evidence about which Cass had no knowledge may exist. No matter, the situation was of enough consequence that someone with extensive trial experience should be involved. As far as Merci was concerned, that someone was Geoffrey Myklebust.

Her thoughts flowed back to the beginnings of her career as a lawyer. First, she'd practiced with her brother, Spencer, in Harlowton. But the town was small, and it soon became evident that the practice wasn't large enough to require the talents of both of them. So, she opened a tiny street corner office in Billings, just herself and a secretary. Merci was the only woman lawyer in town.

At first clients didn't flock to her door. Then she sued a doctor on behalf of a woman whose surgery the doctor had botched and secured a handsome settlement. The word of her success spread. Clients appeared, sometimes with claims of injury to their bodies by others, either deliberately or negligently or damage to their financial situation, all caused by other people. She chose to represent only the ones whose claims were legitimate and compensable. She was successful.

Soon Merci found herself treated with seriousness in the Billings legal community. One day, Geoffrey Myklebust, senior partner of the largest law firm in town, invited her to lunch. She had only met him one time and only then for a brief handshake. So why the invitation? She thought perhaps he was just curious about a woman who dared to practice a profession that most men believed should be theirs alone. For their noonday gathering, she dressed in her professional best.

Myklebust was waiting when she arrived at the door to the dining room of the Highlands Golf Club and stood to meet her as she was escorted to the table. He was over six feet tall and square of shoulder. She knew him to be sixty-one years of age, but his freshly shaven and sculpted face belied the age. His hair, carefully combed and parted far down on the left side, was gunmetal gray. His gray suit was impeccably tailored. A maroon tie complemented it perfectly. He was the picture of a successful professional. Myklebust offered the barest hint of a smile as he reached out a hand and said, "It's nice to see you again, Miss Bruce." His grip

Jim Moore

was firm and his voice, commanding. He pulled a chair from the table and held it for her before seating himself.

The initial conversation about current and professional events was genial. The meal, once served, was eaten in comparative silence. All the while Merci wondered what the purpose of the meeting might be. She found out as they sipped after meal coffee. Myklebust placed his cup carefully on the saucer, raised his eyes and said. "Miss Bruce, your ability as a lawyer has not gone unnoticed at Herman and Myklebust, so I'll get right to it." The man leaned forward. "I'm here to ask if you will join our firm as a full partner, with full benefits."

It took Merci a stunned moment to understand what was being offered. To receive an invitation to join that law firm was unusual. To be offered a full partnership was unheard of. She collected herself, moved her gaze from Myklebust to her coffee cup and back. Offering her most gracious smile, she said, "As you can guess, sir, I'm flattered. Such an offer is totally unexpected."

Myklebust smiled again. "Perhaps. But the offer is genuine. We want you in our firm." When she didn't respond, he leaned back in the chair. "Come with me to our offices. I'll show you the space that will be yours should you decide to join us. We'll provide information about our operations: time requirements, billing, and the manner in which we share the revenues. I'll introduce you to some of the others in the firm. It should help you make your decision."

At the firm's offices, he led Merci about, making comments about office arrangements and taking her from office to office to speak with other lawyers, some of whom she had at least a passing acquaintance.

"We don't need your answer today." Myklebust said as he ushered her to the door. "Give it thought for a few days and then call me."

For seven days she weighed the advantages of an association with other lawyers against the independence she had while practicing alone. She discussed it with her brother. By the end of the seventh day she was no closer to a decision than she had been on the first. Merci was reviewing the deposition of a witness, when the phone ran on the eighth day. She answered to hear Geoffrey Myklebust's smooth voice. "Miss Bruce, my curiosity forces me to make this call and to ask if you've decided to join Herman and Myklebust." He paused. "And, of course, I hope you have."

Without thinking, she blurted out, "Yes, Mr. Myklebust I've decided to accept your very generous offer."

"Wonderful! I can't wait to share the news with others."

It proved to be a good move. She was treated with respect from the beginning and, soon enough, she developed friendships with other lawyers in the firm.

Geoffrey Myklebust was one of the most respected trial lawyers in Montana, and that is exactly what her nephew needed, an excellent trial lawyer. Merci asked his private secretary if her employer could spare a few minutes of his time. That woman smiled at Merci as though she was an innocent asking for a favor from the emperor. Nonetheless, she stepped into the man's office only to return almost immediately with a look of wonder on her face. She waved Merci into a spacious, carefully arranged and tastefully decorated office.

Jim Moore

Myklebust stepped around the desk to grasp her hand. "Miss Bruce, I haven't seen enough of you since you joined us. I understand your practice is blossoming." He led her to a round table away from his desk, held a chair for her, and then settled into another. "You asked to see me. I hope you're not having a problem with something or someone in the office."

"Not at all, sir. I'm here for another reason altogether. It appears that my nephew may be charged with the crime of murder. If so, he'll need the best lawyer he can find." She waited. When he just maintained his intense focus on her, she continued, "He needs you, sir, as his attorney."

Myklebust abruptly leaned back in his chair. When he spoke, his voice was all business. "You must surely know, Miss Bruce, that I haven't tried a criminal case in fifteen years. It would be the next thing to malpractice if I were to do so now. Your nephew needs an experienced defense lawyer."

Merci had anticipated his response and shook her head even as he spoke. "What Cassius needs, sir, is the best trial lawyer. That's you."

He surprised her by showing that hint of a smile. "When all else fails, try flattery. Is that your ploy, Miss Bruce?"

"I'm not offering flattery, sir. Your reputation as an attorney is well known. Both of us know that a criminal trial is, after all, just another trial. Except for a few, the rules are the same as those for a civil trial. Success in a criminal trial, as in a civil trial, lies in the preparation, in knowing the rules, and having the ability to use them to advantage, in having complete knowledge of the facts, and in the preparation and examination of witnesses. All of those are things at which your skills are unmatched."

"You're laying the flattery on awfully thick." Myklebust's smile remained. "All right, what do you want from me?"

"Cassius will be here in my office at nine o'clock in the morning. Would you meet with us, listen to his explanation of the situation? After you hear what he has to say, you can better decide whether or not to represent him."

"Tomorrow is Saturday. What if that's my day on the golf course?"

Merci's face broke into a grin. "I happen to know, sir, that you're here in the office every Saturday morning."

Geoffrey's smile died away. "Why not? It should be interesting to hear your nephew's story."

CHAPTER TWENTY-ONE

Late Friday afternoon, Hannah pulled her pickup and trailer to a stop before the Hetherington house. She'd driven from Bozeman, her trailer loaded with two barrel horses, hers and Summers. Before she could walk to the house to knock on the door, Mrs. Hetherington stepped out onto the stoop.

The many times Hannah had been in that house in the past, Sue Hetherington had been pleasant, energetic, and quick of movement. Now haggard and shrunken, the woman's grief was obvious. She offered no greeting, but stood silent and unmoving except for wiping her hands on a soiled towel.

Hannah shoved her fists into the pockets of her Wranglers, as she walked up the path to the back door. When she stood in front of Summer's mother, she said, "I have Summer's horse in the trailer. Shall I unload him at the corral?"

8 SECONDS

Sue Hetherington's hand wiping stopped. "Might as well. You know where he belongs?"

"Yes. I know where Summer kept him. I'll give him some hay too."

"Please do." Sue turned back to the door saying, "Ephram will have to decide what to do with that animal now."

Hannah was left standing as the wounded woman closed the door quietly behind her.

She muttered to herself as she trudged back down the path to her rig. "That poor lady is really hurting. I hope whoever killed my friend is found. And I hope he's forced to suffer twice as much as Summer's mother."

CHAPTER TWENTY-TWO

The law offices of Herman and Myklebust were on the fourth floor of the Northwestern Bank and Trust building. Saturday morning Cass stopped to read the names painted on the glass next to the doorway. Merci M. Bruce was six down from the top. Cass knew there weren't many women lawyers in Montana. Few had achieved as much as Merci. She ranked in the top ten percent with the national organization that rated lawyers as to capability and professionalism. She was respected throughout the state and was currently the secretary of the Montana Bar Association. Cass was proud of his aunt.

Merci sat behind a huge oaken desk, covered with law books and printed documents. She quickly strode around the desk to wrap her arms around the young man's chest for a long hug. She stepped back to peer at his face. "Well, you don't look any different, despite your latest predicament."

Cass, whose arms had encircled her gently, now dropped

them to his sides. "I may look the same, Auntie, but I don't feel the same."

"Understandable." She looked up at him. "I'm wrong. You don't look the same. Your eyes show your worry. I shouldn't make light of it." Merci pointed to a comfortable chair, one of four around a small table. "Sit. I'll go fetch Mr. Myklebust. Myrtle will bring coffee and donuts. Then we'll talk."

He watched his aunt stride out the door. At fifty years old, she still had the trim figure of her youth. A few fine lines were evident next to her dark brown eyes. Otherwise her face showed little sign of the passage of time. Her cinnamon-colored hair was cut short and worn straight. Today she wore a tan skirt and a tailored jacket over a silken, cream-colored blouse, all set off by a chocolate brown scarf. The picture of professionalism, Merci moved with confidence and grace.

Cass scanned the room. The desk faced away from a large window. Her certificate of admission to the bar hung on the wall to his left. A large framed photograph of a World War I airplane graced another wall. On the credenza, a picture, taken years ago, showed Merci with her brother, Spencer, his wife Eunice, and their two small sons, Thad and Cass.

Cass stood as Merci reentered the room, followed by a tall man who bore the look of poised professionalism.

Geoffrey Myklebust offered a wisp of a smile and shook Cass's hand. "It's nice to meet you. Although, from the things your aunt has told me, I wish it were for a better reason."

"So do I, sir."

When all were seated around the table in the corner, Geoff turned to Merci with an expectant look.

She leaned toward her nephew. "I've asked Geoff to join us because of his experience in the law and because I trust his judgment. I hope that meets with your approval."

"Of course, it does." Cass turned again to the older man. "I appreciate that you're willing to take the time."

"All right, then. Let's get right to it. Begin by telling what leads you to believe you may be charged with a crime?"

Cass looked down at his hands to find that he'd been rubbing them together. He said, "It all seems unreal, like I've had a bad dream." He raised his eyes to look from Merci to Geoffrey. "But it isn't, so here goes." He told of his first meeting with the two sheriffs at the rodeo ground and later meetings where he learned of the death of Summer Hetherington. At last he said. "It's clear to me that they believe I murdered Summer and it's only a matter of time until they'll charge me." Cass slumped farther into the chair.

Geoff asked, "Could there have been someone at the hot springs that you didn't see?"

"Not at the pool. It's wide open with no place to hide."

"How have you gotten along with the others who were at there with you that night?"

"I like them all. And I believe they like me." Cass looked sharply at the lawyer. "I don't believe any of them would have killed Summer." He shook his head. "It appears to the sheriffs that I was the only one who was alone with her, the only one who could have killed her."

"You've mentioned nine people who were there. I take it that those nine comprise the rodeo club, the group of Montana State students who are interested in rodeo. Am I correct?"

"There are several more who have some interest in rodeo and belong to the club but those nine of us are the ones who actually compete." Cass hesitated. "Well, one of the nine that I mentioned doesn't. That's April Menard. She's Justin Madden's girlfriend. There's one person who competes with us who didn't go to the hot springs. That's Wayne Foley."

Geoff asked, "This fellow Foley's part of the group? But he wasn't with you at the hot springs?"

"Right. He and his girlfriend, Doris Hamilton, were there when we talked about it after the Saturday performance, so they knew we were going for a swim. We agreed to gather for the trip at the SUB parking lot, but he didn't show up."

Merci asked, "Was there a reason for that?"

"I guess Doris didn't want to go."

"Was that unusual?

Cass shrugged. "Wayne used to do everything with us. That changed some after he got together with Doris."

"What can you tell us about him?"

Cass thought a second. "He lives on a ranch his family owns on the East Boulder River near Roscoe. Their main home is on the east coast. They're old money. His parents and older sister visit the ranch several times a year. Wayne spent the summers of his high school years on the ranch." He paused. "According to Wayne, he learned calf roping from a ranch hand. After winning some junior rodeo contests, he was hooked. He enrolled at Montana State, even though his family wanted him to go to Harvard." Cass frowned. "Now he has a girlfriend who's really demanding. She probably had something else for him to do that evening."

Merci had been taking notes. She raised her eyes to ask,

"What about the girlfriend? Does she rodeo too? Barrel race?"

"No, the Hamiltons have a general store in Red Lodge. I heard she met Wayne when she worked as a housemaid at the Foley ranch. She got a scholarship to attend Montana State and just finished her sophomore year." Cass turned from Merci to Geoffrey. "Some think the only reason she came to MSU was to catch Wayne Foley."

Geoff asked, "Will she catch him?"

"She already has. He gave her a ring at Christmas. I guess a huge wedding is planned for late summer."

Merci said. "You speak of it in a rather cynical tone."

"I shouldn't. Doris is attractive. She's intelligent and can be charming. She'll make Wayne proud."

"What kind of person is this Wayne Foley?" Geoff asked.

"Wayne's a nice guy. He's smart and personable, has a sense of humor." Cass hesitated. "We all like him. He kind of reminds me of Tyrone Power. He could have the pick of the ladies on campus."

Merci smiled. "Lucky Doris."

Cass nodded. "Yes, lucky her."

Geoff straightened in his chair and launched into a series of questions, not always in a pleasant tone. Cass answered and Geoff went on and on and on until Cass was truly exhausted and began to answer in a peevish manner. The lawyer leaned back in his chair. "I put a little pressure on you to see how you'd react. You handle yourself well. That's good to know if this thing ever comes to a trial."

Cass shook his head. "I watched one of my Dad's trials. I felt sorry for the poor guy he was cross-examining. I hope I never have to go through anything like that."

Merci leaned to put a hand on his forearm. "The first objective is to gather the information needed to assure you are never charged." She looked at her partner. At his nod, she said, "Tell us about the girl, Summer Hetherington. What kind of person was she?"

A soft smile appeared on Cass's face. "Summer? Summer was one of the nicest people you'd ever meet. She always seemed happy and had kind words for everyone." The smile faded as he remembered she was gone. "She was intelligent. Sometimes the big words she used were too much for me and the other rodeo guys. I'm certain she was an honor student. Learning seemed important to her."

Merci asked, "How did she get along with others? Did she ever mention anyone who worried her for any reason?"

"Never. As far as I could tell she got along with everyone."

Geoff asked, "What did she look like?"

"She was lovely, there's no other word that does her justice. Summer was slender but muscular enough to throw a saddle over the back of her horse. Her hair was auburn colored. She wore it long and tied back or braided. Summer's eyes were brown, so brown they sometimes appeared to be black." Cass held a picture of Summer in his mind. "She was ... "he turned to Geoff..."is demure the correct word?" Before the lawyer could answer, he added, "I think it is." He looked from Geoff to Merci. "What else can I tell you?"

Merci looked at Geoff. "OK, let's recapitulate. Summer Hetherington was an exemplary person, one you spent time with. You were not going steady, though the sheriffs want to think you were." She stopped to ask, "Am I right so far?"

"You're right. But when you mention going steady, I have another thought. I've probably spent at least as much time with Hannah Dodson as I did with Summer. And Hannah and I aren't going steady either."

"Well, that's good to know. Will Hannah Dodson confirm that statement if she's asked?"

"I believe she will."

"Good." Merci's quick smile faded. "Then let's continue. The matter of your wallet remains. Your rodeo friends will say you went to the dressing room to get the wallet after everyone but Summer Hetherington had raced to the automobiles. You didn't see her when you picked up the wallet and assumed she was in a car with the others." Merci looked at her nephew. "Is there anything to show that you and that girl were *not* alone together at that time?

"Nothing I know of. I can't think of a thing. There just had to be someone else hiding around there." Cass slumped, his eyes on the floor. When at last he looked up, he begged. "I know why Dad can't represent me. Will you do it, please?"

"Geoff and I have discussed it. My position isn't much different than your father's. In addition, I've never handled a criminal case. That's why I've asked Geoff to take on that responsibility, if you want him to."

Cass turned quickly to her partner. "Will you do that, sir? Represent me, if I'm charged?"

Myklebust spoke earnestly. "It's been years since I tried a criminal case. Nowadays my practice is all civil, and I'm seldom in court. You would be better served by a lawyer whose specialty is criminal law." He paused to let Cass consider. "We can find the best criminal lawyer in Montana and persuade him to represent you."

Cass shook his head. "No. If you're willing, I want you to do it. Merci says you're the best lawyer she knows. I'll feel much more comfortable with you than with someone I never heard of." He waited a second. "Will you do it?"

When the lawyer agreed, Cass asked, "Can't she be involved in some way?" He paused, then added, "No. I suppose not."

Geoff cocked an eyebrow. "Oh yes, she'll be involved. I'm not doing this alone." Turning to Merci, he said, "I'll be the attorney of record, but you will be co-council, handle most of the investigation, prepare documents, and sit at counsel table during the trial—if there is one."

Cass exclaimed, "Wow! That would be great." Then another realization crept into Cass mind. "I haven't the money to cover your fees, but I'm sure my father will take care of it."

Geoff put a hand on Cass's forearm. "Let me discuss that matter with him." He stood and offered a hand.

Cass was on his feet in an instant, grasping the outstretched hand. "It's a relief to know that you'll be looking out for me. I appreciate it more than you can know."

Merci put a hand on his arm. "Now, you've got a rodeo to get to. Try not to worry. Have fun, and win a lot of money."

Cass smiled. "I'll try to do both."

CHAPTER TWENTY-THREE

At ten thirty, Cass stopped at the rodeo office, an otherwise empty storefront, to enter the bareback bronc and the saddle bronc contests. It gave him some comfort that his name meant nothing to the woman at the sign-up desk, and no one in the room gave him a second glance. Maybe news of the death of Summer Hetherington and his connection to it hadn't reached Bridger, Montana.

The day was warm and pleasant as he stepped out the door just in time to find the first of the rodeo parade passing by. Two locals on palomino horses carried the United States and Montana flags. Cass, like all of the other veterans of the recent war, doffed his hat until the flags were well past. The rest of the parade consisted of the king and queen of the rodeo riding in a top-down Cadillac convertible, folks on horseback, politicians waving to the crowd, homemade floats, the high school band, and lots of children wearing western clothing.

Cass watched to the end before turning toward a small café called, "The Lunch Bucket." He'd get something to eat, before the noon hour and the eating places filled up.

The Lunch Bucket was already filled. Several people stood near the door waiting for a table. He gave his name and stepped to wait. Lost in thought, he jumped when a hand touched his arm. Hannah Dodson smiled up at him.

"My parents are here with me, Cass. We have room at our table. Will you join us?"

Still flustered by her sudden appearance, he stumbled with the answer. "Why, uh, yes. Kind of you to ask."

She led him on a wending path through a room crowded with tables. A tall man of late middle age stood as they approached. He was broad chested, with the physique of an athlete that had softened with the passage of time. His thick gray hair showed hints of a once reddish hue. He put out a hand. "I'm Forrest, Hannah's father." He gestured toward the woman seated near him. "And this is my wife, Lillian."

Cass grasped the man's hand. "As Hannah must have told you, I'm Cass Bruce."

"Yup. She's mentioned you." He gestured to a chair across the table. "We haven't ordered yet, so you're just in time."

Before holding the chair for Hannah, Cass turned to her mother. "Hannah and I've known each other for some time. It's nice to meet her parents."

Hannah's mother nodded. "We can put a face to your name now."

A waitress bustled up and asked, "Ready?"

Mrs. Dodson ordered soup and salad. Hannah asked for a

Jim Moore

hamburger with fries and a coke. The waitress turned to Cass who gestured for Forrest to order. The rancher handed the waitress his menu. "Hamburger steak and mashed potatoes. Coffee." After a second he added, "Please."

Cass passed the menu saying, "I'll have what Mr. Dodson's having." The waitress snatched the menus and scurried away.

Cass restarted the conversation. "Hannah told me you have a yearling operation."

Every cattleman likes to tell about his ranch. Dodson leaned forward, elbows on the table. "Yes. I ran the usual cow, calf outfit until a few years ago. But we don't raise much, if any, hay. So we always had to buy enough to feed the cows through the winter months. And we had to hire help, at least during the busiest times. Finally, it seemed logical to dump the cows, buy yearling steers in the late winter and early spring, run them through the summer and market them in the fall. We've been able to get good gains on them each year and we've been lucky with the marketing. The yearlings have worked out really well for us."

"What if you get hit with a bad spring storm?"

"I buy twenty tons of baled hay from a neighbor each fall. If I need it, I can feed it. If not, he buys it back in the spring—at a reduced price, of course. We've been at it for eight years."

Lillian Dodson spoke up. "Forrest's a lot happier with the yearlings. He never liked the plowing and planting and hay-making part of ranching. Just likes to work with the animals." She glanced at her husband and turned back to Cass. "He grumbles a little, though, if he gets caught in a snow or rain

92

storm on horseback a long way from the buildings."

"Do you help him with the horseback work?"

"Sometimes, but not often. I've a big garden, and I try to keep the house, yard, and the other buildings looking good. I want anyone who drives up to the place to understand that we take pride in our belongings."

Hannah added, "Mom's kind of a fussbudget that way. Dad and I try to do our share to keep things tidy."

Before more could be said the food arrived and the conversation quieted as each of them attacked the meal.

When finished, Forrest said, "I understand you spend your summers on your grandfather's ranch near Two Dot."

"That's right. I like the ranch so I get out there as soon as school finishes each year."

"You must know how to work cattle."

Cass laughed. "I like to think I do. It's a cow and calf operation but the offspring are sold as yearlings in the fall. So we nursemaid the cows as they calve in the spring and move cattle from pasture to pasture throughout the rest of the year. I've put in lots of time on horseback. Done the other ranch jobs too—irrigating, haying, and feeding."

"You like that kind of work?"

"I like the work with the cattle best."

The food finished and dishes pushed aside, Hannah said. "My parents know about Summer, of course. They know the law officers think you had something to do with her death. I told them about the problem that's caused for you."

Cass, caught off guard by the remarks, looked from Hannah to Lillian and then to Forrest. He asked, "So, do you want me to stay away from your daughter?"

For a moment, Forrest seemed taken aback, and then he said, "Not at all. Hannah's always said nice things about you, even before this all happened. She insists you're just not capable of killing anyone. We trust her judgment."

Cass turned to Hannah seated in the chair next to him. "It's nice of you to say good things about me, especially right now. There haven't been many who do." He looked from one to another of the Dodson family. "People I've known since I was a child turn away when we pass on the street." He shook his head. "It's hard to take. I'd like to go somewhere far from home. I'll have a degree in business and might get a job with some agricultural company but that process takes time."

Forrest cocked his head. "Every rancher in Montana knows the Bruce outfit—one of the oldest in the state that's still in one family. There must be plenty for you to do there."

"I always assumed that's where I'd end up, but my brother, Thad, graduated a couple of years ago, got married and has been on the ranch ever since. Grandpa spends much of his time caring for Grandma Felicity, so Thad has kind of taken charge of things. He talks with Grandpa, then he gets the ranch hands lined out. He works with them most of the time. He handles most of the business matters too. He doesn't need or want me there." Cass paused for a second. "A couple of years ago I wanted to run the rodeo circuit, see if I could compete with the professionals. Mom insisted I get a college degree. She was right, of course."

Forrest waited for him to go on, so he continued. "I don't want to go to the ranch and mess things up for Thad. Last night I thought of looking for a riding job on a ranch in Wyoming."

94

Hannah interrupted. "It's time to get to the rodeo."

Forrest was quick to grab the check and insisted on paying the full tab despite Cass's protests. On the street, Cass touched Hannah lightly on her upper arm. "I'll be watching you run the barrels. I'll bet you blow the other girls away."

Hannah's smile was a bright as the sun. "Let's hope so."

Dust stirred up by the animals and the crowd greeted Cass as he approached the rodeo arena. He parked his auto in the space reserved for contestants and opened the trunk to extract his gear—saddle, bareback rig, buck rein, chaps and wool pad. It took two trips to move it all to a spot near the bucking chutes. He checked the list tacked to a post near the gate and learned that he'd drawn bareback horse number eight. He walked the length of the chutes checking numbers on the horses. None of those who were busy preparing for the day's performance paid any attention to him.

He spotted Zeke Howard talking with another rider on the other side of the fence and behind the chutes. When that conversation ended, Howard turned and caught Cass's eye. He muttered, "Cass," and strode to the other end of the corral.

Cass was dumbfounded. He and Zeke Howard had rodeoed together, eaten together, even shared a motel room on one occasion. He'd always thought of his fellow rodeo contestant as a friend. That behavior was difficult to understand unless Zeke believed Cass had killed Summer.

He began to notice furtive glances and muttered words being passed among those around the bucking chutes. It didn't take long to figure it out. The Billings Gazette, like every other major newspaper in the state, had reported the killing of the Montana State College coed. Nearly everyone at the rodeo read the Gazette each day. To add to the Gazette articles, someone, maybe Howard, had spread the word that Cass Bruce was the only suspect in the murder.

There was nothing to do but ignore those around him and rig his horse with the assistance of a chute hand, who was obligated to provide the help—even to an accused murderer. When his name was called, he would put on the best ride he could. He went through the usual routine—assure the bareback rig was cinched firmly in place, check the horse's mane for snags, and wait for his turn out of the chute. When it came, the horse kicked high behind but bucked in a straight line, not showy enough for Cass to place as one of the top rides of the day, and he knew it. He gathered his bareback rig and trudged back to his auto, to wait for the saddle broncs.

After a bit he heard the announcer begin to talk about the barrel racers. Cass walked to the fence to watch Hannah make her run. Her horse was big in the chest, so big that her short legs seemed to point out to the side as she spurred him along. Her time was good enough for a fourth-place finish.

Cass didn't return to the bucking chutes until the saddle broncs were ready. By then it was plain that every other contestant and all the chute hands knew about the death of Summer and assumed he had killed her. With help from the same chute hand, he rigged the saddle bronc he'd drawn and then perched quietly on the top rail of the chute until it was his turn to ride. Once on the mount, Cass gave the nod and the gate man jerked the chute gate open. The horse reared on his hind legs to make the turn from the chute. The turn was followed by leaps that were showy, both high and hard. Cass was able to spur in the long strokes that normally scored points. But, on the ground after the ride, it only took one look at the judges, a couple of old rodeo hands, to tell the tale. No murderer would be in the money at this rodeo.

He'd just settled into the driver's seat and turned to pull the door closed when Forrest Dodson caught his eye. The man was coming in his direction and doing his best to hurry. At a wave of Dodson's hand, Cass stepped out of the auto to wait.

Seeing that Cass wasn't about to drive away, the cattle rancher slowed his pace. "I was afraid I'd miss you." He puffed a bit. "Could we visit for a minute?"

"Yes, sir." Noting the man was winded from his hurried walk, Cass asked, "Want to get in the car while we visit, sir?"

Dodson smiled. "No. This will do just fine right here." He leaned against the car's rear fender. "I've been thinking about what you said about getting a riding job in Wyoming."

Cass offered a sheepish smile. "It was just a passing thought. I doubt that I'd really do it."

Forrest nodded. "Perhaps not. But here's the thing. I'm going to have surgery, and I'll be in the hospital for ten days at least. They tell me I can't ride a horse for at least a month after that. I thought I had some help lined out, but that fell through, so I'm stuck." He paused. "How about you? You said you'd consider a riding job, and you know cattle. Hannah assures me that you're reliable. Would you be interested in staying at our place for a couple of months? Take care of the things that Lillian and Hannah can't handle?"

Mr. Dodson's words astonished Cass. Talk of a riding

job had been nothing more than talk. He searched for words. "Mr. Dodson, you don't know me. I'm a suspect in a murder investigation. You must surely wonder if I'm trustworthy."

The rancher's voice showed some impatience. "I know, I know. I've thought of all that. Hannah insists you could never have killed anyone, especially Summer." Dodson stopped and cocked his head. "I guess this really isn't a job offer anyway. I haven't had a chance to discuss it with Lillian and Hannah. Just thought I'd start with you to see how you'd feel about it."

"It's sure an interesting idea. To be at your ranch and learn how you do things would be a good experience for me."

Forrest Dodson pushed away from the auto fender. "Here's what we'll do. You think about it for a few days. I'll talk to Lillian and Hannah. You'll be busy here at the rodeo tomorrow. Maybe we can talk on the telephone sometime next week."

Cass shook his head. "I won't be here tomorrow. I'm heading home. Told the chute boss to turn my horses out. I can't stand all the looks and whispers." Cass pulled his hands from his pockets and said, "OK. Discuss it with your ladies. I'll talk to Dad about it. He's a lawyer. Because of the murder talk he may have some concerns, although I don't know what they could be." After a moment's pause, he added, "Maybe after talking to your wife you'll decide it isn't a good idea after all."

"Perhaps, perhaps not." Forrest reached to slap Cass lightly on the upper arm. "Either way, I'll call next week to let you know my thinking."

Chapter Twenty-four

The courthouse in Livingston was located a block south of Main Street. It was a large brick structure with an extraordinarily tall bell tower, taller by a third than it should be, Merci thought as they approached it. Merrill Hodder's office was on the second floor, across the hallway from the courtroom.

An elderly woman turned from her typewriter as they walked through the door. She put on her professional smile. "You must be the folks from Billings, Mr. Myklebust and Miss Bruce." She rose from her chair. "Mr. Hodder is expecting you." She stepped across the room to a wooden door, gave it one rap, and called, "They're here."

A voice came from within. "Show them in, Mabel."

Mabel pulled the door wide and moved aside to allow the two lawyers entry to a gloomy and cluttered room. The county attorney hurried around the desk with a hand extended to Geoff. "You're Geoffrey Myklebust. It's not often

Jim Moore

that such a distinguished member of the bar appears in this office. I met you once at a meeting in Helena."

Geoff grasped the man's hand firmly and smiled. "Not sure about distinguished, but I remember our conversation at the bar dinner. It was a pleasant evening."

Hodder turned to Merci. "So this is the lady who has upset the old notion that a woman has no place at the law."

Merci extended her hand. "I'm Merci Bruce. I didn't know that I'd upset any notions. I'm just another lawyer, doing my best to be a proper member of our profession."

"So you are and doing it well. AV rating with Martindale Hubble and listed among the best civil defense lawyers in Montana." He made a half turn to gesture toward two hard wooden chairs parked before his desk. "You've traveled far so I won't waste your time in more idle chatter." His callers seated, he sat in his own high-backed chair and he leaned forward with his elbows on the desktop. "You're here to talk about the death of Summer Hetherington. Am I correct"?

"You are," Geoff replied. "Just so you know, we represent Cassius Thaddeus Bruce. From what we've learned, it appears you are certain the girl was murdered."

"Hodder straightened in his chair. "There can be little doubt about it, with an icepick up jabbed under her jaw and into her brain. Our doctor says she was dead in an instant."

"Where did this take place?"

The county attorney raised a hand. "I think we should have the sheriff with us while we discuss all of this. He's the one who gathered the evidence." He called to the lady in the outer office, "Mabel, run down to the sheriff's office and bring Josh. Tell him the lawyers who represent Cassius

Bruce are here." He turned his attention back to Geoffrey and Merci. "The killing took place at Hunter's Hot Springs near Springdale. You would have passed by it on your drive here."

"And the date?"

Hodder didn't answer until Sheriff Waddell appeared at the doorway. He stood for a moment until Hodder waved him to another hard-backed chair. As Waddell moved in that direction Geoffrey, now standing, said, "I'm Geoffrey Myklebust, one of the attorneys representing Cassius Bruce," Waddell merely nodded. Geoff gestured toward Merci. "And this is Merci Bruce, the other attorney." Waddell acknowledged her with another nod and took a seat.

Hodder said, "You asked about the date. It was May 16th. The death must have occurred about nine or ten o'clock in the evening. The lady proprietor of the hot springs found the body the following morning."

Merci leaned forward, "What has she told you about that evening?"

Hodder pointed at the sheriff to answer the question. Waddell said, "She's been very cooperative. Her name is Hilda Stensrud. She said a group of nine young people arrived at about seven o'clock that evening to swim. One fellow paid the cost for the whole bunch. She knows the number because she counted to be certain she was fully paid."

"Did she say who paid?"

Hodder answered the question before the sheriff could speak. "She did not, Miss Bruce. But we've since learned it was Cassius Bruce. He seemed to be the spokesman for the group." The man seemed less friendly as he continued, "You may know him, ma'am."

Merci's voice carried some impatience. "Of course, I know him. He's my nephew. He's the reason we're here."

Hodder nodded. "Yes. He's your nephew. His father is a lawyer, as is his grandfather. I can imagine that your whole family of lawyers is gathering to protect one of its own."

Merci's voice was icy. "Mr. Myklebust and I, as well as those in my family, want to assure that justice is served. Would you have us do otherwise, sir?"

"Isn't the legal representation of a family member in such a serious matter of concern to you? The conflicting demands of such a situation must be obvious."

Geoff Myklebust spoke quietly. "The concern, if there is one, would be ours, Mr. Hodder. But there is no need for such concern. If Cassius Bruce is charged with a crime—and we hope, of course, that such a charge will never be filed—I'll be the one who tries the case. Miss Bruce may assist me." When the county attorney didn't respond, he continued. "For now, we're here to inquire about the investigation. Your remarks make it appear that you're about to charge our client with murder. Perhaps you will share the information that led you to that decision."

Merrill Hodder leaned back and crossed his arms over his chest. "That decision has not been made. Sheriff Waddell and I want to be certain we have all the information available. But I can tell you that your client appears to be the only one who could have committed this horrible crime." Turning to Merci, he continued, "There were nine young people at Hunter's Hot Springs that night. When all of them except Summer Hetherington were out of the pool area and in the automobiles,

Cass Bruce ran back into the building and was out of sight of the others. Miss Hetherington was alive when last seen by others before Mr. Bruce went back into that building. She was found dead in the pool the following morning. Only Cassius Bruce was alone with Miss Hetherington after the others left." He waited a second for comment, then added, "The others who were in the group will testify to that sequence of events. Cassius Bruce killed her when he had the chance. There's simply no other explanation."

Merci leaned toward him. "And why would he do such a thing, sir? Kill another person in cold blood?"

Waddell almost smiled when he answered. "Because she was pregnant."

Sheriff Waddell yelped. "She was pregnant? Why didn't you tell me?"

"I just received the final autopsy report and was about to call you when the lawyers showed up," Hodder said, smiling broadly at the sheriff. "So I'm telling all of you now. No doubt about it. Summer Hetherington was pregnant."

"Well I'll be damned!" Waddell blinked. "That clinches it. Now we know exactly why he killed her." In his excitement he leaned forward and continued with fervor. "She confronted him with the news, and he couldn't stand the thought of taking responsibility or having a blot on his reputation." He seemed downright gleeful as he added, "So he did her in."

When Waddell sat down, Merci asked, "What evidence do you have that he was the one who got her pregnant?"

"The testimony of her friends will convince a jury."

"And the names of those friends?"

Hodder jumped in. "You will get them." He looked from

Myklebust to Merci and back. "If you continue to represent Cassius Bruce, you'll have reason to be in this town in the future. Let me know when, and I'll do my best to provide you with all the evidence we gather. I have no reason to try to conceal any of it. The judge would have my hide if I did."

"That's all we can ask." Geoffrey started to rise then settled back. "If you decide to charge our client, you'll have a warrant issued for his arrest." Turning to the sheriff he added, "Notify me the day the warrant is issued. I'll bring him here to your office the following day at about one o'clock."

Waddell bristled. "Oh no! I'll locate him. I'll bring him in here in handcuffs."

Hodder turned to Waddell. "No need for that, Josh." Back to Myklebust, he said. "I have your word on that, sir? You'll bring him here to voluntarily surrender to the sheriff?"

Geoff answered, "You do." He then leaned forward slightly. "When we bring him to the sheriff's office, you'll have the local magistrate available for an immediate entry of plea and a bail hearing, won't you, Mr. Hodder?"

The county attorney slapped his hands on the arms of his chair and chuckled. "You want it all, don't you?" He looked from the lawyer to the sheriff and back. "The arraigning magistrate, as you call him, is our Justice of the Peace. He's a retired rancher named Willis Tinsman. I can get him here for an arraignment. But bail is another matter. Your client will be charged with murder in the first degree. Bail isn't a given when that's the charge."

"Admitted. But it's not prohibited either. Both you and I can make our arguments as to the appropriateness of bail. The justice will decide." Myklebust stood and reached for

Hodder's hand. The county attorney scrambled to his feet to complete the handshake. Geoff continued. "Thank you, sir, for your cooperative attitude. It will make things easier for all of us." He released the hand. "And thank you, too, for the offer to provide the evidence you gather. We'll take you up on it." He nodded his head to the sheriff, as Merci led him to the doorway. There he stopped. "And I'm sure you'll take the time and make the effort to investigate the possibility that someone other than Cassius Bruce committed this crime." Geoff followed Merci out into the hallway and looked back. "You can expect we will conduct our own investigation, sir. Ours will be thorough."

Hodder, who followed them out, said, "I'm sure that it will be, counselor. I'm sure that it will be." He turned to Merci. "Tell me, what's it like to be a woman in a man's profession?"

She was silent for a brief moment. When she spoke her eyes and voice were cold. "It isn't difficult, sir. When the judge enters the courtroom and says, 'Good morning gentlemen.' I stand up right along with the rest of them."

Chapter Twenty-five

Back in Myklebust's auto, Merci looked sideways at Geoffrey. "Well?"

Her law partner turned toward her. "Now we know. Your nephew will be charged with murder in the first degree one day soon."

"I agree." She turned to look out the window. "The surprise and what they see as the clincher for the motive is the pregnancy."

"Yes. And what they are not telling us is how they will connect that piece of evidence with your nephew. We need to find out as soon as possible."

"It's still hard to believe it's all happening. We need to go back to Harlowton to tell Cass and his parents—and grill Cass for what he knows about this pregnancy. I find it hard to think he knew. He would have told us."

Geoff turned the key to start his Mercury automobile. "Let's just hope the justice of the peace is reasonable and will grant bail." After checking for oncoming traffic, he pulled onto the street that led back to the highway going east. "The charges are sure to be filed sooner than I anticipated. I need to spend time reviewing the statutes and cases on criminal procedure and assign some of my other files to others in the office." He glanced across at his companion. "And you?"

"There's a lot to do. But right now, my time can best be spent interviewing potential witnesses—starting with Cass."

They traveled eastward on the highway from Livingston. The town of Springdale rested around a corner and across the Yellowstone River from a high cliff. Merci turned in the seat to point north. "Hunter's Hot Springs is about two miles up that dirt road."

"One of us will need to spend some time with the woman who runs the place. "

Merci smiled. "That will be me. I'll interview all possible witnesses. Mrs. Stensrud will be high on the list."

They rode in silence for a time. As they approached Big Timber, Merci spoke again. "Stop at the drug store. I can use its telephone booth to call Spencer to warn him of what's coming. I'll suggest that he get the whole family together to support Cass."

Forty-five miles of recently paved highway led northward from Big Timber to Harlowton. There, Spencer's secretary told them the Bruce family had gathered at the ranch. Another twelve miles of pavement west to the tiny town of Two Dot and five more miles of gravel carried them to the Bruce Ranch.

A large white, two-story ranch house stood among several outbuildings. This was where Merci was raised and where her parents still resided. Her father, T. C. Bruce, tall, slender and slightly stooped, met them as they climbed from the auto. After a handshake for Geoffrey and a hug for Merci, he said, "Spencer gathered the whole clan. He didn't tell us the reason. We can guess it isn't to receive good news."

It wasn't often the whole Bruce family gathered in one place. Now everyone settled in the room once called the parlor. Merci's mother, Felicity, rested in a wheelchair close to T. C. Her brother, Spencer, and his wife, Eunice, sat side by side on a davenport. Their older son, Thad, held his year-old son in his arms while leaning against the wall near a front window. Joyce, Thad's very pregnant wife, did the honors by offering iced tea and cookies to the newly arrived lawyers.

Geoff took one sip of the tea before placing the glass on a doily spread across a small stand next to his chair. Sober faced, he swept the gathering with his eyes before settling on Cass who was standing in a corner across the room with his arms crossed. "There's no easy way to tell you this. So here it is. Charges naming you as the one who murdered Summer Hetherington will soon be filed."

Cass didn't move or change expression for a long moment. He simply stared at the lawyer as though he didn't comprehend the words. His body seemed to shrink as he closed his eyes and ran his hands over his face. Of course, he raised his eyes. "I knew it was coming. I just knew it. That sheriff made up his mind the minute he saw me at the Belgrade rodeo grounds."

His mother said, "The sheriff's wrong, Cass. We all know it isn't true."

Spencer leaned forward in his chair as he spoke. "Your

mother is right, son. We're with you and will be no matter what." Then he half turned toward Geoffrey. "Please tell us what you learned from the Park County Attorney. And what Cass can expect to happen next."

"The biggest news was that Summer was pregnant. Did you know that, Cass?"

"Pregnant? No. I had no idea." He stood stunned for a long moment, then added, "That could be why someone would kill her. But who?" Cass looked around the room. "I swear it wasn't me."

"The prosecution will say it was. Do you know of any evidence they might have to pin it on you?" Geoff asked.

"No, but how could there be. I was never with her in that way."

"Son," Spencer said. "This is of grave importance. We must know whether there was even the slightest chance that you could have gotten Summer pregnant."

"I swear, Dad." Cass looked pleadingly at his father. "You and Mom taught me better than that. And Summer wasn't that kind of girl. She had standards. Everyone who knew her recognized that." His disbelief became even more apparent in both his voice and appearance. "Summer expected to be treated like a lady, and she was always treated that way. She never came out and talked about it, but you could just tell. She never sent that kind of signal."

"If it wasn't you, who, then?" Geoff asked. "Do you know of anyone else to whom she may have, as you say, sent that signal?"

"No, I don't. As far as I know, she wasn't dating anyone in particular."

Cass's mother spoke firmly. "If Cass says he didn't have relations with that girl, then he didn't. We not only taught our boys to respect women, we also taught them honesty, and they both learned it well."

"Okay, then," Merci said. "That settles it. I'll see what I can find out from others I interview."

"Anything else?" Spencer asked.

Geoff directed his remarks to Cass. "Rather than wait for the sheriff to arrive and drag you to Livingston in handcuffs, I offered to take you there the day after they notify me that the charges have been filed. We told the sheriff you'd be with us at his office that day at one o'clock." When Cass only stared, he continued. "You'll appear before the local justice of the peace with us at your side for this initial appearance and to enter a not-guilty plea. You'll be photographed and fingerprinted. We'll ask that you be released on bail."

Cass didn't move other than to shake his head almost imperceptibly. Spencer, however, was quick to ask, "Did the county attorney agree to allow our son's release on bail?"

"No. He did not. That's an argument we'll have to make to the justice of the peace." Geoff paused a moment. "Spencer, you might be able to learn something about the J. P. His name is Tinsman. It would be helpful to know more about him so as to understand how he thinks."

Spencer was glad to have some part of protecting his son. "I'll call some folks I know in that part of the world and let you know what I learn."

Cass had been standing with his eyes on the floor. Now, at a break in the conversation, he raised his eyes to ask of Geoff, "What can I expect? Will they take me directly to jail? If that happens, what kind of clothes shall I wear? What should I take with me? Will they let me have any of my stuff?"

"If the J. P. doesn't allow you to be released on the posting of bail, you will be taken to jail. They probably have coveralls that must be worn by all of their prisoners. And they will not allow you to have your own razor or anything else that might be used as a weapon." Geoff offered Cass a smile. "Let's focus on the hearing. We want to present the best possible appearance. That means you should dress in good clothing. A suit would be much better than denim trousers and western boots." He scrutinized his client for a second. "Be clean shaven. Can you get a barber to cut your hair tomorrow?"

"I guess old Baldy down in Harlo will cut it, even if I've been charged with murder." He shook his head. "I can't believe it's really happening."

"It's happening." Geoff stood, followed by Merci. "Now, if you'll excuse us, we must get back to Billings. There's much to do." He turned to Spencer. "If I call to tell you the day when the charges are filed, can you deliver your son to the Park County sheriff's office at 1:00 o'clock the next day?"

"Of course. Eunice and I will do it. We'll be there to give our support to Cassius."

T. C. was on his feet. "Felicity and I will be there too."

Thad asked his brother. "Cass, do you want Joyce and me to be there?"

Cass shook his head. "No. Please take care of things here at the ranch. There's nothing you could do in Livingston but sit around and worry."

Merci stepped across the open space to Felicity's

wheelchair to give her a hug. "We'll be on our way, Mom." She turned to put an arm around her father's waist. Peering upward, she said, "Dad, we'll find the one who actually killed that girl."

While Geoff was saying his goodbyes, she moved to the door with Cass trailing behind. Outside and beyond the hearing of the others, he said, "Auntie, I can't go to jail. I just can't. The thought of it terrifies me."

She put a hand on his arm as she looked into his eyes. "Cass, Geoff is the best lawyer I know. I feel certain that he'll convince the justice of the peace to grant bail. You just have to hang onto that thought."

CHAPTER TWENTY-SIX

County Attorney Hodder, frowned across his desk at Sheriff Waddell. "The pathologist released the body today. It was shipped to Roundup in a freight car. Her parents are clamoring for her belongings. Where are they?"

"I brought them with me, like you told me to when you called." Waddell's face reddened as he explained, "I haven't had time to think about the evidence locker. You've got to remember, I'm new at this."

"It should have been done long ago, but no use getting upset about it now," Hodder said. "Bring it to the conference room, and I'll help you go through it. We just might find the piece of evidence we need to tie that Bruce fellow to the pregnancy. It could give us a motive that can't be refuted."

"I hadn't thought of that," Waddell muttered as he went to drag in a stuffed laundry bag, a box, and a suitcase.

The two men began to go methodically through the contents. "What exactly are we looking for?" Waddell asked, setting a text book aside.

"For one thing, it would be nice to find a diary or a note book with a reference to Bruce and the pregnancy. But look at every item and piece of paper for any kind of evidence."

After several minutes, as Hodder was called to the phone, Waddell found a loose-leaf binder in which Miss Hetherington had taken notes for her classes. He paged through it methodically until he saw the initials W. F. inside a fancy heart shape, drawn in the margin. Waddell frowned and looked for more hearts or similar doodles. If only it said C. B. it might have some bearing. When he found no more, he looked up to be sure Hodder hadn't returned. He tore out the offending page and stuffed it in his pocket. He sure as hell didn't need a distraction to muddy the investigation. When Hodder returned, he said, "Apparently she wasn't one to write her secret thoughts. Nothing but school work here."

They finished the search in less than an hour, repacked everything for mailing and shipped it off to Roundup.

Summer Hetherington's funeral was scheduled for two o'clock in the afternoon on a cold and dreary day. By one thirty, the parking lot at the mortuary was full and cars were lined the length of the curbs of the streets closest to it. The service followed the familiar pattern—prayer led by the minister, singing, a reading by the minister of Summer's obituary, a brief sermon intended to give solace to the parents, and a final prayer. Hannah thought it way too solemn, with none of Summer's liveliness.

The crowd gathered at the cemetery. After a final prayer by the minister, the crowd began to drift away. Those close to the grave sought the opportunity to offer condolences to the bereaved. Among the last of those were the Dodsons. When Forrest offered his hand to Ephram Hetherington, the other man held it for moment to say, "You might as well come and get our daughter's horse. We have no use for him." He glanced at his wife. "The horse is a constant reminder to Sue of our loss."

"I can do that, I guess." After a moment's thought, Forrest added, "That's a good horse. How much do you want for him?"

Hetherington said as he turned away, "Just send me whatever you think he's worth."

CHAPTER TWENTY-SEVEN

Toward the end of the next week, having duly gone over all the elements related to the trial of Cassius Bruce several times, the county attorney called Sheriff Waddell to his office. He reviewed the evidence with Waddell one last time to verify that everything was in order.

Hodder leaned back in his chair, heaved a sigh, and removed his glasses to rub his eyes. He was sixty-two years old but, Waddell noticed, suddenly appeared much older. After replacing the glasses Hodder looked up at the sheriff. "I've held this office for a long time and learned that prosecuting a crime is never easy, Josh. I've never handled a murder case before, but this case, like any murder case, will be hard fought. As certain as you are that the case we have against young Bruce is open and shut, conviction isn't a certainty." He turned and crossed his legs, looking out the window. "That young fellow comes from a family of lawyers. None of those family lawyers will try the case, of course. But

Geoffrey Myklebust has a reputation as the best trial lawyer in Montana. Besides that, the Bruce family reportedly has the resources to do whatever it takes to protect one of their own." He blew out a long sigh before turning to the sheriff. "No, Josh, convicting that lad won't be a walk in the park."

"Are you afraid of losing? Is that what's bothering you?"

Hodder chuckled. "I don't like to lose, any more than you do." His smile disappeared. "No. Fear of losing isn't what I'm trying to tell you. Both you and I just need to understand the task we're about to undertake. We both need to be as prepared as we can be right from the beginning. And we must never quit along the way."

Waddell straightened his back. "I understand. And, by God, I'll do my share. You surely know how important this case is to me."

The county attorney pushed himself up from the chair. "I do, Josh, and I know you will do your best. I'll prepare the complaint and send it to them on Monday. I'll let Myklebust know that he's to bring Cassius Thaddeus Bruce in here for an initial appearance within forty-eight hours as he promised he'd do."

CHAPTER TWENTY-EIGHT

Cass and his family traveled through a cold drizzle in two cars from Harlowton to Livingston. It was the kind of day one might expect in early June. They hurried through the rain into the courthouse where they met Merci and Geoffrey and climbed the stairs and entered the courtroom.

At the front of the room, the county attorney was seated at one of two counsel tables. Geoffrey, Cass, and Merci continued through the small swinging gate in the railing that separated the trial participants from the audience. The attorneys deposited their briefcases on the other counsel table. Merci stood for a moment behind a chair next to the table. Cass placed his hands on the back of a chair next to Merci while Geoff stepped over to Merrill Hodder and put out a hand as the county attorney rose from the chair. "Mr. Hodder."

"Mr. Myklebust."

Geoff turned to the man at Hodder's side. "Sheriff Waddell, if I remember correctly?"

The sheriff muttered, "I am." He didn't offer to shake the lawyer's hand.

Summer Hetherington's parents and some other relatives were seated directly behind the county attorney. The Bruce family contingent filled a bench behind Cass and his lawyers. Neither family acknowledged the other.

Cass, dressed in a tailored slate gray suit, white shirt, maroon tie, and oxfords, glanced around the room. It was much longer than wide, with a high ceiling and three windows along the left side. The judge's bench rested on an eight-inch platform. The witness stand was to the left and on the floor level. The jury box with its twelve chairs, farther to the left, ran perpendicular to the room. The United States and Montana flags draped from staffs behind the judge's bench.

Cass struggled to comprehend his circumstance. He was standing in a courtroom about to be formally charged with murder. He would be tried here. He might be convicted here. He could even be sentenced to death here. For a moment his legs felt as though they would give way. He leaned forward, fists on the table for support, and took a deep breath. He resolved to face the coming proceeding with all of the dignity he could muster.

Geoff took his place next to Cass just as the judge entered the room and climbed to the bench. Justice of the Peace, Willis Tinsman, was tall and lean. He peered down from a bench in the room generally reserved for the District Judge. "Mr. Hodder, you represent the state, do you not?"

The county attorney, on his feet, answered, "As always, Your Honor."

Tinsman glanced at a paper before him. "We're here for the arraignment of one Cassius Thaddeus Bruce. Is that correct?"

"That's correct, Your Honor."

Judge Tinsman turned his attention to the two men and the woman standing at the other counsel table. "And I take it one of you is Mr. Bruce. Am I right?"

Geoffrey Myklebust nodded. "Yes, Your Honor. The gentleman next to me is Cassius Bruce. For the record, my name is Geoffrey Myklebust of the firm of Herman and Myklebust, Billings, Montana. Merci Bruce...," He gestured toward Merci, "and I represent Mr. Bruce."

"So I guess we're all here. Has your client had a chance to review the charging documents?"

Geoff turned to Cass, inviting him to respond. "I've read them, Your Honor."

"Do you wish to have them read to you now?"

Geoff said, "I've reviewed the charges with my client. We wave the reading of the information. Mr. Bruce is ready to enter a plea."

Tinsman said, "Very well. How do you plead, sir?"

Cass's voice was firm. "I plead not guilty."

The Judge nodded as he scribbled a note on the paper. "All right, your plea is noted." He turned to the county attorney. "What else, Mr. Hodder?"

"There's the matter of bail, sir."

"Ah, yes, bail. Always an issue."

Hodder, still standing, continued, "We believe the

defendant should be held without bail. As you know, this was a particularly brutal murder of a promising young woman. It appears to have been both unprovoked and premeditated. The lack of provocation and the apparent premeditation of the attack could lead one to believe it could happen again. Incarceration until trial will assure that such will not be the case." His face took on a look of determination. "We need to keep this killer in jail."

Geoff's voice was measured and quiet. "I hardly need to remind you that Cassius Bruce, the young man standing next to me, has not been convicted of any crime, much less the crime of murder. As to Mr. Hodder's statements that the crime was both unprovoked and premeditated, those are accusations to be proven in court if they are ever to have any consequence. At this time, nothing has been proven." He looked at Cass, standing erect at his side, showing no emotion. "This is an individual who has no record of previous difficulty with the law other than a single parking ticket two years ago in Billings. A parking ticket doesn't indicate that he's such a risk to society that he must be held in jail."

While these exchanges were taking place. Forrest Dodson, dressed in a dark blue suit that was years out of style and carrying his western hat, entered the courtroom. He stood aside so his wife and daughter could slide onto a bench half way to the front of the room.

Hodder was shaking his head as Geoff spoke. "There is nothing in this world to keep that young man from fleeing the jurisdiction of this court. He's finished at the college but has no job waiting for him. His grandparents have a ranch but he's not needed by them. Mr. Myklebust may argue that

Jim Moore

he won't leave his home and family. But that may seem better to him than the verdict he can expect after a jury hears the evidence against him."

Geoff's voice remained calm. "Mr. Hodder has obviously learned a little about Cass Bruce." He paused. "Talk of the things Mr. Bruce could do is the rankest kind of speculation, Your Honor." He half turned toward Cass's family seated in the row behind him. "His parents and his grandparents are here, Your Honor. They will testify, if asked, that Cassius Bruce has never tried to avoid confrontation with a difficult matter. Instead, he meets such situations head on to resolve them in the best possible way." He glanced at the young man and continued. "My client should be released on bail and the bail should be in a reasonable amount."

Before Hodder could speak again, the judge raised a hand to stop him. "Just a minute sir." Turning to Myklebust, he asked, "Does he have a job waiting for him somewhere?"

Geoff looked to Cass who shook his head and mouthed, "Just the ranch." The lawyer faced the judge again. "He's always spent his summers working at the family ranch. His help there will be welcome as always."

One look at the judge's face convinced Cass that working at the family ranch wasn't going to be good enough.

Before the judge could respond there was a loud shuffling sound from the audience section. The eyes of everyone in the room turned as Forrest Dodson struggled to his feet. Peering at the judge and with one hand slightly raised as though asking permission, Forrest asked, "May I say something, sir?"

Tinsman asked, "Who are you, sir?"

122

"My name is Forrest Dodson, Your Honor. I have a ranch near Roundup. I have to have some serious surgery soon."

Looks of puzzlement appeared on the faces of Cass's legal team and the prosecutor and judge. All eyes were now on the rugged, blue-suited rancher. The judge asked the logical question. "Why are you here interrupting these legal proceedings? There's nothing this court can do about your medical problems."

Forrest nodded and cleared his throat. "A few days ago I talked with that young fella," pointing at Cass, "about coming to work for me. He seemed to be interested. I should have made the deal with him right then. Instead I told him we'd discuss it again in a few days."

The judge frowned as he leaned back in chair. "Sir, you're disrupting a court proceeding. Please sit down."

Forrest straightened and forged on. "Your Honor, a moment ago you asked if Cass, there, has a job. He indicated that he didn't. Well, I'm here to offer him the job I should have offered to him when we first talked about it."

Geoff turned an inquiring look at Cass who nodded. He turned to the judge, "Perhaps we should hear what this gentleman has to say, Your Honor. It may influence your decision with regard to bail."

Dodson jumped in. "I believe it will, Your Honor. That's why I'm here. After the surgery I'll be in the hospital for a couple of weeks. And even after they send me home I won't be able to ride a horse for some time. While I'm flat on my back, the cattle and the ranch will still need looking after." He turned to look down at Lillian and Hannah. "My wife and daughter can do some of it, but they'll be with me at the hospital part of the time. There has to be someone there, someone who knows horses and cattle." He directed his next remark to Cass. "That's why we're here, to offer the job to you and in the hope that you'll take it." He looked back at the judge. "And that's why you should let him out on bail, so my family and I can have peace of mind while I'm laid up."

Hodder's voice reflected his exasperation. "Ah, come on. What's going on here?" He pointed at Dodson. "That man has no standing to be speaking in this court. He's nothing but a spectator. Ignore him, Your Honor, and rule that the defendant be held without bail until trial."

Geoffrey Myklebust turned to the judge. "My client is entitled to bail regardless of Mr. Dodson's plea. You, Your Honor, asked if Cass Bruce has a job. That question is answered. He'll take the job with a family that needs his help."

Hodder didn't give up. "This is a set up. You turn that young fellow loose, Your Honor, and he can disappear in an eye blink. How do we know that isn't the plan?"

Dodson grinned. "Sir, if he skips out and leaves my wife and daughter alone with all those cattle, I'll make him wish he'd gone to jail."

There was a chuckle from the few spectators and the judge showed a slight grin. "All right. I've heard enough." He turned to Cass. "If released on bail will you attend each and every court hearing?"

Cass straightened. "I will, Your Honor."

"Will you maintain contact with your attorneys at all times and respond to their requests and suggestions?"

"Yes sir."

"Will you remain at that man's ranch in Musselshell County?"

Geoff raised a hand. "He may need to visit his family in Wheatland County and confer with us in Billings. It's permissible for him to do those things isn't it, sir?"

"Of course." Looking again at Cass, the judge continued. "Just stay where your attorneys can find you at all times." He stopped speaking and stared at Cass for a long minute. "Of most importance, will you do as Mr. Dodson wants, care for his cattle in the manner that he directs, without fail?"

"I'll do my best, sir."

"Your best had better be good enough to keep Mr. Dodson happy." He turned to a paper on the bench before him. "All right. Bail is set at ten thousand dollars. A scheduling conference and a trial date will be set by the district judge and the parties will be notified."

CHAPTER TWENTY-NINE

Geoffrey and Merci began to gather their papers. When the realization dawned on Cass that he would not be in jail, he turned to go to the Dodsons only to have a law officer grab his arm. "We're not finished here. You don't leave until you're booked and bail is posted." The officer led him away.

Ephram Hetherington scrambled to his feet. In an instant he was at the Forrest Dodson's side with a firm grip on his upper arm. "What the hell do you think you're doing? Haven't you thought about our feelings? Sue's and mine?"

Dodson's bewilderment was apparent as he asked, "What are you talking about, Ephram?"

"You invited that…that scoundrel, to come and live in our town—a constant reminder of what he did to our daughter."

Dodson moved the other man's hand from his arm. "Ephram, he'll be at our ranch, not anywhere you're likely to see him." He moved a step away. "Look, man, I can't imagine what you and Sue are going through. And I sure don't want to cause you more grief. I promise you we'll be careful so we don't make that happen."

Hetherington shook his head in disgust and tugged at his wife's arm. "Let's get out of here. So much for someone I thought was a friend."

Forrest Dodson pondered the Hetherington's reaction. Would the others in the Roundup community feel the same?

The Bruce family had discussed the matter of bail before the hearing. T. C. posted enough ranch land to cover it. After Cass was booked, finger printed, and photographed, he found the Bruce family and the Dodsons standing together outside the courthouse. "I see that you've gotten acquainted." He put out a hand to Forrest. "There's no way I can thank you enough for your offer. The thought of jail had me terrified."

Dodson gave the hand a firm grip. "No need to thank me. I hope you meant it…that you'd take the job."

"I meant it, all right. How soon do you need me?'

"As soon as you can get there. How about tomorrow?"

Cass nodded. "Do I need to bring horses?"

"Nope. I've got plenty of horses."

"I'll pack up in the morning and head for Roundup. Should be there by midafternoon. Will that do?"

"That'll do just fine," Dodson said. "We'll be waiting."

Hannah moved quietly to Cass's side. "It will be nice to have you to help at our place, Cass." A mischievous smile appeared. "I'll teach you how to handle cattle."

"Fair enough. I'll try to be a good student."

Merci caught the attention of the group. "We've just been through the first small part of what will be a long drawn out proceeding. Mr. Myklebust and I must head back to Billings to begin preparation." She put her arm around Cass's waist. "Geoff will handle the office part of the preparation, the demand for discovery and a myriad of things that such a trial requires." She glanced at Myklebust and then back at Cass. "I plan to visit as many people as possible in this case." She turned to Hannah. "That includes you, Miss Dodson."

Looking upward into Cass's face she said, "Be strong. And trust Geoffrey to take care of you."

"I know he'll do his best, but I need you too."

She gave him a last hug. "We'll both do our best. And I'm certain you'll be exonerated."

CHAPTER THIRTY

It took most of the morning for Cass to gather the belongings he'd need for an extended stay at the Dodson Ranch. At ten thirty he was on his way eastward along the meandering course of the Musselshell River from Harlowton. The day was gloomy with occasional drizzles of rain. He passed through the tiny towns of Shawmut and Ryegate and stopped for a quick lunch at a café in Lavina. All the while his mind suffered its own darkness as he remembered yesterday's court appearance. The attorney's arguments over bail made him realize, in a way he hadn't before, that he could have been in jail—and that he might someday be in the penitentiary.

In the attempts to drive those thoughts away, his mind shifted to his destination. The idea of a ranch where most of the work required time on horseback was appealing. He always enjoyed the livestock activities far more than the other labors on his grandfather's place—the irrigation, the harvesting of the hay and feeding it in the wintertime. But try as he might to drive away the gloom, it returned with the picture of the inside of a jail cell popping into mind.

As the road dropped down from the hills onto the river bottom, the clouds broke away and sun shone through. That sunshine brightened his day as he entered Roundup, county seat of Musselshell County.

Another ten miles eastward brought him to a junction with a gravel road running northward, the one that Forrest Dodson told him to follow to the ranch. Cass scanned the countryside as he drove. No tall rugged buttes backed by towering mountains of the kind that dominated the scene in the upper Musselshell Valley. Here, low rolling hills and broken ridges were cut at intervals by tiny streams and shallow coulees. There were small groves of Cottonwood trees along the streams and patches of tangled brush here and there among the coulees. South of the river the rounded tops of the Bull Mountains came into view. Only the eastern end of the Big Snowy Mountains in the far distance to the northwest broke what was otherwise an endless expanse of grass. The elevation at Roundup was about thirty-two hundred feet as compared to the forty-five hundred feet at Harlowton. The lower elevation made for longer seasons. Cass noticed the difference in the grasses that covered the landscape. Unlike at home, the grasses here already showed the first dark green and bronze of the maturing process.

About six miles along the road, he came to a large mailbox and a sign that said "Dodson Ranch" He turned from the graveled road to cross a cattle guard and follow a narrow track another mile. Topping a small hill, he came upon cluster of buildings along a small stream and shaded by several tall Cottonwood trees. There were corrals, a couple of barn-like structures, a granary, and a chicken coup. A square two-story house with a nearby garage, both white with blue trim, dominated the scene. A power line alongside the entry road brought electricity to the complex.

As Cass crossed the cattle guard into the fenced barnyard, a collie ran in his direction barking loudly. The noise brought all three of the Dodsons out a door on the side of the house. He could see Forrest call to the dog. It immediately stopped barking and hurried back to receive a pet, first from Forrest and then from Hannah. Lillian, wearing a pleasant smile, stood with her arms folded under an apron.

Cass pulled his auto to a stop next to a pre-war Ford pickup. Forrest greeted him with wide smile and an outstretched hand. "Welcome, young man." He waved toward his wife and daughter. "The ladies have been as anxious for your arrival as I've been."

Lillian grasped Cass's hand in both of hers as she asked, "Have you eaten? We finished the noon meal some time ago, but I saved some for you in case you're hungry."

"Thanks, but I got a bite to eat in Lavina." He turned to Hannah whose smile was as shiny as always. Cass's smile mirrored hers. Neither spoke for a moment, each apparently wondering what to say. At last she giggled and asked, "Are we supposed to shake hands or something?"

With that question, the trepidation Cass had been suffering vanished. He laughed. "Hardly seems necessary after the times we've spent together." He glanced around. "It's nice to see you in your home environment."

Jim Moore

Forrest gestured toward the door. "Come on in. If you like we can share a cup of coffee along with the fresh cookies that Lillian just took from the over. Then I'll show you where you'll be staying."

The conversation was comfortable as they enjoyed the cookies and coffee. At last Forrest ushered Cass out the door and climbed into the pickup to lead the way along a worn track to the top of a small rise. Cass followed in his automobile. In a short distance, a wooden building, longer than wide, with a peaked roof came into view. At one time it might have been a large granary. Now it was carefully sided and painted a dark brown. The framing of the doorway and of several windows reflected meticulous carpentry. An enclosed porch was attached to the front and a small wing had been added on to its south side.

Forrest held the front door and stood aside to allow Cass to enter. Cass was impressed with the neatness of the interior and the careful planning for the building's use. The tiny entryway had pegs along one wall on which to hang coats. Beyond was an open sitting area with two comfortable chairs canted toward one another with a small table between to hold reading material. The previous day's Billings Gazette rested there. A low partial wall divided the sitting area from a kitchen that contained a sink with a drainboard and a long counter with drawers and cabinets below its surface, a refrigerator, an electric stove and a small electric washing machine with wringer. An oval table with four straight chairs held a gathering of wild flowers in a glass jar.

Two doors provided exits from the kitchen, one led to a bathroom, adequate in size and with flushing toilet and shower. Cass pushed open the other door to a room that held a double bed with box spring and mattress. A low end table stood near its head. Through another open door, Cass could see a small closet with rods on which to hang clothing. Shelves for folded clothing ran across the lower portion. Another straight back chair stood near at hand.

The young man turned away from the doorway to face Forrest. "It has everything a person could possibly need." He grinned. "I've been in several bunkhouses. Never saw one as nice as this."

A wry look crossed the older rancher's face. "This old building was sound, so Lillian and I fixed it up and placed an ad for the hunters. Got plenty of response." He blew out an exaggerated sigh. "I soon found out that the ones who arrived needed lots of nurse-maiding. Try as I might, I couldn't do enough to satisfy them, so I quit."

"This place is too nice to sit empty."

"Lillian's brother and sister-in-law drive from Minnesota about once a year and use this building as base to explore the state." Forrest ran his eyes around the room. "Once in a while we have other guests."

"Well, it'll be great for me." Cass said. "I'll unpack and get settled in."

At his pickup, Forrest said, "The horse barn is up by the house. You can store your riding gear there." He reached for the door handle. "Supper's at six. Lillian likes it when people are on time." He slid onto the pickup seat. "Breakfast is at six thirty. After breakfast, I'll take you on a tour of the place. Give you a look at the rangeland and the cattle."

Cass stepped back into the bunkhouse. "Nice place. I can

Jim Moore

make this work."

At five o'clock, Hannah grabbed a jacket and hurried out the door. "I'm going to see if Cass needs anything," she called.

Her mother watched her go, then turned to her husband, seated at the kitchen table reading the newspaper. "Suddenly I'm not so sure having that young man here is a good idea."

Glancing up, Forrest said, "It'll be fine."

"Yes, I hope so."

He gathered the paper neatly together and laid it on the table. "We taught our daughter right from wrong."

"I know," Lilian said. "I trust her. And I believe what she's says about the Cass's morals. I like him. Yet temptation can raise its head as they spend time together." She turned to face her husband. "Have you forgotten the power of attraction at that age?"

"I haven't," Forrest said, smiling. "But I still say they'll be fine. No need to worry about it now."

"You're right, and I won't," Lillian said, turning her gaze back to the window, a frown belying her words.

CHAPTER THIRTY-ONE

Merci traveled westward through the rain along the main highway from Billings to Livingston. She passed through the hamlets of Park City, Laurel, and Columbus before reaching the outskirts of Big Timber at half past noon. A bowl of soup and an egg sandwich with coffee at the old Grand Hotel served for the noon meal. Back on the road she continued westward to the turnoff at Springdale, which rested on the flatland along the bank of the Yellowstone River. She crossed the river bridge, drove through what there was of a town, and continued northward toward the hills beyond. Two miles farther along a gravel road, Hunter's Hot Springs buildings came into sight.

She pulled to a stop next to three other cars in the main parking area and ran her eyes over the principal building. In its beginnings it had been a luxury hotel, with Moroccan style architecture, two stories high and enormous in size. Not much was left of the original grandeur she remembered from

Jim Moore

her youth. Trees and shrubbery, in need of care, remained at tasteful locations around the building and the parking area.

When Merci was young, Hunter's Hot Springs attracted the rich and famous. They arrived by train to "take the waters" and to enjoy gourmet meals and luxurious treatment. People still came to swim but not in the numbers of the past. Merci felt a pang of regret at its obvious decline.

It was nearing two o'clock when she walked into the lobby. An elderly man pushed a broom over the hardwood floor. He looked up as Merci approached and silently jerked a thumb toward a check-in counter. A slender, middle-aged woman of medium height appeared from an office behind the counter. She wore a woolen sweater over a cotton housedress. She asked, "May I help you?"

Merci smiled. "I hope so. My name is Merci Bruce. I came to ask about the young woman who died a few days ago."

The woman stiffened. "She didn't die, she was killed."

"Indeed." Merci nodded. "Were you the one in charge of the pool that evening? The evening of May sixteenth?"

"I'm the one who collected the money for the use of the pool and the charge for bathing suits." The woman rubbed her hands together and frowned. "What's this all about anyway? I've already told the sheriff everything I know."

"One of the young men who was here that evening has been charged with the girl's death."

"That's what I've been told."

Merci straightened. "I'm an attorney representing that young man. As you can guess, I'm anxious to find out exactly what happened." She paused. "May I ask your name?"

"I'm Hilda Stensrud. My husband and I own this place. "

"Please tell me, if you will, what happened that night.

"Not much I can tell you. Nine of them showed up and said they wanted to swim. I was about to lock up because there weren't any other guests." She looked off into the distance for an instant before she added, "That's the problem much of the time nowadays. It was different when I was young." Her attention turned back to Merci. "One of the young men paid for all of them and said he'd collect the money from the others. He was tall and good looking. He called me 'Ma'am.'"

"Mostly men?"

"Three were girls and six were men, all dressed in western clothing. Even the girls were wearing jeans I collected the money, handed them bathing suits that I dug from the closet, led them to the pool and pointed to the dressing rooms"

"Was that the end of your conversations with them?"

"No, in a few minutes the one who paid showed up in the swim suit. My goodness he was a handsome fellow."

"What did he want?"

"Ice. Said they had some pop and beer and wanted to keep it cold." Her face twisted into a wry expression. "It made me kind of mad that they brought their own drinks. They should have bought them from me. But I dug out a small block of ice, dropped it in a bucket and handed it to him. Like I said, he was polite and thanked me properly." She paused in thought. "He asked for an icepick, and I gave one to him."

"Were they noisy? Rowdy?"

"Not at all. They spent their time quietly in the pool. I didn't stay to watch, but from the little conversation I overheard it was plain they were rodeo participants. Even the girls."

Merci asked, "What happened when they left?"

"I was still at this counter as they came hurrying by." Mrs. Stensrud cast a look at Merci from the corner of her eye. "You're wondering if the fellow named Cass Bruce came back a second time." She folded her arms across her bosom. "Yes he did. I've heard that the sheriff believes that young man went back to the pool to kill the girl. It's all that folks around here have talked about."

"How long was he in the pool area the second time?"

"Not long. It seemed like he just hurried through the door into the pool and turned around to come back out."

Merci hesitated before asking, "Was he back there long enough to murder Summer Hetherington?"

"They say he grabbed her and jammed the icepick up under her jaw. I don't know how long that would take." She paused in thought. "But he barely went through that door before he came back out again. It doesn't seem like enough time to do that."

"How did he act when he came from the pool the second time?"

The proprietress smiled. "Polite as before. He was in a hurry, but he gave a small wave as he went by and called out, 'Thanks for everything, ma'am. It was fun.'"

Merci half turned from the counter to look around the lobby. She pointed at a wide doorway. "I take it that's the entry to the pool area. May I take a look?"

"Of course. I'll lead the way."

The pool, long and wide, was surrounded by an expanse

of smooth concrete. Doors providing access to and from guest rooms were spaced at intervals along the walls surrounding the pool. Hilda Stensrud pointed to her right. "Those are the dressing rooms."

The rooms protruded from the end wall into the pool area with a wide space between them. Large signs identified one for men and one for women. The entryway to each of them was to the side rather than facing the pool itself. Merci opened the door to the women's dressing room to peer inside. There were shower cubicles along one wall, lockers in which to place clothing and benches on which to sit. Another wall was lined with sinks and vanities. It appeared spacious and Spartan, now, but in its glory days an attendant or two was probably on hand to provide lavish assistance to the ladies.

The women's dressing room was the farthest from the entryway. It was a walk of some thirty feet from the main pool entry to the doorway into that dressing room. Merci calculated in her mind how long it would take Cass to walk that distance, enter the dressing room, snatch up the icepick and then grab Summer, insert the pick, drag her dead body to the pool and drop it in. A lot more time than Hilda Stensrud said Cass spent back here.

The room was warm and moist and Merci was beginning to perspire. She swept her eyes around the vast room that enclosed the pool one more time. To the left of the women's dressing room was another protrusion, smaller in size than the dressing room, with a door for entry. Merci pointed and asked, "Storage space?"

"It is. I keep mops and brooms and other cleaning supplies in there."

Jim Moore

"Do you keep it locked?"

"There's no need. Nothing in the closet is of any value."

Merci nodded. Back in the lobby, she retrieved a business card from her purse and handed it to Hilda Stensrud. "Thank you for taking the time to show me around and for answering my questions. Please call me collect if you think of anything more that might help us understand what happened the night Summer Hetherington died."

"Even if it shows that Cass Bruce did it?"

"Yes, even if that's the case. I need to know."

When the proprietress looked carefully at the card, she muttered, "Merci Bruce." Eyebrows raised, she said, "You must be related to Cass Bruce."

"He's my nephew."

"No wonder you're so anxious to get him off."

Merci answered in a firm voice. "I'm anxious to show that he didn't commit the crime of which he's accused, because I firmly believe that he didn't."

Hilda took a moment to speak. When she did it was in a quiet voice, "Well, I hope you're successful. It would be shame to ruin the life of such a nice young man."

CHAPTER THIRTY-TWO

At four o'clock Merci was again on the highway going west toward Livingston. She thought briefly about calling upon Park County Attorney Merrill Hodder but decided her time could be better spent with others. The long climb over the Bozeman Pass began outside the Livingston city limits and the highway became steeper and more crooked as each mile went by. Not far from the summit she found herself stuck at the end of a line of cars, all of them creeping along behind a heavily loaded cattle truck. The truck driver pulled to the side of the road at the top of the mountain and put his arm out the window to wave for those behind him to go by. Merci was relieved when the traffic moved again at a decent speed only to be slowed again by the twists and turns through the narrow Rocky Canyon.

In Bozeman at last, she followed the main street to a parking place in front of the Baxter Hotel. She checked into a room. At the sight of a comfortable chair in a corner by

Jim Moore

the window, she realized how tired she was. Some of the weariness came from the long drive but most resulted from the events of the past few days. She'd reviewed client files she would turn over to other lawyers while she concentrated on Cass's predicament.

She slumped into the chair, kicked off her shoes, dragged a light blanket from the foot of the bed to cover herself and closed her eyes.

After a short refreshing nap, Merci scrubbed the sleep from her face and straightened her clothing. A glance at her watch told her the day was all but gone.

It was Merci's first time in the Bacchus Pub, the eatery on the hotel's ground floor. Unique gargoyles were aligned along the wall just below the ceiling. They all seemed to be smirking. Booths along the walls, tables in an open area to the rear, and a long bar down the middle furnished the room. The patrons included businessmen, some college folks— both students and staff—and a couple of farmers with dirt on their boots. She was ushered to a table toward the back and seated near two women who were engaged in lively conversation. Their voices were loud with no evidence of concern that others might overhear what they said.

Merci decided they were college employees, probably secretarial staff. Merci tuned out the sounds from the adjoining table as she scanned the menu. She placed her order and was waiting for her food to arrive when the name, Cass Bruce, penetrated her consciousness. Her attention immediately focused on the women's conversation.

"Of course, I've heard about Cass Bruce. I'm told he's a tall, handsome rodeo guy that the coeds all swoon over," the

142

dark-haired woman said.

"Tall and handsome he may be, but from talk around the ad building, he's a murderer." The speaker had blond hair. "They say he got Summer Hetherington pregnant and then did away with her." Her expression was more leer than grin. "The president, of course, is worried about how it will affect the public perception of the college."

Dark hair nodded. "And the Dean's afraid that the rodeo will reflect poorly on the College of Agriculture." After a pause to sip her drink, she asked, "What do you hear about her, Summer Hetherington?"

"I'm told she had a figure to knock 'em dead. The guys all thought she was the best-looking woman on campus."

"Were they going steady? Summer Hetherington and Cass Bruce?"

Blondie pushed an empty coffee cup to the side. "Maybe. You know how rumors spread. I've heard she may have been going with Wayne Foley, another rodeo guy."

Dark hair was quick to respond. "Not likely. Wayne Foley's family has money. He's engaged to Doris Hamilton from Red Lodge. I used to live there, so I know her and her family. She waits table at the Student Union. Two summers ago, she got a job cleaning house at the Foley ranch and has been chasing Wayne ever since."

Blondie grinned. "I guess she caught him."

"Yes. They've planned a huge wedding at the Foley family compound on Long Island in the fall." Dark hair showed a wry smile. "Doris keeps a close watch on Wayne Foley. She's not about to let any other woman mess up the life that marriage to him will give her."

"Maybe, but someone said that Foley took Summer for an airplane ride."

"Not likely. Doris would never allow it."

Blondie pushed back from the table. "Let's get the check. I have things to do before I go home."

As they walked out the door, Merci dug into her purse to retrieve a small note pad on which she wrote, "Wayne Foley."

CHAPTER THIRTY-THREE

Merci's first stop after breakfast was at the office of the Gallatin County Sheriff. Abel Parsons' huge hand enveloped her small one. "It's nice to make your acquaintance, Miss Bruce." He gestured toward the door to the right. "We can visit in here." With Merci seated on a hard chair before his desk and he behind it, the sheriff began. "I'm sure it's the Hetherington matter that brings you here. But what do you want from me?"

Merci nodded. "Anything you can tell me will be helpful."

The sheriff turned his chair to cross his legs. "Ordinarily I wouldn't discuss any criminal investigation with a defense attorney without clearance from the county attorney." He paused. "But you'll quickly learn everything I know, so there's little sense in wasting your time as well as mine." Parsons smiled. "So what, specifically, do you have in mind?"

Jim Moore

Merci smiled. "You conducted the first interview with most of those who were at the hot springs the evening of the girl's her death. And you've had time to reflect on the things they said. Surely, you've had thoughts about it all. Would you be kind enough to share those thoughts with me?"

Parsons settled back into his chair and smiled. "My thoughts aren't worth much, ma'am. But it looks as if your nephew was the only one who had the opportunity to kill that poor girl." He paused. "I'm sure you'd like to hear something else but there isn't anything else to tell you."

Merci nodded. "What have you learned about Summer Hetherington? What kind of person was she?"

The sheriff shook his head. "I know nothing of substance about her. You should talk to the sorority house mother."

Merci leaned forward. "I'll do that. While I'm here, perhaps you can tell me about your involvement in the matter."

The sheriff nodded and began at the beginning when Josh Waddell had come to him with the news. He told of interviewing Cass Bruce, the first contestant they'd come to.

"What did you learn from him?"

"He was forthcoming. Led us to believe that he wasn't aware that anything had happened to the Hetherington girl. He was entered in the bareback riding, so he was in a hurry. We asked him to make a list of all who were at the Springs the night before and bring it to the jail after the rodeo ended."

Merci's smile continued to show. "Did he do that?"

"Yes, he did, ma'am."

"When he arrived, what else did he tell you?"

"Not much more. He told us that nine of them traveled

146

to Hunter's Hot Springs in two cars. Summer Hetherington was in his car when they went out. She wasn't in his car when they left to come back. But he claimed he thought she's gotten in the other car for that trip."

Merci's smile was replaced by a frown. "Were you suspicious of him at that time?"

Parsons looked squarely at her. "I wasn't."

"What about Sheriff Waddell?"

The officer cocked his head. "I believe he was suspicious, even then."

Merci raised an eyebrow. "Even then? What do you mean by that?"

"It wasn't until the next day that a girl who was in the group gave us information that showed Cass Bruce had the opportunity. She said that Cass Bruce, after he got to his car, yelled that he forgotten his wallet and ran back to the dressing room to get it."

"And you think he killed her in that short time?"

"It's not what I believe that matters. Merrill Hodder, the Park County Attorney must believe that's the case. He's charged Cassius Bruce with murder."

"Indeed, he has." Merci rose while reaching out for the customary handshake. "Thank you, Sheriff Parsons." When he released her hand, she added, "May I have a copy of the names of those you interviewed about the happening at the Hunter's Hot Springs?"

"Of course." The sheriff extracted a piece of yellow paper from a desk drawer. "I knew you'd want the list. This has the names of all who were there. The ones I've talked to have a check mark beside the name."

Jim Moore

Merci glanced at the paper in her hand. "Thank you again, sir. My law partner and I may want to visit with you again."

"It would be my pleasure, ma'am."

She stepped toward the door to the office but stopped when the sheriff, now standing, spoke again. "Miss Bruce, I hope you find that your nephew didn't commit that crime. He was forthright in the things he told Sheriff Waddell and me each time we talked with him. He just never acted like a guilty person."

Merci smiled again. "It's kind of you to share that thought, sir. Since I'm certain he isn't guilty, I'll keep poking around. Some information may turn up to tell us who really did it."

CHAPTER THIRTY-FOUR

The Chi Omega sorority house, an older, carefully designed and well-maintained residential building, was located near the campus on the north side of Cleveland Avenue. Merci parked her auto on the street and trod up the walkway to the front door. A tall attractive woman about sixty years of age answered the knock. "May I help you?"

Merci introduced herself as a lawyer representing Cassius Bruce and asked if they could visit about Summer Hetherington. The woman stepped back from the doorway and led Merci to a large sitting room where she waved Merci to one of two comfortable chairs. She took the other.

"I'm Eloise Newman, the housemother for this sorority. How can I help you?"

"As I said, I represent Cassius Bruce. You must have heard that he's been charged with the Hetherington girl's death."

"Yes, everyone knows that." The housemother's eyes dropped to her hands. "What a tragedy!" She pulled a handkerchief from the sleeve of her blouse to wipe at an eye.

Merci waited for the housemother to regain her composure before asking her to tell about Summer Hetherington.

A wistful smile replaced the tears. "She was lovely." The smile faded. "Summer was of average height, a little on the tall side. She had the figure every young woman wishes for. Her long hair was caramel-colored. Her eyes, brown. She had a small nose that some might call pert." The lady looked at Merci. "Is that what you want to know?"

Merci nodded. "It is. But I also need to know what kind of person she was."

"What kind of person was Summer?" Mrs. Newman shifted in the chair. "She was a remarkable young woman. Intelligent, personable, warm, and friendly. She was seldom anything but happy and smiling. Everyone liked her."

"Sounds like someone extraordinary."

"Indeed, she was." The wistful smile disappeared. "It's difficult to sit here and speak of her as no longer with us."

Merci leaned forward. "As the kind of person you've described, there must have been a young man or maybe several young men in her life."

"Oh yes! She was popular with the fellas. She was always getting calls for dates. But she was selective. She went out with different men from time to time. But only two or three seemed to be of much interest to her." A small frown creased her brow. "One of them was your client, Cassius Bruce."

"What can you tell me about him?"

The frown disappeared. "That boy is a charmer." She

paused for a second. "He's nice looking, as I'm sure you know. He's perfectly polite. He always addressed me 'Mrs. Newman.' And in casual conversation he called me 'Ma'am.'"

"Did Summer and Cass spend much time together?"

"As much as she spent with any one man. As you no doubt know, she kept a horse at the fairground and participated in the college rodeos. She didn't have a car. The fairgrounds are on the north side of Bozeman, not within easy walking distance. I know he took her down there quite often to care for the horse." She paused, looking into the distance. "Those two, Summer and Cassius, seemed more like friends than people pursuing a romance."

Merci said, "You said there were two or three who interested Summer Hetherington. Who were they?"

"I guess there was only one besides Cass Bruce. Wayne Foley. I understood that he was another rodeo contestant."

"What was he like?"

"Wayne Foley was polite too. Just like Cassius. But it wasn't in the same warm and friendly way. He was more standoffish, if I can use such a term to describe him."

"Did Summer spend much time with him?"

"Not until recently. And not as much as with Cassius. I would know he was here to get her because he drove that big Buick Roadmaster. It's only in the last two or three months that Wayne has come around."

"Was Foley's interest in Summer one of romance?"

"How am I to know? But it's probable, isn't it?"

Merci said, "I'd like to talk with some of Summer's sorority sisters, if possible. Are any of them about?"

"I'm afraid not. It's the end of the school year and they've left for home."

"Can you tell me the names of those Summer was closest to?"

"Ella Brown, her roommate. But the one she seemed to feel most comfortable with was Donna Hathaway."

"Where do they live?"

"Ella lives in Whitehall and Donna in Townsend."

Merci stood and put out her hand. "I appreciate the time you've taken with me. You've given me a better insight into Miss Hetherington's life."

The housemother held the door as Merci stepped out onto the stoop. "I hope they find that someone else committed this awful crime. Cass is such a nice boy, I can't believe he did it."

Merci drove to Whitehall, arriving at the Borden Hotel at seven o'clock. She was given a comfortable room for the night. After a quiet meal in the dining room she bathed, climbed into bed and reviewed the things she'd learned that day.

Chapter Thirty-five

Cass's first day at the Dodson ranch arrived with bright sunshine. He knocked on the kitchen door at six thirty in the morning. Hearing a loud, "Come in," he pushed into the kitchen. Forrest, seated at the table in the middle of the large room, removed his spectacles and set aside a copy of *The Drovers Journal*. He greeted Cass with a hearty, "Good morning."

Lillian, flipping pancakes, flashed a smile over her shoulder. Hannah pointed toward a chair next to the table, set for four. She grabbed the coffee pot from the stove, filled a cup for Cass and said, "You may need this. Dad plans to take you over the whole ranch today."

Cass smiled from Hannah to Forrest. "I'm looking forward to it."

Forrest explained, "Lillian or Hannah can show you where different things are located while I'm in the hospital. I'd better show you the entire outfit the first thing so I can answer any questions you have about the operation."

Talking ceased when platters of food appeared on the table. The ladies joined the men. Forrest turned to Cass. "We ask a blessing at this house." With that he bowed his head. Cass followed suit as Lillian recited, "Bless us Lord and these thy gifts which we are about to receive from thy bounty. Through Christ Our Lord. Amen."

When finished eating, Forrest pushed his plate to the side and clambered to his feet. "Let's go." Cass offered quick thanks for the meal to the ladies and followed his new employer to his pickup.

As they traveled, Forrest described his operation in detail. Cass looked as he listened. He was impressed by the fences— four wires, well braced and stretched tight. The condition of the range showed no evidence of overgrazing. They traveled slowly over the low hills and shallow coulees, passing from pasture to pasture with Cass opening and closing the tight gates with lever latches at each fence line. Forrest kept up his monologue about the water sources and other features of each pasture, with only an occasional question from Cass.

Turning eastward and veering south, they went through a gate to come upon a scattering of yearling steers grazing along a hillside. Most were white-faced Herefords with a few blacks and black white faces. The rancher told Cass there were about two hundred fifty yearlings in the pasture. The next two pastures held about the same number. He explained the rotation throughout the year and from one year to the next to prevent overgrazing.

It was close to three o'clock when they again approached the ranch buildings, having traveled several miles over open country. Dodson explained that his wife was patient with him and would have a late meal ready. And so it was. When they finished eating, Forrest said, "Get your saddle and riding gear ready. Tomorrow we'll introduce you to some of the horses."

Hannah chimed in. "You'll like the horses. But just remember, you don't get to ride my barrel horse." After a moment, she added, "Or Summer's."

At the dawn of another warm Montana, June day, Cass met Hannah and Forrest at the horse barn, a short distance from the main house. Twelve horses were in one of three small pastures adjacent to the barn. They all drifted toward the corrals when they saw people at the barn. Cass soon learned what drew them there. Forrest and Hannah scattered oats along troughs that lined portions of the corral fence. When Hannah opened the gate, the horses traipsed to the troughs each seemingly accustomed to his own place.

Cass recognized both Hannah's and Summer's barrel horses among the rest of the young geldings. Hannah poured each of them a tad more oats than she gave any of the others.

Forrest stood next to Cass while the animals chewed the oats, telling him all about the horses. When they finished the oats, he said, "Let's saddle up. Try that dark red horse. I call him Ketchup. I think you'll like him."

After Cass mounted, he noticed the twist of pain on Forrest's face as he pulled himself into the saddle.

They rode about two miles to a much larger set of corrals constructed of metal panels fastened to solid wooden posts. Cass noticed a squeeze chute and a set of livestock scales. He could see that the corrals were laid out for the easy working of cattle. Forrest explained. "In April of each year, an order buyer begins buying yearling steers for my account and has them delivered here. Our veterinarian checks them over as they arrive and we brand them." He pointed. "They go first into that pasture until they settle down. Then we move them on and out of the way for the next load."

Dodson turned to Cass. "I don't like to cowboy the livestock unless it's really necessary. When we find a yearling that needs attention—sick, bad feet or whatever—we bring him in here to treat it. We don't rope and tie them out on the range unless, for some reason, the animal can't be moved." Dodson lifted the reins. "Let's move along. We should check the water pump in the southwest pasture. It's a diesel pump that was acting up for a while. It's been working fine lately but we don't dare let the cattle run out of water."

They arrived back at the barn in mid-afternoon to find that Lillian was waiting again with dinner. Cass concluded that late midday meals might be an ordinary thing on the Dodson Ranch.

The next evening, Forrest said, "Tomorrow's Saturday. We need to go to Billings for things we can't get in Roundup. Saddle one of the horses and use the day to look the outfit over. On Sunday we go to church. You're welcome to join us if you wish."

"I haven't been much of a church goer, so I'll take the day to get settled in, maybe wash some clothes."

Forrest continued, "I'm to have a pre-surgery physical on Monday. Lillian and Hannah are going with me, so you'll be on your own. Take the pickup and spend more time just getting acquainted. Check fences as you go and take a look at the water tank in the southeast pasture."

Mrs. Dodson said, "We won't be back until late. I'll leave stew and some other things to eat in the refrigerator, so you shouldn't go hungry."

Cass rose from his chair. "I'll do fine. If I write down a list of staples could you pick them up for me on your shopping trip? Then I can feed myself when you are away."

Hannah laughed. "You can cook?"

Cass turned to her with a smile. "I can cook the necessaries. I don't pretend to cook any fancy stuff."

"Maybe you'll let me sample some of it someday."

"Whenever you think you can stomach it."

Away from the others and back at the bunkhouse Cass found visions of the penitentiary clouding his mind. They had become almost a constant.

CHAPTER THIRTY-SIX

Merci learned that Ella Brown worked at her father's bank and decided it would be best to let the banker know the purpose of her visit. Seated in his office, she said, "You must know of the death of Summer Hetherington, your daughter's college roommate."

The man's smile disappeared. "Of course, I know about it. She and Ella were more than roommates; they were good friends. Our daughter has been terribly upset."

"I'm trying to learn all I can about Miss Hetherington. It would be helpful to visit with your daughter. May I do so?"

The banker asked, "What's your interest in the girl's death?"

"You may know that they've charged a young man with her murder. I'm an attorney who represents Mr. Bruce."

"Didn't you just tell me that your name is Bruce?"

"Yes, I did. Cassius is my nephew."

Grover straightened in his chair. "Isn't that some kind of

a problem? A lawyer representing a relative?"

Merci offered her charming smile. "A different lawyer is the lead counsel for Mr. Bruce. I'm working with that lawyer. There'll be no ethical problem with my activities."

The man shrugged. "Well, if there's a problem, it won't be mine or Ella's." He stood. "Give me a minute. I'll get her."

Merci could hear murmurings as he spoke to his daughter and then called another woman to work the teller booth in her place. Soon, the banker returned with a young woman.

Merci, when the banker introduced his daughter, put out a hand that Ella Brown held for only an instant.

Her father held a chair for Ella. "I told Ella you want to visit about Summer."

Ella's face contorted into a frown. "Dad said you're trying to save Cass Bruce. You won't get any help from me."

The fierce tone of her voice took Merci by surprise, but she responded in measured tones. "Yes, I represent Cass. To do that job properly we need to know as much as possible about the night of her death and about Summer Hetherington. You roomed with her for two years, so you must know her as well as anyone. I hope you'll tell me what kind of person she was."

Ella slumped in the chair while staring downward to pick at a fingernail. At last she raised her head, took a breath, and finally spoke in a rush. "Summer was one of the smartest and nicest people you could ever meet. She deserved to live a long life, to get married, to have kids, to watch them grow up. She sure didn't deserve to be killed."

"Just so you know, I don't believe Cass murdered her, but despite my belief, he's charged with the crime. As you surely understand, our laws allow him to defend himself against the charge. I'm seeking information that may help in that defense. You're not obligated to share your thoughts about Summer with me, but I hope you will." She leaned forward for emphasis. "Just to be certain that justice is served."

Ella sighed. "All right. Summer was the golden girl, the best looking, the one with the nicest personality, and the smartest. She could do no wrong. Summer was easy to room with. Everything of hers was neat and tidy." She smiled. "My style was a little different. But Summer never complained about the messes I made."

"How about her study habits?"

"Good grades were important to her, so she spent a lot of time at the library. And she got good grades."

"Did you two do things together other than at the sorority house? Maybe double date?"

"No, certainly not double date. Summer could be out on a date every night if she chose. Her dates were jealous of their time with her. They didn't want anyone else around."

Merci crossed her legs and smoothed her skirt. "All of this has been helpful. What else can you tell me about Summer?"

"Nothing much." Ella blinked at a sudden thought. "Well, one thing. Even though Mom and Dad provided me with all the nice clothes I could desire, she didn't seem at all jealous. She would often compliment me on some new dress, but she never seemed to wish for more than she had."

"No envy?"

"Never."

"You make her seem like someone too good to be true."

"Yes, but that's the kind of person she was."

"Did Summer have a special boyfriend?"

"She spent time with Cass. But I wouldn't call him her boyfriend."

"And others?"

"She went out a few times recently with Wayne Foley. He's another of the rodeo guys."

"Were she and Wayne Foley going steady?"

Ella shook her head. "No. He was just another guy who caught her fancy for the moment." She added, "He had a big fancy Buick I think that car is what Summer found most impressive about Wayne."

Merci rose from her chair, and the others followed suit. With a reach for the banker's hand, she said, "Thank you, sir, for allowing me to take up a part of your day." She turned to his daughter. "And thank you, Miss Brown, for sharing your thoughts with me."

CHAPTER THIRTY-SEVEN

From Whitehall it was a slow drive over a narrow highway that followed the many curves of the Jefferson River back to the town of Three Forks. Forty miles over windswept roads northward from Three Forks took Merci to Townsend, another small county seat town along the Missouri River. After eating a solitary lunch in a quiet café on Main Street, she said to the proprietress, "I'm looking for Donna Hathaway. Can you tell me where I might find her?"

The woman answered while counting out Merci's change. "Actually, Donna's working at the hardware store up the street a block. You can't miss it."

Merci gave her thanks, dropped a generous tip on the table and left the café. At the hardware store a bespectacled young woman manned the cash register. She handed change to an elderly man and turned to Merci. "May I help you?"

"I hope so. My name is Merci Bruce. I'm hoping to find Donna Hathaway. Might that be you?"

8 SECONDS

The young woman's brow went up in a look of inquiry. "I'm Donna. What do you want with me?"

"I've been told you and Summer Hetherington were friends at Montana State."

A cautious look appeared. "Yes, we were friends. Why?"

"I'm an attorney who represents the young man accused of the crime. Is there somewhere that you and I can visit?"

Miss Hathaway glanced around the room. "I'm working and can't talk to you now."

"I understand. Is there a time when we could talk in private? I won't bother you for long."

Donna Hathaway appeared close to tears. "It's hard for me to think about what happened to Summer, much less talk about it." She shook her head, eyes on the ground. "It's just so wrong."

Merci waited a second before saying, "I'm sure you want the one who killed her to pay the price."

Donna raised her head. "That's Cass Bruce."

"He's accused of the crime. But whether he's guilty or not will be decided by a jury."

"There doesn't seem to be any doubt. Everyone says he's the last one who was alone with her at Hunter's Hot Springs."

Merci spoke in a patient manner. "What everyone says and what actually happened may not be the same." A man holding a shovel approached the checkout counter. Merci asked, "Do you take a midafternoon break? If so, could I meet you somewhere. I'll buy some refreshments."

"I'm off at three o'clock for half an hour. I'll meet you at the Busy Bee."

Jim Moore

The Busy Bee, located on the highway leading to Helena, was an ice cream parlor that served a limited offering of meals. Donna Hathaway, appearing frazzled, hurried through the door and saw Merci standing by a table with one hand raised to attract her attention. She dropped into one of the chairs without a word, picked up a menu, scanned it for a second, put it down and looked at Merci. "I don't know why I bother. The food never changes."

If the food never changes, perhaps you can tell me what's good here."

"Oh, everything's good. It's just that it's always the same. I like their strawberry milkshakes."

"That will do for me." Merci put the menu aside. "As I told you, I'm one of the attorneys representing Cassius Bruce."

After a teenage waitress took their orders, Merci asked, "What about Summer and the guys?"

Donna smiled. "Since the veterans returned from the war there have been more men than girls on campus. Lots of men wanted to date Summer." The grin faded. "But the only man Summer spent much time with was Cass Bruce. He'd show up and they'd go off and do things together."

"What kind of things?"

"He helped her with her horse a lot." Donna paused to think. "They went to a movie, but mostly just daytime dates."

"Did any other man interest Summer? Someone she thought of in a more romantic way?"

Donna stirred the milkshake with a straw and frowned. "The last few months she was seeing a fellow named Wayne Foley. He's tall, really good looking and supposedly has lots of money."

"How did they get acquainted"?

"He's a rodeo guy, too. I guess that's where they met."

"Did he help her with her horse like Cass Bruce? Was that what brought them together?"

"Oh no!" Donna shook her head. "The first time he came to get her, she got all dressed up and was waiting for him. He parked that big car at the curb and knocked on the door. Mrs. Newman let him in. I guess he was polite enough with her but rather impatient and anxious to get going. No small talk."

"Did Summer tell you where they went... what they did?"

"No, she didn't. That was different. She would often share stories about funny things that happened on dates." She frowned. "With Wayne, it was different. She didn't want to talk about the things they did together."

"It sounds like you had concerns. Was there something about Wayne Foley that bothered you?"

"For one thing, he was engaged to be married."

"Did Summer know about it?"

"She must have. It was common knowledge."

"Did you talk to her about it?"

"Just once. She told me to mind my own business." Donna looked across the table. "I don't know what it was that she found so attractive in that man. Maybe it was his good looks or the big car or the large ranch his family is supposed to have. I just don't know."

"Did Cass Bruce know about all of this?"

"If he did, it didn't seem bother him. He'd still help Summer with her horse and they still did some other things

Jim Moore

together. But not in the evenings. Those were saved for Foley."
Donna straightened, looked at her watch and hurriedly
sucked up the last of the milkshake. "I have to get back to
work." She grabbed her purse. "I hope this has been helpful.
I don't like to think bad things about Cass but everyone says
he's the only one who had the chance."

CHAPTER THIRTY-EIGHT

Merci spent Friday at the office and reported all she'd learned to Geoffrey, The next day, she drove to Ennis to interview Lyndon Welch, a saddle bronc rider and one of the nine who were at Hunter's Hot Springs. Welch recited his remembrance of the events of the night: the decision to go, the time spent in the pool, and the rush to leave. He had a vague recollection of Cass going back to retrieve a wallet. His comments about Summer Hetherington were all complimentary. Merci dutifully reported it all to Geoffrey.

Two days later she made the drive from Billings to Lodge Grass to visit with Zeke Howard. He worked in a feed store and agreed to talk with her in a storage room during his work hours as long as she understood that he'd have to wait on a customer if one arrived. He was a heavy set young man with a ruggedly handsome face and dark hair and eyebrows. During the conversation he explained that he didn't live on a ranch but was able to keep his calf roping horse in the store owner's feed lot. Otherwise he wouldn't be able to rodeo.

In answer to Merci's questions about the events at the hot springs he had little news to offer. Some of his remarks about Cass seemed to indicate his feelings for his fellow rodeo hand were less than positive. "Cass was the one who decided we should go to Hunter's Hot Springs. He didn't even ask the rest of us." And, "As usual, he took charge when we got there and collected the money." And "I've always thought he had his eye on Summer but she didn't seem to think too much of him."

The interview with Zeke took less than thirty minutes, so Merci stopped in Billings to meet with her senior partner. Geoffrey gestured to some chairs next to a small table where coffee and rolls awaited. Refreshments were not customary, but welcome. They would serve as an early lunch. Merci told of her conversation with Zeke Howard and of his apparent dislike of Cass Bruce.

"Will he be a problem for us at trial?"

"Perhaps, if the county attorney can figure out a way to show that his feelings are relevant to the murder."

"That, it seems, would be difficult."

They spent a brief time visiting about the affairs of the law firm before Merci stood to go. She still had a three-hour drive to the Madden ranch near Stanford.

"I'll be interested in the things you learn," Geoffrey said. "Thank you for checking in with me. I appreciate our brief times together."

A telephone call to Justin Madden had confirmed that he could meet with her in midafternoon. On her arrival at the ranch in the Judith Basin, Justin greeted her with an easy smile and an invitation to join him in the kitchen. He introduced his father, mother and younger sister, each of whom offered a hand in welcome before settling into chairs at the kitchen table, already graced with a plate of cookies. Wilbur Madden, Justin's father said, "I guess you want to talk with Justin about the death of that young woman, right?"

"Yes, sir. I do." She turned to his son. "It would be helpful if you would tell me all that you remember about the day that Summer Hetherington lost her life."

Mr. Madden interjected, "Lost her life? Hell, she was murdered."

Merci acknowledged him, saying, "That's correct, sir." She turned again to Justin. "Please begin, if you will, with the decision to go to Hunter's Hot Springs. Who suggested it?"

Justin's face twisted slightly as he thought. With his eyes on the wall behind Merci, he proceeded to give the same details of the evening she'd heard many times from Cass and others who were there.

"Did everyone go?"

"No, Wayne Foley said he couldn't. He had things he had to do." Justin gave a slight grin. "I'd hoped he'd go and drive his big Buick. It's a lot more comfortable than either my car or Cass's."

Merci asked, "Anyone else who didn't want to go?"

"Foley's girlfriend, Doris Hamilton. She never lets Wayne out of her sight."

Merci, nibbling on a cookie, turned to Mrs. Madden. "These are delicious."

Jim Moore

Justin's mother put a hand her daughter's arm. "Lucie baked them. She likes to cook."

"I made lots. Eat all you want," Lucie offered.

Merci broke another corner from a cookie and popped it into her mouth before shifting her attention again to Justin. "I'm most interested in the time when you left. What do you remember?"

Justin straightened in the chair, a pained expression on his face. "When someone—I believe it was Harry Croswell—hollered that it was getting late, we all scrambled out of the pool. As soon as I dressed, I beat it out to the car. Zeke Howard was right behind me, and Hannah Dodson not far behind him." Justin stopped to think. "I started the car. April wasn't in the car yet, so I waited."

"What did you do while you waited?"

"I watched for April. My car was parked on the far side of Cass's. I could see some of the others getting into his car. Finally, April came running, opened the car door, stood beside it for a minute, then climbed into the front seat beside me. That's when I put the car in gear and took off."

"Could you see if Cass was following you?"

Justin thought again. "Not right away, I guess, but when we reached the highway, he was there."

Merci leaned in his direction. "We're told that you and April Menard went to the sheriff in Bozeman to say that Cass Bruce got to his auto, then went back to get his wallet. You also said Summer Hetherington was still inside when he did it. Were Cass Bruce and Summer Hetherington alone in the pool area?"

Justin frowned. "They might have been, I mean, that's

what April says happened." He leaned slightly toward Merci. "Look, I don't want to accuse Cass of anything. April was the one who said she saw Cass go back for his wallet; I didn't. She insisted on telling the sheriffs, so I took her to the jail to do it."

"It's helpful to know that. I expect to visit with her soon." Merci placed her hands on the table, ready to stand. "Anything else stick in your mind about that night at the hot springs?"

"No ma'am. If I think of anything, can I call you?"

"You can, and I hope you will." She stood and extracted a business card from her purse. "That's the number."

Merci offered her hand to Mr. and Mrs. Madden. "You are gracious hosts."

Finally, she reached for Justin's hand. "Thank you sharing what you remember with me. Cass will appreciate it as well."

The young man's last words followed Merci to her auto. "Tell Cass I'm sure he didn't kill Summer."

CHAPTER THIRTY-NINE

The Dodson family returned to the ranch Monday evening. The doctor's report was not good. Forrest's hernia had worsened. Emergency surgery was scheduled for Tuesday afternoon. All three family members would leave for Billings the next morning and would be away from the ranch for at least a couple of days. The responsibility for the care of the place would fall on Cass much sooner than any of them had contemplated. Could he handle it?

Cass assured them he could. "I'll do my best. It doesn't seem that much could go wrong in such a short time."

"Well, if something does go wrong and you need help, call our neighbor to the north. He is a good friend and will come running if you holler."

Shortly after breakfast Tuesday morning, the three Dodsons offered Cass their hurried goodbyes. Hannah was last into the car with Cass holding the door for her. She placed three fingers on his wrist and spoke softly. "I'll be back as soon as I'm sure Dad's going to be OK. You already know that I can handle a horse. I'll prove to you that I can cook."

Cass watched until the car disappeared over the hill. Only then did the import of his situation fully register. The responsibility for their ranch was now his alone, at least for a couple of days. For a moment he was at a loss, wondering what he should do. He looked around, rubbed his face, then decided the first and most important thing was to check on the cattle. He found the keys to the Dodson pickup on the seat, climbed in and was about to start the engine when a sudden and deep sense of gloom overwhelmed him. While the need to care for the Dodson cattle was important to them, it was of little personal consequence to him. He was still charged with the crime of murder. He could be convicted and sentenced to life in the prison at Deer Lodge. Or worse. The thought of standing on the gallows waiting for the drop through the trap door flashed across his mind. That mental picture was so stark as to make his stomach turn. For an instant he thought he would retch.

He forced the picture from his mind. He was not in court. Today was today and his obligation to the Dodsons remained. He punched the starter, pulled the pickup into gear and began the drive through the pastures, one by one. All seemed to be as it should be. There was water at the watering places. The fences were erect and stretched tight. The grass was green and lush. The cattle seemed content. By the time he'd reached the farthest point from headquarters, his optimistic nature had again taken control of his mind and feelings. It was a glorious day to be doing the things that he enjoyed doing.

Jim Moore

At two o'clock he parked the pickup in its usual place. Time to get something to eat. His first thought was to prepare something in the bunkhouse. The Dodsons had brought the staples he needed to feed himself. Then he reminded himself that Mrs. Dodson had said there were enough leftovers in the refrigerator for a meal or two. Cass trudged up the walkway to the kitchen door, reached for its handle and then stopped. It seemed like trespassing to barge into the Dodson house when there was no one there to greet him. But he had to eat and food intended for him was there. The feeling that he was intruding didn't leave him until he'd had his fill of food and scrubbed the dishes clean. As he left the house and closed the door behind him Cass resolved to keep to the bunkhouse.

The next morning, he was up at five, cooked breakfast and then saddled a dark bay horse to check on the cattle more carefully than he had the day before. This day was cold and dreary. In each pasture the yearling steers had drifted toward the southeast to seek shelter from the wind. They stood hunched up behind clumps of trees or brush with their heads lowered. The hair on all of them looked rough and the misery they suffered was evident. Nothing like the warm days before. It reminded Cass of how quickly the weather—and other things—could change.

The elements were no more merciful to Cass than to the cattle. Dressed warmly, he still suffered a chill each time a wind gust caught some opening in his clothing. His fingers were numb when he at last returned to the buildings and dragged the saddle from the horse. It took a while for the stove to heat the bunkhouse. Cass hunkered by it with his hands extended toward the heat.

And so, Cass established a routine. Up early, eat breakfast, travel the ranges, check the cattle, and handle any problem that arose. In the late afternoon tidy up the bunkhouse, wash clothes when needed, and prepare an evening meal. He ended most days by reading from a novel by Ernest Haycox, Walt Coburn, or Luke Short.

Dark thoughts of prison intruded constantly. He did his best to push them aside, with little success. And so, three days passed without any word from the Dodsons. He hoped the surgery went as planned.

Cass spent the days with no company but the cattle that he visited each day. He spent long hours on horseback, inspecting every acre of the Dodson ranch until some of the cattle in each group became distinct and recognizable.

Late in the afternoon on the fourth day, Lillian and Hannah drove up to the bunkhouse. Cass was out the door before they clambered from the auto. Lillian spoke first and her face revealed the worry that her words expressed. "Forrest's surgery hasn't gone well at all. The surgical wound's become infected." She shook her head.

Cass turned to Hannah, whose face was as grave as her mother's, and then returned his attention to Lillian.

She wiped her face on her sleeve to brush away a tear. "The poor man is worried about you being here all by yourself, so he made us come home to make sure you're all right."

Cass said, "I drove the whole place one day after you left and I've ridden the pastures to check all the cattle each of the other days. Nothing's gone wrong so far."

Lillian shook her head. "I'll tell him. It'll make him feel

better to hear what you've done. But I'm sure he'll continue to worry."

"What can I do to give him some reassurance?"

She smiled a wisp of a smile. "Nothing. It's just the way he is." Mrs. Dodson stood looking at the ground. At last she raised her eyes to say, "Forrest and I've decided that Hannah should be here. She can't do anything to make things better for him by sitting around in the hospital. But she knows how to do things here at the ranch."

Hannah, who'd been standing silently to the side, spoke at last. "I agree. At the hospital I'm just a bother. And it costs money for me to stay there."

Lillian nodded before turning to the auto. "I have to get back to Billings tonight, but first, we've got to wash clothes."

She climbed into the driver's seat and reached for the door. Cass stopped it with his hand. "You need to eat. How about I fix some supper here in the bunkhouse for all of us?"

Hannah spoke. "You'll cook?"

"Be here at about six o'clock."

For the first time since their arrival both women smiled as Hannah answered, "We're brave. We'll try it."

Supper was a hamburger loaf, baked potatoes, canned corn, store-bought bread and packaged pudding. They ate mostly in silence, each lost in private thoughts. The meal finished, Mrs. Dodson turned to Hannah. "Honey, please go fill the auto with gasoline. I don't want to run out on my way to town." Hannah patted her mother's hand, pushed away from the table and left.

When her daughter was safely out of hearing Lillian faced Cass. Her look and the serious tone of her voice were different than he'd seen before. "Having you and Hannah here alone on the ranch raises a new concern for me. Please understand. I find you to be a fine young man. But that's the problem. I remember well what it's like to be the age of you and Hannah, young and vital. I know you are 'just friends,' but that could change and a more intimate relationship…"

Cass interrupted, "But…,"

Lillian stopped him with a squeeze of his arm. "Hear me out. With you and Hannah here alone together, your admiration for each other may grow. One thing could lead to another without either of you intending for it to." She leaned so close to him when she next spoke that he was tempted to lean away. "What I'm saying is, I don't want you and my daughter to even think of engaging in any kind of romantic activity." She squeezed his arm even harder. "Is that completely clear?"

Cass was so startled by Lillian's remarks, he was speechless. At last he leaned back in his chair and said, "Mrs. Dodson, Hannah and I are friends. We enjoy each other's company and like to do the same kinds of things." He leaned forward. "But I've never thought of her that way."

"You don't find her attractive?"

"Of course, she's attractive." He flashed a quick grin. "She has plenty of male admirers, and I'm sure she's never wanted for dates. But she's never shown any romantic interest in me. Your daughter and I are good friends, and I hope we can always be friends."

They heard door slam as Hannah returned with the car. Lillian spoke hurriedly, "I believe you, and I do trust you both, but I just had to say something to relieve my concern."

Jim Moore

The object of their conversation breezed through the door saying, "The wind's come up. Looks like it might rain. We'd better get up to the house. You have a long way to go, Mom, and it takes a while to finish the wash."

Cass held the car door for Lillian. He turned to Hannah to ask in tentative tones, "Breakfast at six thirty?"

"Supper wasn't bad. I'll be here."

CHAPTER FORTY

The Menards lived in a neat two-story house in the northwest part of Lewistown. Merci called the evening she arrived after driving from Stanford, explained who she was and arranged for a visit with April. The young woman said she went to work at the dry goods store at ten o'clock but would be glad to answer the lawyer's questions if Merci could be at her house at nine. At Merci's knock, promptly on the hour, Mr. Menard opened the door, introduced himself and led her to the kitchen where the family of five had gathered. They settled into chairs around a Formica-topped table. Merci acknowledged the usual offer of coffee and treats then turned to April to say, "I'm here to ask what you remember from the evening at Hunter's Hot Springs, the evening that Summer Hetherington lost her life."

The young woman didn't say a word or change expression for a long moment. At last she shifted in the chair

Jim Moore

and heaved a sigh. "I feel so bad about Summer that I've tried to put it from my mind."

"I understand." Merci spoke quietly but then persisted. "As I'm sure you know, Cass Bruce is accused of killing her. I'm trying to learn all I can about the events that night especially how it happened that none of you realized Summer wasn't in a car when the rest of you left."

April remained quiet for a moment before saying, "I don't know where to begin."

"How about at the beginning. You and the others went to the Hunter's Hot Springs. Was it a common thing for the rodeo group to do such things together?"

April shook her head. "No. Not at all." She shifted in her chair. "There's a rodeo club for those who compete, but there are others who spend time with them." She placed a palm on her chest. "I don't rodeo, but I like to be with those who do."

One of her two younger brothers piped up. "What she means is that she likes to spend time with Justin Madden. He's her boyfriend."

Merci smiled. "I visited with Justin yesterday." Returning her attention to April she said, "So the trip to Hunter's was a one-time thing for the nine of you?"

"Yes, but it wasn't uncommon for three or four of us to get together from time to time—at the student union for a coke or downtown for a burger. A couple of times some of us went to the movies and sat together. One of those times it was Cass and Summer, Wayne Foley and Doris Hamilton, and Justin and me, of course."

"Cass and Summer?"

"Yes, they were a couple. I don't know for sure if they

were going steady, but it sure seemed like it to me."

Merci moved on. "Was Wayne Foley one of the regulars?'

"Well, yes, as regular as any of us. He's a calf roper, so he spent some time doing things with the other contestants."

"Then how did it happen that he didn't go with you?"

"At first it seemed that he would go and take his big Buick. But then Doris said something, and he changed his mind."

"Doris?"

April frowned. "Doris Hamilton is Wayne's girlfriend. It seems they're always together."

Merci placed her coffee cup on the table. "I've been told that you all left the pool in a hurry. Is that correct?'

"Yes. Harry Croswell hollered that we'd better get going or we'd miss the curfew, so we all scrambled out of the water and into the dressing rooms. There were just us three girls in the women's room: Summer, Hannah Dodson and me. Summer mumbled something about a shower, and I told her we didn't have time. She got in the shower anyway."

"Who was first to leave?"

"Hannah. She changed in a hurry and ran out the door."

"That left you and Summer in the dressing room."

"Yes. When I left Summer was pulling on her clothes. I didn't look back but assumed she'd follow me out the door."

"What did you do then?"

"I went out to Justin's car and looked inside to see who was in the back seat. It was getting pretty dark, so it took a minute for me to see Zeke and Hannah. I figured the other guys were in Cass's car and maybe Summer, too. "Just as I was about climb into the front seat, I heard Cass holler that he'd forgotten his wallet. He ran back to get it."

"Did you see him come back from the pool?"

April shook her head. "I'd gotten into the seat and pulled the door shut, so I didn't look back to see if he'd come back yet. Justin put the car in gear and drove away." She shook her head. "We just left poor Summer there. I wish I'd waited for her to finish dressing. If I had maybe what happened wouldn't have happened." She dabbed at her eyes.

"I'm so sorry for your loss," Merci said, pushing her chair back "Thank you for helping me understand what happened that night." She put out a hand. "I may wish to visit with you again." Before turning to the kitchen doorway, she shook the hand of each of the other members of the Menard family.

Mr. Menard escorted her to the door and held it for her. "Our daughter wants to be sure the one who killed that girl is punished. If it was your client, she may not be of help to you."

Merci half turned. "I'm sure she'll just tell the truth. That's all Cass and I ask."

Seeing she had time for one more interview, Merci used a pay phone to call Greg Lovell. She left Lewistown shortly after noon to drive south through the Judith Gap, then westward to White Sulphur Springs. She'd arranged to meet Greg at the Truck Stop after he finished the day's labors.

She arrived early, found a table and ordered coffee while she waited for his arrival.

Lovell, wearing work-worn western clothing, spotted Merci as he walked in. He snatched his hat from his head and hurried to the table. He apologized for being late. Merci waved the apologies aside and pointed to a chair. He sat, dropped his hat on the floor, and said with a smile. "So, you're Cass's aunt? He's spoken of you."

"I hope his remarks have been kind."

"Oh yes. He thinks you're great. Says you can handle a horse better than any woman he knows."

"Nice compliment." Merci rested her arms on the table top. "You surely know that Cass has been charged with killing Summer Hetherington. What can you tell me about her?"

Lovell's head cocked to one side as she thought. "Summer? She was a sorority girl, and I wasn't a fraternity guy, so we didn't run in the same circles. I wouldn't have known her at all if she hadn't been a barrel racer."

"Of those in the rodeo group, whom was she closest to?"

"The other barrel racer, Hannah Dodson. They grew up in the same town and traveled to the rodeos together."

Merci leaned toward him. "What about the men?"

"I know that she and Cass dated some." He hastened to add, "But she was a popular girl. She could have had a date every night of the week."

"Any others beside Cass who stick in your mind?"

Lovell looked away for a second. "Come to think of it, she seemed to kind of hang around Wayne Foley lately."

"What do you mean, 'hang around?'"

He faced Merci directly. "Lately, when we've been at the fairgrounds taking care of the horses, she seemed to stick close to Wayne. I don't remember her doing that until recently."

"How did Wayne Foley react?"

"Wayne's a nice guy and a gentleman. He treated Summer

just the way you would expect, always friendly and polite."

"Did you see any sign of a romantic interest between them?"

Lovell laughed. "Not a chance. Doris Hamilton has poor Wayne roped and tied. She isn't going to let another girl get close to him."

Merci shifted the conversation. "How did it happen that Summer was left behind at Hunter's Hot Springs?"

Lovell shook his head. "I just don't know how that happened. Those of us in Cass's car assumed she was with Justin. The other girls were. Justin must have assumed she was with us."

Merci pushed from the table. "I don't want to take too much of your time. Please call me if you think of anything that might help us find the one responsible for Summer's death."

"You don't think Cass did it?"

"I'm certain. Cass could never kill anyone."

"I'm glad to hear you say that. I don't think he did it either," Greg said as he held the door for her.

CHAPTER FORTY-ONE

Hannah was quiet while they ate their breakfast of eggs and sausage the morning after she returned to the ranch. It was cloudy and cool when they saddled the horses. The sun broke through the clouds as they rode through the cattle, sometimes side by side, sometimes separately in order to check the far sides of different hills. Hannah enjoyed the pastoral scenery—the shimmering tree leaves, the varicolored browns and greens of the curing grass, the gray sage, and the healthy red of the cattle in contrast with the white of their faces.

Cass, on the other hand, had another disturbing matter crowding his mind—one beside the all but constant specter of time in the penitentiary. He found himself viewing Hannah in a new light. Because of Lillian's admonition, he felt a strange discomfort around her.

In early afternoon, as they walked from the corrals to the house, Hannah said, "I'll fix a couple of sandwiches to tide us over until supper and put a roast in the oven for tonight."

"You don't need to feed me. I've been doing pretty well by myself."

She turned to face him. "Look, we're here together. There's no reason for us to eat alone—unless you'd rather."

"The roast sounds great," he conceded. "I have some apples. How about I make a pie."

Hannah's laugh was lyrical. "You're acting like a girl trying to convince some boy that she'd make a good wife."

"Nonsense. I'll bring the pie. You can eat it or not."

Hannah set the roast, mashed potatoes and gravy and fresh peas on the table. Neither spoke much as they ate. Cass cut the pie and each of them poured thick cream over a slice. After the last of the pie was swallowed, Hannah crossed her arms to rest them on the table and looked directly into Cass's eyes. "Mom gave you the talk, didn't she?"

"She did."

Hannah heaved an exasperated sigh. "I knew she would do that. It's because of what happened to Summer."

"That's understandable."

"Look, Cass. I know you have no such ideas about me, but any testimony I could give about your relationship with Summer won't be worth anything—because of the time you and I have spent together."

"What kind of testimony would you give?"

Hannah held up her hand and pulled down one finger. "One—that you aren't the kind of guy that would push himself on a girl. I know because Summer and I talked about you."

"Oh?"

"Of course. Girls talk about guys, and we were good friends."

"What else?"

"Two," She pulled down another finger, "even though you've had your eye on Summer, like forever..."

Cass crossed his arms. "What are you talking about?"

"Cass, it was obvious—to me at least. Whenever she came around you'd get all google-eyed."

"Nonsense!"

"Come on. Wherever Summer was, you were there, always standing close by." Hannah grinned.

Cass sat silent for a long moment. Then he shrugged. "All right. I may have had feelings for Summer. I thought it would be nice to have something more with her than just friendship. But she wasn't interested."

"That's what I was getting at, Cass. She just wasn't interested in settling down with you or any other ranch guy. She longed to get away from Montana—far away. She wanted to go to the top of the Empire State building, listen to Big Ben chime, visit the Coliseum. It wasn't that she wanted money. She just wanted more out of life than a ranch house and a boring husband."

Cass, looking into the distance, muttered, "Perhaps."

"I'm sorry, Cass. I know you miss her," Hannah said, touching his arm as tears filled her eyes. "I do too, so I know how you're feeling, except that you have the worry of the trial on top of everything."

Cass blinked back tears. "Thanks, Hannah."

"The accusation that you killed Summer will go away. You'll get on with life and someday someone else will capture your heart."

"It's hard to think that right now."

"I know."

"Thanks for being a good friend, Hannah. You don't know how much that means to me, right now."

They ate breakfast in the bunkhouse before saddling horses for the daily ride through the cattle. The sun shone. The grass was lush and the cattle seemed to smile in contentment. And so, the daylight hours passed.

It became they're habit to sit side-by-side on the bunkhouse stoop as the air cooled in the evening, engaged in conversations with no particular focus. And so, Cass Bruce and Hannah Dodson settled into a relationship that each of them found pleasant and comfortable.

Chapter Forty-two

Wayne Foley had agreed, reluctantly, to meet with Merci at the family ranch near Roscoe. He suggested that Doris Hamilton join them, a suggestion that Merci readily accepted. She would need to talk with the Hamilton girl at some point. This arrangement would save time.

The entry road led to the top of a small hill from which the buildings of the Foley ranch could be seen spread across an expanse of flatland next to the East Boulder River. All of the buildings were constructed of logs and painted a dark brown with a lighter brown trim. The main house, which seemed to stretch forever, was surrounded by a carefully groomed lawn interspersed with trees, shrubs and plants. Merci parked on the graveled area before the front entrance.

The young man who answered the door was movie-star handsome, about six feet two, and slender with a muscular upper body. Moving with lithe grace, he led Merci to a room dominated by a large office desk in one corner. Two of the walls were lined with bookshelves. A wide window gave a view of the grounds leading down to the river with mountains in the far distance. A huge stone fireplace took up much of the third wall. In another corner were four comfortable chairs surrounding a round table on which were a plate of fancy cookies, three cups and a carafe. A tall, attractive young woman with the figure of a fashion model stood with her arms crossed near one of the chairs. She remained sober faced and only nodded when Wayne introduced her as his fiancée, Doris Hamilton. She was wearing an engagement ring that bore a large diamond with a small sapphire on each side.

Foley held a chair for his guest before suggesting that Doris do the honors with the coffee and treats. When each of them was seated with a cup filled with coffee, Foley turned to Merci. "We understand that you're Cass Bruce's aunt and that you're a lawyer, providing legal help to Cass now that he's been charged with murder."

Merci couldn't help but smile at his blunt approach. "That about covers it." She reached for a cookie. "In an effort to learn as much as I can about the death of Summer Hetherington, I've visited with most of the others who've participated in the college rodeo program. Each has told me something that provides a better picture of the kind of person she was." She focused on Wayne. "You've been one of the rodeo group. I'm told you may be the best of all of the collegiate calf ropers, good enough to compete with the pros."

Foley didn't smile. "I do my best."

"You must have gotten to know Summer over the last

two or three of years. What can you tell me about her?"

Wayne glanced once at Doris who remained unsmiling. He turned again to Merci. "You say you've talked to the others, so you know she was an attractive and pleasant person." He waited for Merci to respond. When she didn't speak, he asked, "What more can I tell you?"

"Who were her closest friends? Who did she spend time with? What were her interests besides running the barrels?"

Foley was shaking his head before she finished speaking. "I can't answer those questions. She had her own life away from the arena and I had mine." He gestured toward Doris. "Much of my time has been with Doris."

Merci turned to the young woman. "I understand you're engaged to be married." She nodded toward Doris's hand. "I like the ring."

Doris seemed eager to discuss something other than the Hetherington killing. She uncrossed her arms and held the left hand out to better display the ring. "We visited Wayne's family last Christmas. He gave the ring to me while we were there." She wiggled the finger. "It pleased his grandmother. She seems to have taken a liking to me."

Wayne's face clouded. "My grandmother, Imogene Foley, is the family grande dame and likes to believe she controls the rest of us. When she was here a couple of summers ago, she met Doris. Doris charmed her."

Doris's eyes lit up as she spoke. "She insists we have the wedding ceremony in the Catholic Church on Long Island where she was married more than sixty years ago. The wedding will be in October."

Wayne waved a hand as though to brush the conversation

away. "None of that's of interest to you, Miss Bruce. What else can we do to help you?"

Merci thought a moment. "As you can guess, I'm certain that my nephew wasn't the one who murdered Miss Hetherington. Do you know of anyone else who might have had a reason to do so?"

Foley shook his head. "As I said, away from the rodeos, Summer and I didn't travel in the same circles. I know nothing of any others she spent time with."

Merci turned to Doris. "How about you, Miss Hamilton? What can you tell me about her?"

"I would sometimes see her when I went to rodeos with Wayne. During the school year we'd see her at rodeo club meetings but not at any other times. She and I seldom spoke." The liveliness Doris had shown when discussing the wedding was gone. Once again, she seemed tense and was sober faced.

Merci looked from Foley to Hamilton and back. "What can either of you tell me about the relationship between Summer Hetherington and Cass Bruce?"

Neither responded as they exchanged glances. Doris answered first. "They spent time together. Everyone knew that. Some said they were going steady."

Wayne shifted in his chair, blew out a breath. "Look, we've all heard that she was pregnant. You want to know who's responsible, and you're wondering if we'll say it's Cass." A hint of anger came into his voice as he leaned forward. "We won't say it's Cass. How would we know?"

Merci, who had been holding a cup, smiled in response to the outburst and placed the cup on the saucer. "Perhaps we'll learn the answer to that question as the investigation goes along." She brushed at her skirt as she stood. "Your cooperation has been helpful. As you might guess, your testimony may be needed at the trial. May I call if I need to visit with you again?" When Foley nodded his assent, she turned for the door. "Thanks for your hospitality."

In her car, she sat for a moment in thought. Wayne Foley must surely realize that his relationship with Miss Hetherington is known to others. Perhaps he couldn't bring himself to admit to that relationship in the presence of Doris Hamilton.

Wayne wandered back to the den with Doris trailing behind. He dropped into a chair, placed his elbows on his knees. "God! What am I going to do?" He blew out a big breath, eyes still on the floor, "That woman knows I spent time with Summer. It will all come out."

Doris sat on the arm of the chair and placed one hand on his shoulder. "Yes, Cass's lawyers and everyone else is going to find out about your dates with Summer Hetherington." Her voice bitter, she continued, "But they won't find out what you did with her in the back seat of your fancy car. Summer can't tell. No one can force you to tell. I sure as hell won't tell." She rose to her feet to stand in front of him. "You've told me before, but I'll ask again; you haven't told anyone else, have you?"

Wayne shook his head, eyes still on the floor "No, Doris, Just you."

"So you said the day after Summer told you she was pregnant. When you, poor fool, told me you had to do the right thing, break our engagement and marry her." She pulled one of the other chairs around so she could sit facing him with her hands resting on the arms of the chair. "How did I react, Wayne? Remember? I could have raved and cried. I could have told you to go to hell. I didn't do anything like that did I? I told you to put it out of your mind. I reminded you that it could be someone else who got her pregnant. Probably Cass Bruce. He might have thought the baby was his and killed her." Doris leaned back in the chair and crossed her arms again. "We can have a good life together, Wayne Foley. Don't admit to anything."

He sat unmoving, just staring at her as she talked. Once in a while he blinked but showed no other response. Doris began again. "You know your grandmother's ideas about sex before marriage. And her feelings about me. She likes me, Wayne. She's decided that I'm the right one for you. If she learns you had anything to do with Summer Hetherington, she'll cut you off in a second. And she'll see to it that the rest of your family does the same. There'll be no more access to the Foley fortune for you. You'll find out how the rest of us live. You'll have to get a real job, go to work."

Wayne dropped his eyes. "So what? If it comes out that she and I were getting it on, those lawyers will argue that I got her pregnant and killed her."

"No one but you and Summer knew what you were doing together. She isn't able to talk about it, and you don't have to. When it comes out that you'd spent time together, you can say there was nothing to it but two college students innocently enjoying the company of one another. No sex involved." She waited again. "Who's to contradict that? No one can."

Wayne Foley heaved a sigh. "I guess not."

"The authorities know she was pregnant. They've charged Cass Bruce with the murder, so they've concluded he was the father of her child." Doris stood to look down at him, still slumped in the chair. "You told me you didn't kill her. That's the truth isn't it?"

Wayne shook his head again. "Good God, Doris. I didn't kill her. I couldn't do something like that."

"Then keep you damn mouth shut and let them convict Cass. Then you'll never have to think about it again." She touched his cheek with one finger. "We'll get married, Wayne. You'll become involved in the family business just like your grandmother has planned. We'll travel, we'll enjoy her lavish parties at the mansion on Long Island. We'll have children— perfect children." Doris put her arm around his shoulder to pull him toward her. "Don't mess it up, Wayne."

Chapter Forty-three

In her room that evening, Doris thought back to the day she met Grandma Imogene. Like everyone else in the area, Doris knew of the Foleys and their ranch over the hill near Roscoe. One day, in the spring of her junior year in high school, she heard that the Foley family was looking for a house cleaner. Already a hard worker with ambition, she'd developed her own house-cleaning service. She put on her best dress, borrowed her father's car, and drove to the Foley ranch. Not knowing what else to do, she knocked on the front door. When the door opened she found herself facing a tall elderly woman, with a royal bearing. The woman looked her over from head to toe and barked, "What do *you* want?"

Doris, caught by surprise mumbled, "I'm sorry, ma'am. I must have knocked on the wrong door. I came to tell someone that I'm a good house cleaner and to ask for a job."

Doris never knew what the woman saw in her other than a frightened youngster, but apparently it pleased her. The woman swept her hand to indicate that Doris should come in. Her gravelly voice now carried a note of kindness. "You should have gone to the servants' entrance."

Doris bobbed in a kind of bow. "I'm sorry, ma'am. I didn't know." She took a step back. "Please excuse me."

The old woman clutched her arm and pulled the young woman inside. With the door closed, she released her grip and stepped back to look carefully at Doris. "My goodness, such a pretty girl and well-mannered too."

Doris, not knowing what to do or say, stood silent and unmoving.

"Come along with me." The old woman led her to a sitting room and eased herself into one of the chairs. She gestured for Doris to take another. Doris settled gently onto the very edge of the cushion. Her hostess rested for a moment. At last she spoke in a firm, raspy voice. "I'm Imogene Foley. Everyone calls me Grandma Imogene. You came because you want a job. How good a house cleaner are you?"

Doris blinked. "I'm sorry. I didn't tell my name. I'm Doris Hamilton from Red Lodge. To answer your question, Ma'am, I'm the best house cleaner you will ever find. And if I get the job, I'll prove it." She stopped and held her breath.

A wide smile wreathed Grandma Imogene's face. "Not afraid to toot your own horn, are you."

Doris didn't return the smile. She remained all business. "I'm just telling the truth, ma'am. I know how to clean, and I enjoy it doing it right."

Grandma Imogene coughed out a harsh laugh. "Well! I like people with confidence in their own abilities."

At that moment a tall, middle-aged, austere man strode

into the room. When he saw the two women he turned to leave, muttering an apology. Grandma Imogene stopped him. "Clifford, I want you to meet Doris. She's here to ask for work cleaning the house." She turned back to Doris. "This is my son Clifford. He manages the family businesses."

Doris was on her feet in an instant and, once again, dipped her upper body in a half bow. "I'm pleased to meet you, sir."

"Ah, yes. Nice to meet you too." His attention returned to his mother. "Let Morris deal with the help, Mother. Just tell her where to find him. He'll decide if there's a place for her."

"Do you know if we need someone to help clean this house?" She waved her cane to point around the room as she asked the question.

Clifford led her to Morris in the kitchen, gave him the order to hire her, and left. Morris took her to a large closet where cleaning supplies were stored. Then he led her to a bathroom larger than the biggest room in her home. The tub first caught her eye. It was built into the wall along one side of the room and was long and deep. A shower head, far up on the wall, protruded over it. A glass-like partition with a sliding door provided bathing privacy. A long counter with two washbasins built into it ran along another wall. The fixtures were gold in color. The toilet in the corner of the room was enclosed with a swinging door to allow access. A window at the far end of the room provided light. Cabinets, some with mirrors, lined the wall above the counter with drawers opening below.

Morris pointed to a small patch of dirt on the tile near

the door to the toilet. "Miss Alicia saw that this morning and complained about the condition of the room. She's one of the Grandma Imogene's granddaughters, so we try to keep her happy." Morris backed out of the room. "All right. Have at it. We'll see if you know how to clean."

An hour and a half later Morris found Doris on the floor scrubbing with a brush at the corner where the wall meets the floor. He scanned the room. "Well! You told the truth. You do know how to clean."

Thereafter Doris Hamilton traveled over the hill from Red Lodge to the Foley ranch every Saturday and Sunday until school ended in the spring. During that summer, she spent five days a week cleaning what at first seemed to her an endless number of rooms. Over time she came to know the Foley family. Grandma Imogene reigned with unquestioned authority. She had two children, a son and a daughter. Clifford was the father of Wayne, a first-year student at Montana State College who lived at the ranch during the summer. Grandma Imogene's daughter, Deborah, was married with two daughters, ages ten and twelve.

Even over the hill in Red Lodge, Doris had heard that Wayne was the best-looking young man one could imagine. Not long after he returned to the ranch for the summer she passed by the sitting room where Grandma Imogene had first questioned her. Wayne was standing before his grandmother in an attentive pose while holding a western hat in one hand. She appeared to be giving him a lecture and he kept nodding his head. Doris could hear him mumble over and over, "Yes, Grandma." She hurried on by the doorway but was able to get a good look at Wayne Foley. She liked what she saw.

Jim Moore

Grandma Imogene kept a close eye on Doris. One day she asked the young lady, "Have you met my grandson, Wayne?"

"No ma'am." She dropped her eyes. "There isn't much occasion for us to be in the company of one another."

Grandma Imogene pushed herself straight in the chair. "Well! You two should get acquainted."

Doris smiled. "Ma'am, I'm sure your grandson knows plenty of girls. He wouldn't be interested in me."

The lady now leaned forward. "First of all, you're to call me Grandma Imogene from now on. No more 'ma'am'" She waited, then asked, "Understand?"

"Yes, ma'am." She let out an embarrassed giggle. "I mean yes, Grandma Imogene."

"Good. Now, I'm going to make sure that you and Wayne get to know each other. When you meet him, it wouldn't hurt to turn on the charm. Do you know how to charm a boy?"

Doris had charmed her share of boys in her school, but she just said, "I try to get along with everyone."

Grandma Imogene stood. Doris was immediately on her feet. The old woman's face took on a stern appearance. "Charm. When you meet Wayne, turn on the charm." She pointed to the tile. "I interrupted your work. I'll let you finish." She walked to the bedroom door where she stopped and looked back. "I'm Grandma Imogene, remember. And don't forget the charm."

The next Friday evening, Doris trudged to the employees parking area. Rest was on her mind. Getting to know Wayne Foley was not. He caught up with her just as she reached the car. He pulled the western hat from his head. "Grandma

Imogene mentioned you'd like to go to a rodeo." His smile was warm. "There's a one-day show at Forsyth this coming Sunday. Would you care to go?"

Doris knew immediately what precipitated the invitation. The old woman, who controlled everything and everyone, had ordered her grandson to offer the invitation. Her first inclination was to decline, not impose herself on him when he'd probably prefer to go alone. But then she thought, why not? It would be nice to be seen in the company of such a sophisticated, good looking young man. "I hadn't meant to bother you or your grandmother with my wish to watch you at a rodeo. But it you really mean it, I'll take you up on it."

And so, Doris accompanied Wayne to a rodeo, and she turned on her charm. She listened with interest to his every comment as they ate lunch at a street front café. She watched him unload his horse from the trailer and throw the saddle onto the animal. She followed along as he rode to an area away from the arena to warm his horse. She cheered when he roped and tied his calf in the fastest time of the day and complimented him on his each and every move.

Wayne ate it up. It was the beginning of many dates—until the fall semester began at Montana State College.

Doris realized the limits of her understanding of business matters, national politics, world affairs and other matters that interested the Foleys, she began to read the Billings Gazette each day and looked for chances to discuss important issues with adults even as she went to school and work.

When Grandma Imogene returned, she immediately called for Doris. Very soon, Wayne Foley was asking her out again and including her in all Foley family outings. He was unceasingly attentive. Doris enjoyed a life completely foreign to her.

Whenever Wayne dropped her off after one of their evening excursions, he would lean across the car seat to kiss her good night. But he never pushed it beyond the one kiss. Once, when he'd parked the car in front to her house, she slid across the seat to cuddle. He didn't move for a moment but then put his arm around her and pulled her closer. When she lifted her face for the kiss, she received more than a chaste peck. The kiss was hard and filled with passion. Doris responded with passion of her own. She pressed her breast against his chest. He pushed her backward until she was half lying along the seat of the auto.

But then he stopped. He shoved himself upright as though her body had burned him. With his back to the door and his eyes looking into the distance, he said, "We can't do this."

"Why not?"

"We just can't." He got out and hurried to the passenger's side and reached for her hand to help her from the car. "You'd better go now."

Doris was numb. Certain she'd made a foolish mistake, she cried in a way she hadn't done for a long time.

Doris found Grandma Imogene to be her usual inquisitive self. "Did you and Wayne have an enjoyable evening?"

"Yes, Grandma Imogene."

The lady smiled. "My grandson appears to be smitten by you."

"Smitten, ma'am?"

"Yes, smitten. I believe he may propose marriage. If he

does, will you accept?"

Doris was dumbfounded. Wayne wasn't in love with her. She knew that. If he proposed it would only be because his grandmother forced him to do it. But marriage to Wayne Foley would take her to the life she dreamed of. She answered, "Grandma Imogene, if Wayne asked me to marry him, I'd accept in an instant. He's all I could hope for in a husband."

The days and nights flowed on to the end of another summer. The dates with Wayne continued but he didn't propose and he was careful to never again get too close to her in the automobile.

When Doris graduated from high school, Wayne appeared with a gift—a necklace with a diamond pendant. She was so astonished, she pulled his head down for a kiss. He let the kiss linger for a second before straightening to ask, "Like it?"

The summer followed the pattern of the previous year. Doris cleaned the lady's rooms, followed Wayne to rodeos, and joined him at family functions.

August arrived. Wayne would soon be back at college. Grandma Imogene's time at the ranch was also near an end. Doris was mopping the bathroom floor when the lady appeared at the door. She gestured for Doris to follow her to the easy chairs. "What are your college plans?"

Doris hesitated. "I don't have enough saved for tuition plus room, board and books. I plan to be a cosmetologist."

"Nonsense!" Grandma Imogene leaned forward as she spoke. "You're a good student. There are scholarships that will pay the cost. Have you looked into any of them?"

"No" She looked down. "Perhaps I should have."

Jim Moore

"Well, it's not too late. If you look, you'll find the Aberdeen Entrepreneurial Scholarship. I happen to know it's still available. Apply for it. Enroll in the business curriculum at whichever college you choose."

Doris's application for the scholarship was approved. It provided all of her collegiate monetary needs, including registration fees, room, and board. She enrolled in the business curriculum at Montana State College. Wayne introduced her to his social world. She had many male admirers, but she focused on Wayne. She knew what he had to offer. She soon learned that the Aberdeen Entrepreneurial Scholarship was funded by the Foley family. She should have known.

In early December, Wayne said, "Our family gathers at the house on Long Island at Christmas time. Grandma Imogene suggested that I ask you to join us this year."

And so, she found herself in a New York mansion in December. At the gift exchange on Christmas Eve, when all eyes focused on Wayne, he knelt on one knee in front of her. "My love, will you marry me?"

Of course, she accepted. Later, alone in her room, she spread her fingers to peer at the large diamond. When Wayne handed her the ring, the dreams of life as the wife of a member of the Foley family seemed on the verge of coming true.

Now, his foolishness with Summer Hetherington threatened it. But it didn't have to. All Wayne needed to do was keep his mouth shut. They'd convict Cass Bruce of murder, she would become Mrs. Wayne Foley and would make Wayne the happiest man in the world—a member in good standing of the Foley empire.

CHAPTER FORTY-FOUR

Merci and Geoffrey attended a scheduling conference for Cass's trial. As is usually the case, the lawyers quarreled about discovery, evidence disclosure and, finally, the trial date. The quarrels ended, as all such discussions must, with promises by each side to abide by the disclosure schedule established by District Judge Nathanial McNair. The judge also set a trial date.

County Attorney Merrill Hodder argued for an early trial date. Geoffrey Myklebust tried to convince the judge that they needed several months to prepare. It would take time to interview witnesses, to review and address the material delivered to them under the discovery order and to conduct the research and document preparation required for such a serious legal proceeding.

Judge McNair, spectacles resting low on his nose, spoke quietly. "Mr. Myklebust, I like to keep my trial calendar clear. In this district the parties in every proceeding are given adequate time for preparation but no more than that. Then we set a trial date. This is a simple case with a limited number of witnesses and few exhibits. The trial shouldn't take more than five days. I have an opening on my calendar in early September. The trial of State vs. Cassius Bruce will begin on Monday, September eleventh." The judge peered at Geoff over the spectacles. "Be here, Mr. Myklebust, and be prepared."

CHAPTER FORTY-FIVE

It was late on a hot summer afternoon when Forrest Dodson, rid at last of the worst of the maladies that had plagued him, was able to leave the hospital and come home. Cass was standing on the stoop to greet him when the car pulled to a stop. Both Lillian and Hannah scrambled around to the passenger side to offer assistance. The man pushed the door open, waved their offers aside and eased himself to his feet.

Cass was shocked. Forrest, vigorous and robust when he left, seemed shrunken, pale and devoid of vitality. In response to Cass's greeting he offered a wave and a wan smile. Each of the women held an arm to walk with him the short distance to the doorway. Once there Hannah turned to face Cass. The usual lilt in her voice was missing. "At least he's home."

Cass just shook his head but spoke to Forrest with a smile. "I'm sure you'll feel better in your own house with your wife and daughter to care for you." He turned to Lillian.

Jim Moore

"You don't need me here right now. And I won't bother you with supper this evening. I'll come by for a visit when it's convenient for Forrest."

"He'll want to see you tomorrow," Hannah called after him as he walked away. "Don't plan on me for breakfast. I'll eat here with my parents."

As Cass saddled a horse the next morning, Hannah came to tell him, "Dad's up and had breakfast. He wants to visit with you."

After putting the saddle and the horse away, Cass followed Hannah to the house. Forrest spoke from his easy chair. His color had improved and his body seemed to have regained some of its vigor. He offered Cass a firm handshake before gesturing to another chair. "All right, tell me. Has anything happened that I need to know? Anything kept from me while I was sick?"

"Not that I know of, sir. Hannah and I've been looking after things as best we can. I hope you'll find the place in decent shape."

Forrest's smile was genuine. "That's what Hannah's been telling me." He scooted forward in the chair, ready to stand. "How about we get in the pickup and take a look."

His wife was at his side in a second. "No, Forrest. You've got to regain your strength. Hannah and Cassius have both said nothing requires your attention right now. Rest today. Tomorrow might be better."

"We'll just take a look at some of the cattle in the closest pasture." He pushed himself to his feet. "This ranch is my life, Lillian. Cass can drive. I'll just ride along and size things up."

Hannah spoke up. "I'll drive. Cass can open gates. You, Dad, can give us orders as we go."

It was one of those pleasant late-summer days when the ranch land appeared at its best. Hannah traveled slowly to give her father time for a good look at the cattle as well as at the range. The yearling steers showed appropriate weight gain. The hair on their red bodies and white faces was so shiny as to appear recently washed. They all appeared healthy and content. The sight brought a smile to Forrest's face.

Before long, however, weariness forced him to suggest they return to the house. He'd seen enough to assure himself that the ranch was in decent condition. Standing with one hand on the open pickup door, Forrest faced Cass. "Thank you for everything you've done. Hannah's been telling me that you two had it under control. It's nice to see for myself." He pushed on the door to begin the walk to the kitchen doorway. "Give me a few days and I'll be back on horseback."

Cass grinned. "The sooner the better."

Forrest Dodson's recovery was steady thanks to his wife's good food and tender care. There soon came a day when he, Cass and Hannah traveled together on horseback to check watering places and to assure that the fences remained tight and sound. But Forrest's stamina was slow to recover fully. Most days he simply had to return to the house before they'd finished the planned activity. There were even days when he wasn't able to ride at all and remained in his comfortable chair. And so the summer passed steadily by.

CHAPTER FORTY-SIX

The never ending pressure of a law practice filled the summer days for Merci Bruce. While she devoted most of her time to preparation for the Bruce trial, she couldn't completely ignore other clients. Each client believed his or her legal problem was the most important one and expected Merci to treat it as such.

Geoffrey Myklebust was buried under the discovery demands of a suit filed by a farmer against his client, a combine manufacturer. Geoff's thoughts weren't on Cass Bruce until late in August when the combine suit was ultimately settled. The morning after the settlement was finalized, he rapped on the open door to Merci's office. She was deep in a review of court decisions on the burden of proof in homicide cases and was slow to raise her eyes. When she did and saw who was standing in the doorway, she pushed the material to the side of her desk, rose to her feet, smiled and waved him into the room. Neither spoke as Geoff settled into a client chair in front of her desk and she dropped back into her chair behind it. He said, "You've been busy, and so have I. But it's time to concentrate on your nephew's upcoming trial."

"It is."

Geoff waited for her to say more. When she remained silent, he asked, "What do you see as a defense strategy given the facts as we know them?"

Merci looked across at him with raised eyebrows. "The defense? Someone else did it. That's the only defense we have." She leaned forward to place her crossed arms on the desk top. "And, as you know, there isn't any other person we can point to—at least right now." She shook her head. "We're faced with the fact that Cassius had the means to kill Summer—the icepick was at hand. He had the opportunity to do so—the trip back to the pool area to get his wallet when no one but he and Summer were there. As to motive, the prosecutor will argue that Cass got Summer Hetherington pregnant and felt he had to get rid of her."

Geoff nodded. "And so far, we know of no other person who had the means, the opportunity, and the motive."

"That's correct."

"So, for a defense we must rely almost entirely on the testimony of Cassius Bruce."

Merci said, "Not entirely. We can muddy the water with testimony from Summer's sorority sisters about her relationship with Wayne Foley."

"That testimony will show that Miss Hetherington spent time with Foley. It won't show that Foley had the opportunity or the means to commit the crime."

Jim Moore

"That's true. But we should be able to get him on the witness stand."

Geoff's facial expression hadn't changed when he rose from his chair. "There is that much. But it's a slim reed for Cassius Bruce to rely on. It's time to get our client in here. He needs to learn how to handle himself on cross-examination."

Late one afternoon in August, Merci called on Cass. They faced one another across the small table in the bunkhouse. "Your homicide trial is scheduled for September eleventh, as I said in my letter. It's time to begin serious preparations that involve you." When Cass didn't respond, she said, "First, you must spend lots of time with Geoffrey Myklebust and me. We'll go over your recollections of the night Summer Hetherington died. We must do this more than once. There can be no sudden last-minute remembrances, something damning that others told the prosecutor and you didn't tell us. We must prepare you to be a witness at the trial. We want to impress upon your memory the words and mannerisms that give support to your testimony as well as the ones that cause jurors disbelief." She paused, then hurried on. "You may or may not need to testify. If you do take the witness stand your testimony must be convincing. To assure that it will be, we must go over your testimony, time after time. As part of that preparation, you'll be subjected to simulated cross-examination. Whoever does it won't treat you nicely. But neither will Merrill Hodder when he cross examines you in court."

When Merci waited, Cass heaved a sigh. "The thought of the trial keeps me awake at night. I try not to think about it but it's always there, haunting me."

"You must think about it now. Your trial is scheduled to begin in little more than two weeks. You'd better plan to spend several days in Billings, beginning Monday."

Cass dropped his eyes and ran his hand through his hair. "Forrest Dodson's condition is much better, but he still isn't back to his old condition. I hate to leave him right now."

Merci stared hard at her nephew. "You don't have a choice, Cass. Think about it. Your life is on the line." Merci stood. "Now, I have to get back to Billings." Cass followed her to her auto and held the door. Through the open window she said, "Be in my office at ten o'clock Monday morning."

At supper that evening, he told the Dodsons of Merci's visit. The news wasn't unexpected. Forrest, seated at the head of the table, waved a hand in a dismissive gesture. "We need to adjust to things without you. Might as well begin now."

"I hate to leave you before you've recovered completely."

Lillian wiped her hands on a dish towel. "Don't you worry yourself about us." She pushed the towel over a hanger before turning to face him. "We'll miss you though. It won't seem right without you at the table."

Cass's brow had been scrunched in worry. At her kind words his face softened and he glanced from one to the other. "It sounded like I'll only need to be in Billings on certain days. The other days I'll be here, if it's alright with you."

Hannah stood by the stove with her hands stuffed into her pockets. "When does the trial begin?"

Cass turned to face her. "It starts September eleventh."

Hannah looked from Cass to her parents. "As you all know, I've been subpoenaed. But I'd be there anyway.

Jim Moore

Summer was a good friend, and I was at the hot springs the night she died. I have to know what really happened to her."

"You'll probably be a witness for the state."

She smiled. "If so, maybe I can help you."

Forrest spoke from his chair. "We wish we all could be there. You've helped us. We want to do all we can to support you." He struggled to his feet. "How long will it last?"

"I don't know. Merci didn't say."

Forrest pondered. "I can't leave this place for more than a day or two. But Hannah has to be at the trial and Lillian can go with her." He turned to his wife. "Call the Park Hotel and make reservations for two for six days. That should cover it."

Cass frowned and spoke to Lillian. "Six days is quite a while for you to leave your husband. I appreciate your concern but there's no need to create difficulties for yourselves because of my problem."

Lillian had been staring downward at the table top. "We'll just see how things go and then decide."

CHAPTER FORTY-SEVEN

Cass came out of the bunkhouse carrying a canvas bag filled with the clothes he'd need while in Billings. He looked up to see Hannah hurrying along the road from the main house. He dropped the bag into the trunk of his Chevy and then waited, his hand on the car's open door. She stopped by the side of the vehicle and caught her breath. The seriousness that shown on her face told him she wasn't there just to say good bye. It was emphasized when she jammed her hands deep into her pants pockets.

"Cass, I've spent a lot of time trying to remember everything that happened at the Springs. Last night, before I went to sleep, I thought again of the way we left the pool on our way to the cars—who went first, who was last." She stopped and looked upward to his face. "I left the dressing room before both Summer and April. When I got to your car, Harry was already there. I could see Zeke climbing into Justin's car. Then Lyndon got in the back of your car just as Greg climbed into your front seat. I went to Justin's car. Justin was in the driver's seat waiting for April, so I climbed into the back with Zeke."

"So?"

"So, you and April came out of the door to the hot springs after that. She was behind you."

Cass crunched his brow. "I don't remember that."

"Well, that's what happened." She released her grasp on his arm and stepped back to look at him again. "While she was getting in Justin's car, according to what she said, you ran back to get your wallet."

"So what?"

"Don't you see? The sheriff assumes that you were the one who killed Summer because you were the last one who was alone with her that night."

Understanding appeared like a blossom on Cass's face. "You're saying the sheriff's wrong? That April was alone with her in the women's dressing room after everyone else had left and before I went back to get my wallet?" He paused. "Are you saying April might have killed her?"

"I'm saying she had the opportunity."

Cass shook his head. "No one will believe that. April's too nice a person. Beside there wouldn't have been enough time for her to do it."

Hannah tugged at his shirtsleeve. "Think about it. From the time I finished dressing and left the women's dressing room, those two were alone together. Plenty of time to do it. More time than you had."

Cass looked off into the distance, then pulled his eyes back to Hannah. "But what possible reason could she have to do such a thing?"

"Who knows? Probably none. And to tell the truth, I don't believe she's the killer. But Merci needs to know."

Cass brightened. "You're right. The lawyers will know what to do with it. I'll tell them."

Three days later Merci and Geoff, alone in her office, considered this information. Geoff asked, "Your thoughts?"

"It gives us someone to point to beside my nephew, someone willing to testify to the exact order of events," Merci answered. "By April's own admission, she was in the dressing room alone with Summer, at least briefly. What we didn't know was that she was the only one in the pool area at that time."

Geoff shook his head. "It's too convenient, too late to use her testimony. Hannah and Cass have been living and working together at the same ranch ever since it happened. People, including the jurors, will believe they cooked up that story."

"How will the jurors find out about their work and living arrangements?"

"As soon as we finish our direct examination of Hannah, Merrill Hodder will bring it out on cross."

Merci wouldn't give it up. "Some of the others, including April remember the order similarly."

"What would she say if pressed?"

"Probably that Summer was still in the shower when she left not far behind Hannah."

Geoff rose from his chair to end the conversation. "It doesn't help us much, I'm afraid."

CHAPTER FORTY-EIGHT

Cass was tired. He had answered questions, given explanations, and told them, repeatedly, everything he remembered of the night Summer Hetherington lost her life at Hunter's Hot Springs The questioning had gone on for three hours. Geoffrey Myklebust was relentless in his pursuit of more precise and detailed information. And Merci had shown no sympathy. Instead she badgered him with questions and demands of her own. The latest question from Geoffrey was too much. "Isn't it true that you and Miss Hetherington spent lots of time together? Time to develop a romantic relationship as others think you did?"

Cass's face reddened as he sprang to his feet. "I've answered that question already," he yelped. "Yes, we spent time together. I have no way of knowing what others might think." He stopped speaking, breathed a couple of heavy breaths to calm himself. "I understand your need to know everything that might come up in the trial. But we've been over all of this stuff time and again. My recollections aren't going to change." He fell back into his chair. "I'm sorry for the outburst. It's just that these questions are wearing me down."

To his surprise, Geoffrey responded in a soft voice. "Of course, they are. We've been pounding on you for a long time without a break. There's a reason. You need to know how it will feel to be a witness at the trial. Believe me when I say the county attorney will treat you with less kindness than we have." Cass remained silent, eyes downcast. Geoff said, "It's noon. You two eat lunch without me. I have an appointment that will take some time. Let's meet back here at three o'clock."

They ate in the Grand Hotel restaurant mostly in silence. When finished Merci pulled several pages of paper from her bag and passed them to her nephew. Cass scanned the first pages, a summary of Merci's conversation with Zeke Howard.

"I didn't know he felt that way about me," Cass said.

Cass read through the rest of them. "They all seem to remember things the same way. No surprise."

Merci pulled another sheaf of papers from the bag and handed them to Cass. "How about these?"

He looked at the name on the first page and thumbed through rest. "I don't recognize either of these people."

"They were Summer's sorority friends. Read what they had to say."

Cass's eyebrows raised as he read. "They both think Summer knew that Wayne Foley was engaged to be married,

Jim Moore

but she was going out with him anyway."

"Seems that way. What do you know about it?"

Cass shook his head. "Nothing. I didn't know they ever saw one another, except at a rodeo or the fairgrounds."

"Who else would know if Summer and Wayne had moved beyond friendship?"

Cass frowned. "I don't know of anyone. They traveled in a different circle than the rest of us on the rodeo team."

"Could Foley be the one who got Summer pregnant?"

The thought brought a sour look to Cass's face. "I suppose. Somebody did. And it sure wasn't me."

Merci pointed to the stack of papers. "Take them with you. Review them carefully. If anything new comes to mind, let me know." She rose from the chair. "Now we need to get back to the law office."

"How long is this questioning going to continue?"

"Until the end of the trial—which begins in a few days."

CHAPTER FORTY-NINE

The Livingston courthouse was three stories high and constructed of stone. Entry to the large courtroom on the second floor was through doors at the rear. A wide aisle between wooden benches led to the low barrier separating the working area from the spectator's space. The judge's bench rested on a raised platform with the state and national flag behind it. A jury box with seats for twelve jurors was to the judge's left with the witness stand also to his left. Two rectangular tables filled the area before the bench.

Cass Bruce, dressed in a dark blue single-breasted suit, gave the outward appearance of quiet confidence, belying his inner turmoil. For the past several days, anxiety over the impending trial had left him no respite. Today, the eleventh day of September, he was numb, as he followed Geoffrey Myklebust through the courtroom door with Merci close behind. As they passed into the room, the chatter among prospective jurors and spectators ceased. Cass's family filled the bench behind the defense counsel table. Cass put his hand on his father's shoulder as he passed. His father gave it a pat.

Cass followed as Myklebust pushed through the little swinging gate, dropped his briefcase onto the counsel table and stepped to his left to grasp Merrill Hodder's hand. The two exchanged brief but pleasant words, a formality akin to knights saluting before the joust.

Seated between Geoff and Merci at the council table, Cass's stomach continued to churn until the bailiff shuffled through a door behind the bench to call, "All rise."

Judge Nathaniel McNair, about sixty years old, his black robe flapping around his slender frame, strode into the room and up to the bench. He rapped the gavel once before dropping into his chair to say, "Please be seated." Satisfied that the principals were in place, he addressed those seated beyond the barrier. "We have a large number of prospective jurors who need to be here in the courtroom. If you are not one of those jurors, please vacate your seat to make room for one who is." He raised his voice. "Bailiff, please make certain the jurors are all in the room and on the benches."

When the potential jurors were seated, the noise abated. The judge looked up from the file he'd been scrutinizing. "We are here for the matter of the State of Montana versus Cassius Bruce." He looked at the county attorney. "Mr. Hodder, you represent the State. Is that correct?"

Hodder was immediately on his feet. "It is, Your Honor." He pointed at the man next to him. "I've asked Sheriff Josh Waddell, who conducted most of the investigation, to join me at counsel table throughout the trial." He nodded in Geoffrey's direction. "Mr. Myklebust has indicated he does not object."

"Is that correct, sir?"

Geoff rose to his feet. "It is."

The judge smiled. "Nice, for a change, to begin with some agreement." A ripple of laughter arose from those in the room. The judge turned to the defense counsel table. "You are Geoffrey Myklebust and represent the defendant. Correct?"

"That's correct, Your Honor. I represent Cassius Bruce." He turned his head to his client. "Mr. Bruce is here at my side." Cass stood, solemn faced and unmoving. Geoff pointed to Merci. "I'm sure you remember my co-counsel, Merci Bruce."

The judge's demeanor brightened. "How could I forget?" He relaxed against the seat back. "It's nice to have a member of the fair sex grace this courtroom. I doubt that it's ever happened before."

Merci didn't smile. Sober faced, she replied, "Let's hope it becomes a common thing, Your Honor."

"Well, I suppose that might happen." The judge said, "First, we must select a jury." He turned to the clerk. "Please take the role of prospective jurors."

As the clerk droned names and mutterings of "here" and "present" could be heard in response, Merci looked at her nephew and took a deep breath. At long last, the trial that would forever define his life was underway.

It took all morning to go through the selection of the jury. In the end that panel seemed to fairly represent the community. There were three men who labored in the railroad repair yard, a retired woman schoolteacher, two cattle ranchers, the abstractor, a gas station operator, the town librarian, two ranch hands, and a bank secretary. The two alternates were a housewife and an automobile dealer. They all stood to take the usual oath to do their duty.

Throughout it all, Cass heard words flow about the room. But the words were merely sounds. Seated, unmoving, hands clasped together on the table, the same thoughts scrolled over and over through his mind: he did not belong here; there had to be some mistake. Maybe he would wake up to find it all a bad dream.

During the jury selection his mind briefly escaped that bleak reverie. His attorneys passed notes back and forth in front of him and leaned across him to whisper thoughts to one another. While doing so, they made decisions affecting his entire future. He became irritated that they didn't consult him even once. After all, it was his future they were deciding. But he remembered his instructions and remained silent.

Judge Nathaniel McNair's voice interrupted his musings. "It's close to noon. Court will be in recess until one thirty this afternoon." He turned to those chosen as jurors. "You are directed to refrain from discussing anything about this morning's proceedings with your fellow jurors or anyone else. In fact, you may not discuss anything about this trial with anyone until I give you permission to do so. That won't be until all of the evidence is in and you go to the jury room to deliberate on a verdict." He was quiet for a moment as he ran his eyes the length of the jury box. "Do you all understand?"

He smiled when the head of each of the jurors bobbed up

and down in assent. "All right. Get a good meal and be back here before one thirty." The judge banged the gavel on the bench and barked, "Court's in recess."

CHAPTER FIFTY

Rooms had been reserved for the Bruce family contingent at the Murray Hotel. Two additional rooms had been converted to offices in which Geoff, Merci and a paralegal could deal with trial matters during breaks. They all gathered in a private dining area that they soon began to call the Bruce Family Room.

After waiters took orders for a mid-day meal, Geoff spoke to the group. "We have a jury. Any thoughts?"

Spencer said, "This town is neutral territory. Neither Miss Hetherington nor Cass ever lived here. None of those on the jury should bring community prejudices with them."

Geoff nodded. "True." He looked at the others at the table and asked again, "Any thoughts?"

Cass's grandfather, T. C. Bruce, said, "The real question is are you and Merci satisfied with the jury?"

Merci said, "I am, Dad. They're about as neutral as we can

hope to get." The food arrived. Cass, silent since they arrived in the room, left most of his on the plate.

In opening statements, the county attorney, speaking with passion, asserted that evidence would prove Cassius Bruce murdered Summer Hetherington in cold blood.

Geoffrey Myklebust, quiet and reserved, asked the jurors to pay careful attention to the testimony. If they did, they would find that there was no evidence that Cassius Bruce committed the crime. Inferences weren't enough to convict a person.

"Mr. Hodder, you may call your first witness."

"The state calls Sheriff Joshua Waddell."

The Park County sheriff, his badge pinned to his vest, rose from the chair and moved with purpose to stand before the bench, hand upraised. The clerk read the oath. "Do you swear to tell the truth, the whole truth, and nothing but the truth, so help you God?" Waddell responded with a vigorous, "I do."

Hodder gave him a moment to settle into the witness chair. "Please state your name, sir."

"Joshua Waddell" It sounded like a harsh bark.

The crack of the sheriff's voice brought Cass out of his dark musings. It was the speaking tone Cass remembered from his earliest encounter with Waddell, the one at the Belgrade rodeo arena, the one that caused all of this to begin. If he'd walked away from the sheriffs, would he be here now?

The county attorney asked, "And your position, sir?"

"I'm the sheriff of Park County, Montana."

"Sheriff Waddell, how did you first learn of the death of

Jim Moore

Summer Hetherington at Hunter's Hot Springs?"

"Mrs. Stensrud, the lady who runs the place, called our office to say she had a dead woman on her hands."

"What did you do?"

"I called Doc Winters." Waddell turned to the jury. "He's the county coroner."

Hodder continued. "Tell us what you did then."

"I headed out there to the hot springs as fast as I could. Mrs. Stensrud led me back to the pool area." He inhaled and then puffed out his cheeks. "She pointed to the dead girl lying on the bottom of the pool."

"What did you do then?"

"Well, we had to get her out of the water, so I called for my deputy to come and bring help." When Hodder didn't ask another question, he added, "Doc showed up and the boys lifted the body out onto concrete at the side of the pool."

"What did you observe that was of special interest?"

The sheriff's brow crunched into a deep frown. "There was an icepick stuck up under her chin, clear up to the handle." He demonstrated by pointing beneath his chin with his index finger.

The county attorney asked, "Did you take photographs of the body at that time?"

"I didn't. Doc had a camera, and he took some."

"Have you seen the pictures?"

"Yes. Doc gave them to me after they were developed. I gave then to you." Hodder turned to the counsel table for some Polaroid pictures and handed them to the witness. "Please look at these and tell me if they're the photographs you've just mentioned."

Josh Waddell shuffled through the pictures. "They are."

"Sir, do these pictures accurately reflect the appearance of the body as it was taken from the pool that day?"

The sheriff glanced again at one picture. "Yes, sir, they do."

"And the icepick you told us about. Is it visible?"

Waddell thumbed the pictures again. "It's visible in two of them."

The county attorney asked the clerk to mark the pictures as State's exhibits. At the same time he handed copies of the pictures to the judge and to Geoff. When the clerk handed them back, Hodder turned to the judge. "I offer the pictures as State's exhibits, one through four, into evidence."

The judge looked down from the bench at Geoffrey and Merci, perhaps expecting an objection. Geoff thumbed slowly through the pictures before passing them to Merci. Cass averted his eyes as the pictures went by. He'd seen them. Geoff spoke for the defense. "No objection."

Hodder retrieved the pictures from the clerk and handed them to the juror in the seat closest to the clerk's desk. Merci watched the reaction of each juror as the pictures were passed from hand to hand. She saw frowns, pinched lips and head shakes but no other kind of emotional reaction. The appearance of the body with the icepick protruding was distasteful to view but could not be called gruesome.

"Did Doctor Winters examine the body at that time?"

"He did. Then Doc said we had to get her to the pathologist, so the boys loaded her up and we sent her away."

Hodder asked, "Sheriff, what did you do after that?"

"I found out as much as I could from Mrs. Stensrud. She

told me that a group of kids from the college had come there after the rodeo in Bozeman the night before. She thought the dead girl was one of them. Then I headed to my office before going on to Bozeman. I thought I should find out who they all were and learn as much as I could about them."

"What did you do when you got to Bozeman?"

"I went to see Able Parsons. He's the sheriff of Gallatin County."

"Why did you go to him?"

Waddell leaned forward as though he'd been challenged. "That's his bailiwick. I felt I should let him know I was nosing around in his county. A matter of courtesy." He straightened. "Besides, I thought he might be of some help."

"Was he?"

The sheriff nodded. "Yes. He took me up to the college. We learned the name of the dead girl and talked to the woman who runs the place where she lived. After that we went together to the rodeo arena out at Belgrade."

"What happened when you got to the arena that's of importance here today?"

"Well, we wanted to find one of those who were at Hunter's Hot Springs. Walking along the arena fence we came upon that young fellow." He pointed to Cass. "He was putting spurs on his boots. It seemed possible he might be one we wanted to talk to. Or if not, that he might know who they were."

Hodder shifted in his stance. "What did you do then?"

Waddell looked from the county attorney to Cass and back. "I jumped him out about it."

A pained look crossed the county attorney's face, but he

continued. "What do you mean, 'jumped him out'?"

"I told him we knew about the party at Hunter's Hot Springs the night before and asked if he was one of the partiers. He told us he was."

"Did he want to know why you were asking?"

"Yes, he did, but we didn't tell him. Instead I told him who we were and asked him if a girl named Summer Hetherington was with them at the hot springs."

"What was his response?"

"He told us that she was with them. He also told us she was a barrel racer and should be at the other end of the arena getting ready for the day's show."

"He spoke as though she was still alive?"

"That's right."

"Then what happened?"

Waddell looked at Cass. "He told us he didn't have time for us. When he started to walk away, Parsons asked him to come to his office after the rodeo and bring the names of those who were with him at the hot springs."

"His response?"

"He said he'd be there."

Hodder stood silent for a long moment. "Did you ever tell him why you were asking all the questions?"

"Not at that time."

"Did he seem to know the reason for your interest, that the Hetherington girl was dead?"

"I thought he might have known about her, but was pretending not to."

"Did the defendant show up at the sheriff's office later that day?"

Jim Moore

Waddell nodded. "He got there at about six thirty."

"Did he bring the names of those who were at Hunter's Hot Springs the night the Hetherington girl was killed?"

"Yes, he had the list." The sheriff looked once at Cass. "And by that time, he wasn't pretending he didn't know she was dead. I'm sure he knew it even before we told him."

Geoff was on his feet. "Objection." His voice was soft but carried throughout the courtroom. "There is no evidence Cassius Bruce was pretending at any time. This witness can only speak to things of which he has direct knowledge. His beliefs are not facts about which he is allowed testify."

The judge was quick to respond. "Sustained." Turning to the jury, he added, "The last statement of the witness is not evidence and you must disregard it." Looking at the sheriff, he said in a stern voice, "You are to speak only of facts. Just answer the question that is asked. Don't embellish."

Waddell lowered his head. "Sorry, Your Honor."

Judge McNair looked at the clock on the back wall. He rose to his feet. "We'll take a fifteen-minute break." Turning to the jurors he said, "Remember my admonition not to discuss anything about this trial with one another." Lastly, he rapped the bench with the gavel. "Court's in recess."

Chapter Fifty-one

Back on the bench after the break, the judge spoke to the county attorney. "You may continue sir."

Hodder stood, relaxed, before the witness stand. "Sheriff Waddell, what more did you do in your investigation of the death of Miss Hetherington?"

The sheriff appeared to be confused by the question. At last he muttered "Well, the body was sent for an autopsy to determine the cause of death."

Hodder put his hand up to stop him. "The pathologist will speak to that." He dropped his hand. "Did you interview the other college cowboys and cowgirls who were also at the hot springs?"

"Most of them went to the sheriff's office in Bozeman during the next day or two. Sheriff Parsons took their statements and shared them with me."

"Did any of those statements provide information that was helpful?"

"Oh, you bet." Waddell pushed forward as he spoke. "One of the other girls; her name is April Menard, told what happened. She said they were hurrying to get back to Bozeman. They all ran from the pool and climbed into the two cars, ready to go. None of the others noticed that the Hetherington girl wasn't in either car. Then that fella," the sheriff jerked his head again Cass's direction, "hollered that he'd left his wallet, got out of his car and went back into the building." The sheriff stared intently at the county attorney as he said, "Summer Hetherington never got in either of the cars, so she still had to be there when he went for his wallet. They were in that place alone—just the two of them." He looked at Cass. "That's when he must have used the icepick on her."

Geoff's voice filled the room. "Objection. The witness is speculating. There's no evidence before the court to support his last statement."

The judge said, "Sustained." Looking at the sheriff, he added, "Only speak to the facts as you know them, sir."

Again, Waddell lowered his head. "Sorry, Your Honor."

Hodder spoke quickly to move the jurors' thoughts away from any wrongdoing by the witness.

"Sheriff Waddell, did others confirm this?"

"Yes. Others did in their statements to Sheriff Parsons."

Hodder stepped closer to the witness. "Sheriff, in your investigation have you been able to identify any other person who was alone with the victim at the time of her death?"

Waddell straightened, looked once at the jurors, and then back at his questioner. "No, Mr. Hodder, I have not."

The county attorney looked to the judge. "I have no more

questions for Sheriff Waddell, Your Honor."

The judge turned to the defense counsel. "Mr. Myklebust?"

Geoffrey rose slowly and stood for a moment without speaking. The sheriff shifted nervously in his chair as he waited. Geoff spoke in his usual quiet voice. "Sheriff Waddell, it's possible that somebody else—someone beside the nine college students—was at Hunter's Hot Springs the night the young girl was killed, isn't it?"

The sheriff contemplated the question. "Possible? I suppose anything is possible. But I made a real effort to find out if anyone else was there. I never found anyone."

"That's a huge building, isn't it? It has rooms for guests and innumerable storage spaces here and there throughout. Can you say with certainty that the nine students and Mrs. Stensrud were the only ones in the building that night?"

"As I said, I tried to find out if anyone else was there. Mrs. Stensrud said she'd locked the whole place up."

"I'm sure we'll hear from Mrs. Stensrud later." Geoff continued in his measured manner. "How about the area around the main building? There are several small sheds and a garage near at hand, are there not?"

"Yes, sir. There are."

"Even the shadows from one of those buildings would have provided a hiding place, wouldn't it?"

The sheriff was losing patience and shook his head to show it. "As I said, anything is possible." He turned to the jurors. "But I did my best to find some other person who could have killed that girl and didn't find one."

"The fact that you didn't find one isn't proof that no one

Jim Moore

else was around, is it?"

Waddell slumped back into the witness chair. "Maybe not. But I'm satisfied that no one but the fella sitting over there," he said, pointing to Cass, "is the killer."

Geoff turned to the judge. "Move to strike that last statement, Your Honor. It was gratuitous, without any basis. In fact, it was prejudicial and self-serving."

The judge nodded his head in agreement. "All of those, indeed." He looked across at the witness. "Sheriff, you should know by now that you can only testify as to facts. You may never offer your opinions as evidence." He paused for effect. "Don't let it happen again." He then addressed the jurors. "You are directed to ignore the sheriff's last remark. It is not evidence. Remove it from your minds."

Fat chance of that, Cass thought.

Judge McNair looked back at Geoff. "Do you have more questions of this witness, sir?"

"Yes, sir. I do" Geoff had been standing at the counsel table. He walked with deliberate steps around the end of the table to stand directly in front of Sheriff Waddell. "You decided that Cassius Bruce was the one who killed Summer Hetherington when you first talked to him, didn't you, sir?"

Waddell straightened and scowled. "No, sir. That isn't correct."

"Well then, when did you decide he was the killer? That same evening at the Bozeman sheriff's office?"

"I became suspicious that evening."

"When did those suspicions become certainty in your mind? The next day?"

Anger crept into the sheriff's voice. "Probably the time

he was in Parson's office. We were asking him a few more questions when he got mad as hell and stormed out of the building. He was afraid we'd figure it out—that he was the one." Then the law officer crossed his arms and clamped his lips together, a defiant look on his face.

Geoff stood in silence for a moment. When he spoke again, his voice was as quiet as always. "And from that time on, you never tried seriously to find the real killer, did you?"

Waddell jerked forward to bark, "He did it, damn it. There wasn't any reason to look for someone else."

Geoff waited. The sheriff realizing what he'd done, slowly settled back into the witness chair. Only after Waddell's breathing returned to normal did the lawyer ask his next question. "You've insisted that there was no one other than the college group at the pool that night. But that isn't correct, is it?"

"What do you mean?"

"Mrs. Stensrud was also alone in the building with Summer Hetherington after the others left, wasn't she?"

The sheriff reacted by straightening his back and grabbing at the arms of the witness chair. After a moment his face contorted into a fierce show of anger. "Mrs. Stensrud? Kill that girl? You're out of your mind. That lady's lived here all her life. She wouldn't harm a flea."

"Perhaps, but your own testimony tells the jury she was in the building after all the others had left. You can't say with absolute certainty that Cass Bruce was the last one alone with Miss Hetherington that night, can you?"

The sheriff's frustration was reflected in his answer.

Jim Moore

"Damn it, Hilda Stensrud didn't harm that girl." He pointed at Cass. "He did it."

Geoff stared at the man for a long second before turning to the judge. "I have no more questions for this witness, Your Honor."

"Redirect Mr. Hodder?"

"One, Your Honor." The county attorney stood behind his table. "Do you have any evidence that Hilda Stensrud committed this crime? Anything at all?"

"No, sir. I don't"

"No more, Your Honor."

The judge seemed to be relieved. "It's near the end of the day. Court will be in recess until nine o'clock in the morning." He turned to the jury. "Sleep well and be back here on time, refreshed and ready."

CHAPTER FIFTY-TWO

Geoffrey, Merci and Cass stood without speaking until both the judge and jury cleared the room. Merci moved around the counsel table. She put a hand on her law partner's arm. "The sheriff's outbursts shouldn't help Merrill Hodder's case with jury."

Geoff answered, "No, but it doesn't change the evidence."

Cass had turned to his parents, seated directly behind him in the spectator section. His father was quick to step forward, reach across the rail and put a hand on his son's shoulder. "How are you holding up?"

Cass cocked his head slightly to one side. "I suppose I could be worse."

Spencer Bruce dropped his hand. "Foolish question."

Cass showed a wan smile. "Not important." He turned from his father to lean across the rail and wrap an arm around his mother's shoulder. Her face was worn from long months of worry. Sitting on the hard bench listening to the testimony only increased the stress. "Mom, you shouldn't be here. Go home. There's nothing you can do, and I have to get through this all by myself"

"We're here to give support, if nothing else" she said firmly. "None of us will leave."

Spencer added, "Of course, son. We'll all see it through together."

Merci moved them toward the door. "Nothing more we can do today. Let's get ourselves to the hotel to eat and relax."

At the Murray Hotel they made their way to the Bruce family room. Cass's mind drifted away while the meal was ordered. Conversation after that flowed around him with little of it penetrating his consciousness. He was numb.

The following morning, with the jurors back in place, Judge McNair turned to Merrill Hodder. "Call your next witness."

Hodder stood. "The state calls Hilda Stensrud."

The manager of Hunter's Hot Springs walked forward to take the oath and then moved purposefully to the witness stand. Once seated, she cast a glance at Cass before turning her attention to the county attorney. Waiting for the first questions, she seemed calm and composed.

"Please state your name and address."

"My name is Hilda May Stensrud. My mailing address is Springdale, Montana." Her voice was not loud but carried well throughout the room.

"Where do you live?"

"I live at Hunter's Hot Springs. It's about two miles north of Springdale, here in Park County."

"What is Hunter's Hot Springs?"

8 SECONDS

Mrs. Stensrud rubbed her hands along the arms of the witness chair as she spoke. "It's a resort. There's a hot water spring there. The water that flows from the spring is beneficial to the health. Years ago, my grandparents built a large complex at the site, with a big swimming pool and a couple of smaller pools for children. They're all enclosed and under a roof. There are accommodations for guests: rooms and restaurant service." She paused. "I continue to operate it."

The county attorney dropped his arms. "Were you open for business on the night of May thirteenth of this year?"

"I was."

"Did you have any paying guests that night?"

Mrs. Stensrud sighed. "No guests to stay the night." She turned to the jury. "Business isn't like it once was. When I was young—before the depression of the nineteen thirties and the war—the place would be full of people who came to enjoy the waters for a day or for several days. Not anymore."

Hodder nodded. "Did any guests show up that evening?"

Mrs. Stensrud faced him. "None early. I finished the cleaning and walked through the place to make certain everything was buttoned up for the night."

"Then what happened?"

"At about a quarter to eight, some young people walked in. They wanted to swim. They said they'd been at the college rodeo and needed to soak away the dirt and the bruises."

The county attorney moved around the counsel table to stand closer to the witness. Hands again clasped behind his back, he asked, "How many were there in the group?"

"There were nine of them."

"Is one of them in the courtroom right now?"

She nodded and pointed. "That one over there was one of them. His told me his name was Cass Bruce. He seemed to be the spokesman for the rest."

"What do you mean?"

"Well, when they first came into the lobby, he was the one who introduced himself and asked if they could swim. He asked for swim suits for each of them and paid me." She glanced at Cass again. "After a while he came out of the pool area to ask for some ice to cool their pop and beer. I gave him a block of ice in a bucket and an icepick to use to break it up." This time her eyes lingered on him as she continued. "He was very polite, very gentlemanly."

"How long did the young people stay in the pool?"

"It was after nine o'clock when they came rushing out of the pool, hurried through the lobby and out to their cars."

"All in a group?"

"Oh, no. Strung along one after another but fairly close together."

Hodder stood silent for moment, now with a thumb under his chin and a finger alongside his cheek. "Do you remember which one was the last to come out of the pool?"

"I'm not sure except for Mr. Bruce." She glanced at Cass again. "The first time he went out he stopped by the registration desk where I was standing. He said, 'We left the swim suits in the bucket.' He thanked me and left."

Hodder frowned. "You said you weren't sure who was the last one out except for the defendant. What do you mean?"

"That was the first time Mr. Bruce came from the pool.

Some others, I don't remember how many, maybe one or two, came after that. Then he," she moved her head in Cass's direction, "came back by my desk."

"Did he say anything then?"

"He just said, 'I forgot something.'"

"Then what happened?"

Mrs. Stensrud shrugged. "He came back out of the pool, thanked me again and left."

"Did any of those young people come from the pool after that?"

Her head was moving from side to side before he finished speaking. "No, sir. I heard the cars start, and they drove away." She stopped, dropped her eyes to her lap, rubbed her hands together for a second before raising her head. "I didn't count them. I thought they were all gone. I didn't know about the young girl who was left in the water."

Merrill Hodder allowed a moment of time for the members of the jury to absorb the picture. "When did you find out that one of the girls didn't leave with the rest?"

The witness dropped her eyes. "Not until the next morning when I began the daily cleaning." She glanced at the judge then back to the county attorney. "She was just there, lying on her stomach, at the bottom of the pool."

Hodder gave the jurors time to hold that picture in their minds. "What did you do?"

"I immediately called the sheriff's office to tell them. It wasn't long before the Sheriff Waddell showed up."

"For the benefit of those who've never been to Hunter's Hot Springs, please describe it. Begin with the main building."

Hilda Stensrud cocked her head to one side a though

trying to decide how to begin. She looked briefly at the jury and then returned her attention to the county attorney. "Well, the main entrance is on the south east end. It's a wide double door that leads into an open lobby. The lobby has a registration desk near to the entry. To the left and some distance across the lobby is the doorway to the pool area. There's another desk by that door. That's where we take payment for entry into the plunge. If the guests need swimming suits, they rent them there."

Hodder asked, "What about the pool area? What's it like?"

"The entire building is constructed around the swimming pool." She paused. "The pool is rectangular, one hundred twenty feet in length and fifty feet across. It's made of concrete and is surrounded by a smooth, flat concrete surface. The whole pool area is covered by a roof. It's kind of like a huge amphitheater."

Hodder interrupted. "Is it wide open in its entirety?"

"It is." Mrs. Stensrud went on to describe everything in great detail, just as Merci had seen it when she'd first visited.

Hodder glanced once toward the jury. "Tell us about the dressing rooms."

"Inside the plunge, or pool area, the dressing rooms stick out from the walls about twenty feet. There are two, one for men and one for women. The dressing rooms have showers. There are lockers for guests to store clothing. Filling the space between the dressing rooms is a large storage closet. We keep cleaning supplies and other such things in it."

"Where are the doors to the dressing rooms located?"

"They're at the side of the rooms, facing ninety degrees

from the pool."

Hodder gave her a moment before saying, "You told the jury that there were no other guests at your place on the night when Summer Hetherington lost her life. Were there any other people about? Anyone at all?"

Mrs. Stensrud straightened and spoke with resolve. "No, sir. I'm quite certain that there were no others there that night." Hodder started to speak but she lifted a hand a couple of inches to stop him. "Let me explain. Both the man who helps with the maintenance and the grounds keeper were long gone. I'd walked the entire building just before the college group arrived and checked the doors on each of the rooms to be sure they were locked. No one was in any of the rooms or in the hallways. All the exit doors except the one to the lobby were locked. I'm sure there wasn't any person in that building but me, until the rodeo bunch arrived."

"Is it possible that someone was outside and sneaked in after you did your rounds?"

"I suppose there could have been someone hiding somewhere. But how could that person get into the building? All the doors except the one into the lobby were locked."

Hodder moved back around the counsel table to his chair and stood silently for a long moment. "You were in the building, of course, after the college people were gone. There's been some inference your presence there gave you the opportunity to kill that girl. What about it?'

Mrs. Stensrud gasped. "Me? Why would anyone think I killed her?"

"Did you?"

She scowled and shook her head vigorously. "Of course

Jim Moore

not!" Her indignity at having to even answer the question was evident.

Hodder remained quiet for less than a second. "No more questions for Mrs. Stensrud, Your Honor."

The judge pushed his chair back from the bench and announced a fifteen-minute break.

CHAPTER FIFTY-THREE

The two defense lawyers and Cass huddled outside the courthouse. Cass groaned. "Unless it's possible to show that someone beside Mrs. Stensrud was at the pool that night, the jury's bound to think I did it. No one will believe she's a killer."

"I agree that no one will believe she committed the crime." Geoff answered, "Theoretically it's the burden of the state to prove there was no one else around. But, unfortunately, your assessment is correct." He glanced at Merci and back. "Mrs. Stensrud isn't finished yet. Your aunt will cross examine her. As you've learned, she's good at her work."

A frown crinkled Merci's brow. "I'll ask the questions but don't put the entire burden on me."

Cass smiled. "Auntie, I did that when all of this began."

"So you did."

At the end of the break, Hilda Stensrud was back in the witness chair. Looking down from behind the bench, Judge

McNair muttered, "Mr. Myklebust, you may cross examine."
Geoffrey turned to Merci, who was already on her feet. "I'll
do the cross, Your Honor."

"Well, then, get on with it."

Mrs. Stensrud watched warily as Merci walked slowly
around the counsel table to stand before her. She relaxed a
bit when the first question came with a warm smile. "Mrs.
Stensrud, we've met before haven't we."

The smile and the tone of the question seemed to alleviate
Hilda's concern. "Yes, you came to the Springs to look at the
pool and to ask about the night the girl was killed."

"You were most accommodating. I appreciated it then
and still do. It gave me a better understanding of the way
things occurred." Mrs. Stensrud showed a small smile. Merci
continued. "You've described the main building for the
benefit of the jury. But what about other buildings? Aren't
there service buildings and sheds here and there about the
premises?

"Oh yes, there's a garage where we store the service
truck and the snow plow. And there's a shed to store the
lawn mowers and other gardening tools and equipment."

"I think I saw at least six buildings of various sizes, most
of them in the area out back. Am I right?"

"Yes, that's about right."

"They all have doors, do they not?"

Mrs. Stensrud frowned. "Of course."

Merci shifted her stance. "When you told the jury that
you locked every door, that wasn't quite correct was it? You
didn't lock the doors to all those sheds did you?"

"No, I'd locked the shed with the gardening equipment

a couple of weeks before that. I didn't lock the others. There was no need to. There's nothing of value in them."

"It's possible that someone could have been hiding in one of the sheds at the time you made your evening rounds, isn't it? And you would not have known that person was there? Isn't that right?"

Judge McNair raised a hand, palm to Merci. "That's three questions, Miss Bruce. Ask only one question and then allow the witness answer it."

"Of course, Your Honor." Merci turned back to Mrs. Stensrud. "Is it possible that someone was hiding in one of those sheds that night?"

Mrs. Stensrud pursed her lips. "Anything's possible."

Merci nodded her head. "You told the jury you were certain there was no one else at the hot springs that night. You really can't be sure of that, can you?"

"As I said, anything's possible." She rushed to add, "But how would that someone get into the pool to kill that girl? All of the doors to the main building were locked."

"Let's think about it. How secure are the locks? Are they all new?"

"No. Most of them have been there for some time. But they're all secure."

"How long is some time?"

Mrs. Stensrud squinted her eyes as she thought. "We put new locks on the front doors and some of the others two years ago."

"Why did you do that?"

"Someone tried to break in. Whoever it was didn't get in but made a mess of the door latch while trying."

"When were the locks on the guest room doors installed?"

"I'm not sure. Must have been when the place was built."

"They're not state of the art, are they?"

"They aren't new, if that's the question."

"It wouldn't be difficult for someone to jimmy the lock to one of the doors, would it?"

Mrs. Stensrud crunched up her mouth and shook her head. "Look, I've told you that anything's possible." She continued in a louder voice. "But I'm sure there wasn't anyone but those nine college kids in the pool that night."

Merci didn't give up. "Were you able to watch the front doors during the time the college rodeo people were there?"

The lady cocked her head slightly to the side before answering. "I was there at the reception desk except for the time it took me to get the bucket and icepick."

"So, if the main doors were untended for that period of time, someone could have entered without your knowledge. Right?"

Hilda Stensrud slumped back in the chair. "I wasn't away from the front very long. But I suppose it's theoretically possible that someone could have sneaked in during that time."

Merci glanced at Geoff. The nod of his head was barely perceptible. She looked to the judge. "No more questions, Your Honor."

"Redirect, Mr. Hodder?"

"None, sir."

The clock on the wall at the back of the courtroom showed eleven thirty. Judge McNair banged the gavel. Court was in recess until one thirty.

CHAPTER FIFTY-FOUR

Hodder stood at counsel table. "The state calls Abel Parsons."

The Gallatin County Sheriff, dressed in a loosely fitting suit but with his badge pinned to his shirt pocket, smiled at the clerk as he hoisted his hand in the air and swore to tell the truth. He nodded once at the judge and smiled at the jury. Finally, he lowered himself into the witness chair. Parson's face was sober when he focused on the county attorney.

Hodder assumed his accustomed posture, hands clasped behind his back. "Please state your name and address."

"My name is Abel Parsons. I live over the hill in Bozeman, Montana."

"Your occupation, sir?"

"I'm the sheriff of Gallatin County."

"In your capacity as sheriff, did you have occasion to help with the investigation into the death of a young woman named Summer Hetherington?"

"I did."

"How did that come about?"

Parsons looked at Josh Waddell seated at the prosecution counsel table before returning his attention to the questioner. He detailed the conversation with the Park County sheriff, his offer to help in the investigation, their visit with the house mother of the sorority at the college, and finally, their trip to the rodeo grounds in Belgrade.

"What happened there, at the rodeo grounds?" Hodder asked.

Parsons looked briefly at Cass. Facing the county attorney, his pleasant demeanor remaining, he said, "We came upon that young man, Cassius Bruce, near the bucking chutes. He was kneeling in the dirt, putting on his spurs, getting ready for the show."

"Am I right that you talked to him?

"We introduced ourselves. Sheriff Waddell asked if he'd been one of a group who were at Hunter's Hot springs the night before. He said he was. He also said that a girl named Summer was with them." Parsons waited a moment for Hodder to speak. When the attorney was slow to do so, he added, "Young Bruce said that Summer Hetherington was a barrel racer and should be somewhere at the other end of the arena getting ready for her run."

"What did you do then?"

"Josh explained that we needed to talk to him about the hot springs visit. He told us he was up in the first section of the barebacks and needed to get ready for the ride. One of us —I think it was me—asked if he'd come to my office after the rodeo to answer questions and to bring with him the names of all of the ones at Hunters. He said he would."

"Did he show up?"

"Yes. He got there about six thirty. And he had the list." Parsons paused for a split second. "By that time, it was obvious that he knew something bad had happened to Summer Hetherington."

"He knew she was dead?"

Parsons shook his head. "I don't think so. He seemed shocked to hear it."

Apparently not expecting that answer, Hodder frowned and quickly moved on. "What more happened at your office that night?"

"We asked some more questions." Parsons stopped, glanced at Waddell. "Josh explained that only the nine were at the pool when Miss Hetherington was last seen alive. He said that it led him to believe one of them might have been the killer."

"The defendant's reaction to that?"

"Well, Josh flat out asked him if he was the one who did it." He jerked his head in Cass's direction. "That young fellow seemed to lose his temper and stormed out of the room."

"What more did you do to help Sheriff Waddell with the investigation into the death of Summer Hetherington?"

"Over the next couple of days, the others who were at Hunter's Hot Springs with Summer Hetherington came in to my office. I listened to what each one had to say, took notes, and asked questions for clarification. After each session I reviewed the notes of the things they'd told me for accuracy."

"What became of the notes?"

Parsons smiled. "I gave them to Josh, and I believe he gave them to you to use in this trial."

Hodder flashed a smile in return. "He did, and they've been helpful." He turned to take a couple of sheets of note paper from a file on the counsel table. With them in hand, he asked, "Did one of those in the group have something to offer that shed additional light on Summer Hetherington's murder?"

Parsons' eyebrows went up in inquiry. "You mean what April Menard told me?" When the county attorney nodded his head, the sheriff continued. "The next morning, a young man and a young woman came to see me. They introduced themselves as Justin Madden and April Menard and said they were in the bunch at Hunter's Hot Springs."

"Did they have something to offer that was new?"

The sheriff nodded his head. "Oh, yes."

"And what was that?"

"The young woman, April, said she thought they were all loaded in the cars and ready to leave but Summer Hetherington was still in the dressing room. That's when Cass Bruce hollered that he'd left his wallet and ran back to get it."

"What was the significance of that?"

Up went the sheriff's eyebrows again, as though to wonder why anyone would need to ask. "It showed that Cass Bruce was the last one of the group who was alone with Summer Hetherington before the others left for Bozeman."

"The inference was that he had to be the killer, is that it?"

"He had the opportunity."

"You shared this information with Sheriff Waddell?"

"I did."

Hodder stepped back and turned to the judge. "No more questions for Sheriff Parsons, Your Honor."

"Questions for this witness, Mr. Myklebust?"

"None, Your Honor."

The judge smiled at Abel Parsons. "You're excused, sir." He straightened in his chair and looked at the clock on the rear wall above the exit. "I have another matter that demands my attention, and it will take some time. We'll recess until tomorrow morning at nine o'clock." He turned to the jury. "You're admonished to refrain from discussing anything about these proceedings with anyone—not your fellow juror, not your spouse, not your best friend, not even your dog." There was a brief chuckle from the folks in the room. "I'll tell you when you may do so." He pushed his chair back from the bench. "Please be on time." He banged the gavel. "Court's in recess."

CHAPTER FIFTY-FIVE

The jurors were in place and Court was in session to begin the third day of the trial. Judge McNair said, "Mr. Hodder, please call your next witness."

"The state calls Doctor Henry Winters."

The doctor, about sixty years of age and slightly stooped, took the oath and moved with purpose to the witness chair. Hodder allowed him a moment to get himself settled.

"Please state your name and address, sir."

"My name is Henry B. Winters. I have my office at 224 West Park Street here in Livingston, and I live in an apartment in the back."

"Your profession, sir?"

"I'm a medical doctor."

Hodder asked a series of questions, the answers to which detailed the doctor's education, training and additional qualifications. Even though Merci had explained the purpose of the questions—to qualify the doctor to testify as an expert medical witness—it seemed to Cass an unnecessary waste of time. The man was a doctor. That's all anyone in the room needed to know. The questions and answers droned on until at last, the county attorney asked, "Were you called to Hunter's Hot Springs on the morning of May fourteenth of this year?"

"I was. The sheriff sent word for me."

"What did you find when you arrived there?"

"I was met by Mrs. Stensrud. She led me to the pool area."

"What did you see when you got there?"

"I saw the body of a young woman lying at the bottom of the swimming pool."

Hodder, standing a short distance from the witness chair, asked, "What did you do then?"

"Sheriff Waddell had called for some help. A couple of young guys arrived and climbed down into the pool to lift the body from the water."

"Doctor, were you able to determine the cause of death right away?"

Winters glanced at the jury and said, "My preliminary determination at the time was that the death was caused by an icepick that had been driven upward under the woman's chin and into her brain."

"You say the determination was preliminary. Was there a later, more certain determination?"

"Oh yes. The body was sent to a pathologist. After a complete examination the pathologist came to the same conclusion."

The county attorney retrieved the small photographs of the dead woman that he had previously introduced into evidence. He handed them to the doctor who took a second to shuffle through them before looking up at his questioner. Hodder asked, "Do you recognize those pictures?"

The doctor gathered them together into a group. "Yes, I recognize them. These are pictures of the body as it appeared after it was removed from the pool."

"Is the icepick about which you spoke shown in any of the pictures?"

The doctor fingered the pack to extract one of them. "It's shown clearly in this one." He turned to his left and held it up for the jurors to see.

The county attorney looked to the judge. "May I pass it to the jury again, Your Honor?"

"You may."

Hodder took the picture from the doctor and handed to it the nearest juror who held it only a second before passing it to his neighbor. Turning again to the doctor he reached for the remaining pictures. "I'll take those." He walked the pictures back to the clerk before again taking his stance before the witness chair. "Doctor, in what possible way could that icepick been impaled into the victim?"

Winters didn't answer for so long that it appeared he hadn't heard. At last he turned to the jury. "I suppose there are a variety of ways, perhaps some of them mechanical. But with the information given to me by Mrs. Stensrud, I have to believe the pick was driven into the body by another human being."

"And what is the information to which you refer?"

"She told the sheriff and me that a group of young people came to swim. No one else was in the pool area from the time young folks arrived until she found the body the following morning. Nor was there any mechanical device that might plausibly be used to impale the pick as it was found."

Hodder nodded his acceptance of the statement, dropped his eyes to the floor and stood in silence as he framed the next question. "How would one person go about thrusting an icepick into another in the manner that is shown in that picture?"

The doctor paused. "I've thought about it a lot. It would be almost impossible if the victim was in a position to resist. That being the case, it seems the attacker would have to approach the victim from behind, grasp that person's hair and pull the head sharply back. That would lift and expose the victim's chin." The doctor reached with his left hand to the back of his head to demonstrate. Speaking with his head leaning back, he continued. "The killer would then drive the pick upward with all his might through the skin under the chin and on upward until it pierced the membrane upon which the brain rests." With his right hand he demonstrated the thrust.

Winters ended his explanation and looked again at the county attorney. Hodder gave the jurors a short minute to consider the word picture the doctor had painted. At last he asked, "How much strength would it take for one person to do that to another?"

The doctor shook his head with vigor. "It would not be easy to do, especially to drive the pick through the membrane that supports the brain and on upward into the brain itself. Only a person with considerable strength could do it. But more than that, it would also take someone with significant coordination, a person with the ability to complete the two tasks almost at once—the head pull and the pick thrust—quickly, in rapid succession and with great force."

The attorney glanced at Cass and back. "An athletic young man?"

The doctor's eyes didn't follow those of Hodder as he answered without hesitation. "It would seem so. Certainly, a diminutive young woman couldn't do it."

Merrill Hodder turned toward the counsel table then immediately turned back to say, "You said that a pathologist examined the body. Did he do a complete autopsy?"

"He did."

"Did that autopsy disclose anything else of significance?"

The doctor ran his hands along his pant legs as he answered. "It disclosed that the young woman was pregnant."

Hodder allowed the jurors time to absorb the information. "Did the autopsy report disclose the length of time she had been pregnant?"

"About a month and a half."

In Cass's mind, Hodder's walk around the corner of the counsel table to his chair resting behind it seemed to take forever. Time for the jury to contemplate the two items of importance in the doctor's testimony. First, Summer was pregnant. Second, some athletic young man must have killed her. They were bound to tie the two together. Four of the jurors showed it in the surreptitious glance each of them cast at him.

Standing before his chair, the county attorney looked at the judge. "No more questions for Doctor Winters."

8 Seconds

Judge McNair looked at the clock and then pushed back his chair. "We'll take a fifteen-minute break." He rapped the gavel once. "Court's in recess.

CHAPTER FIFTY-SIX

A small cubbyhole of an office, available for use by trial attorneys and their clients, was located off a hallway away from the courtroom. Merci, Geoffrey, and Cass huddled there. Cass spoke as soon as the door closed. "The things the jury just heard are enough to convince them that I got Summer pregnant and then killed her."

Merci gestured toward a chair and took one for herself. "We've known all along what the state's case would be. The things we heard were no surprise."

Cass remained standing. "I understand. But listening to it pour out in that courtroom makes me wonder if anything can be done to counteract it."

Geoffrey seated with his hands in his lap. "The defense, as we've always agreed, has to be that someone else was there and did it." He paused. "It would be perfect if we knew of another person who was there or might possibly have been there. But we don't, so we have to settle for less than perfect and try to shift the burden. We must convince that jury that it isn't enough for the prosecution to say they couldn't find anyone else out there that night. We must convince them that they cannot convict you unless the state produces proof that no other possible killer exists." Geoff was still for an eye blink. "That will be difficult unless we learn something more from other witnesses as we go along."

Cass asked, "What can you do about that doctor's testimony. It seemed damning."

Geoffrey got to his feet to head for the courtroom. "Try to scatter a little doubt."

The doctor, back in the witness chair, waited in seeming patience. The judge looked at Geoffrey. "Do you have question for this witness, Mr. Myklebust?"

Geoff rose to his feet to stand erect, hands clasped at his waist. "One question, Your Honor."

Both the judge's and the doctor's eyebrows rose as though to ask, "Only one?"

Still standing behind the table, Geoff said, "Doctor Winters, when asked what kind of person could drive the icepick into the brain of Summer Hetherington you said, and I quote, 'only an athletic young man could do it.'" Geoff waited a split second for the doctor to recollect. "Isn't it also possible that an athletic woman—not a diminutive young woman, as you mentioned, but a well-developed, solidly-muscled young woman—could thrust the pick into the throat of Summer Hetherington where it was found?"

The doctor leaned back in the chair as he contemplated the question. At last he turned his eyes from Geoff to the jury and back. "Well, yes, I suppose that's possible. It would just have to be someone with significant strength and agility. The gender wouldn't matter."

Geoff lowered his head slightly in a single nod. "No further questions for the doctor."

As the doctor slowly made his exit from the courtroom., Judge McNair said, "Mr. Hodder, call your next witness."

"The state calls Gregory Lovell."

A young man in western dress entered the court room, walked the length of the aisle to stand before the judge's bench. He swore to tell the truth and took the witness stand.

Hodder began, "Please state your name and tell us where you live.

"My name is Gregory Lovell. I live in White Sulphur Springs." The way he rubbed his hands along the arms of the chair revealed his nervousness.

"That's Montana, isn't it?"

"Yes. About seventy miles north of here."

Hodder then posed a series of questions that led him to tell of the happenings the night of Summer's death—the decision to go, the time spent in the pool and the rush to leave. He said he'd heard about Cass and his wallet but had no distinct memory of Cass going back to retrieve it. "He couldn't have been gone long, if he did."

His comments about Cass as well as Summer were complimentary.

The county attorney finished the direct examination. Geoff rose to his feet. "No questions of this witness, Your Honor."

Judge McNair intoned, "Once again, I have to attend to

another matter, so we'll recess until nine o'clock tomorrow."
A bang of the gavel brought the session to an end.

CHAPTER FIFTY-SEVEN

Geoffrey, Merci and Cass stood quietly as the jurors moved slowly through the door to the jury room, and the spectators, including Cass's family, paraded out the main entryway, followed by Hodder and Josh Waddell. When the three were alone at last, Merci touched Cass on his upper arm to turn him in her direction. "How are you holding up?"

Cass's response was accompanied by a slow shaking of his head. "All the things that have been said so far seem to be true." He looked squarely at his aunt's upturned face. "But it was all so innocent. I can't help but wonder how I ended up being accused of doing such a horrible thing."

Outside the courtroom Geoff spoke to Cass. "Go with your family. They'll want to visit with you. Later they'll have questions for Merci and me." He moved on to Cass's father. "Your sister and I have matters to discuss first thing. Your son needs a little time to rest and refresh, as do the rest of us. May I suggest that we all meet in the Bruce Family Room at about six o'clock? We can order dinner. After the meal's finished we can discuss today's testimony and the things we might anticipate for tomorrow."

Spencer said, "Sound's good."

They had learned that wind was a constant in Livingston, Montana. This day it tore at their clothing as they all hurried from automobiles to the hotel lobby. Geoff and Merci were last to the elevator. In the rooms used as their office, Merci dropped the files on a table, kicked off her shoes and settled into the chair next to her work station. She smiled at Geoff. "Your thoughts?"

Geoffrey showed no emotion. "There was nothing in today's testimony to surprise us." He looked off into the distance for a second. "It appears that Mr. Hodder will present his case in a linear fashion—line it out in a way that will be easy for the jury to follow."

"He'll want to finish with the most compelling testimony. Who will be the final witness and what will that person's testimony be?"

"We can only guess," Geoff said, "but probably one of the others who were at the hot springs that night. We both need to relax and clear our minds. If there are matters you and I need to discuss before tomorrow's session, let's do it after we've eaten. Right now, I'm going to my room and stretch out on the bed for half an hour of rest before making some calls to the office. You may wish to do the same."

"Best idea yet."

In the hotel lobby Cass escaped from his parents and other well-wishers to his room. As he locked the door and turned to the bed, exhaustion overcame him. He shed his suit coat and shoes before lying flat on his back. His eyes drooped shut, short flashes of memory crossed his mind before he tumbled into a deep dreamless sleep. The next thing he heard was a knock on the door and his father calling him to dinner.

Cass sat between his parents; his grandparents sat across from him. Merci sat at one end of the table and Geoffrey at the other. They ate with none of the banter common at the Bruce table on every occasion Cass could remember.

At last Geoffrey pushed his plate to the side and looked at Cass's father. "Spencer, you're a lawyer. You're bound to have comments or questions."

Spencer finished a last swallow of ice cream. "Not many. There was nothing unexpected in the testimony of the witnesses today. Is that your impression?"

Geoff looked toward Merci who gave the response. "Geoff and I agree." She reached with one hand palm down across the table in the direction of T. C. Bruce. "How about it, Dad? You're a lawyer too. What do you think?"

The old man responded by smiling and patting her hand. "It's been years since I was in a courtroom, but nothing said today was a surprise." He looked at Myklebust. "None of it seemed controversial, just statements of facts that really aren't in dispute."

Geoff nodded slowly. "I believe we're all in agreement." He ran his eyes from one to another around the table. "What about those of you who aren't lawyers? Any questions before we leave here to rest up for tomorrow?"

Cass's grandmother asked, "How long will this last?

Merci smiled at her mother. "The standard answer to that question is, 'It will last as long as it lasts.'" The smile disappeared. "Geoff and I can't predict with certainty how long this one will take. But my guess is about three days."

Geoff spoke in his quiet voice. "It's just a guess." He pushed his chair away from the table. "If you will excuse me, I'll go to my room, prepare a couple of things for tomorrow and get some sleep."

Merci was on her feet. "I'm off to my room as well." She walked around the table to put her hand on Cass's shoulder. "Get some rest. Tomorrow will be a long day."

Cass flashed a wan smile at his aunt. "I just hope I can sleep." Back in his hotel room he wondered if there was a way he might have done things differently to somehow change things so that this day and this place had never arrived.

CHAPTER FIFTY-EIGHT

The remaining seven of those who were at Hunter's Hot Springs on the night of May thirteenth, minus Summer and Cass, had been subpoenaed by the state to appear at the Park county courthouse for the Bruce trial. None of the seven came alone. Most were accompanied by at least one family member. Hannah was among them. Her mother was with her, having reluctantly left Forrest alone at the ranch. The state also subpoenaed Wayne Foley and Doris Hamilton. The defense had subpoenaed them as well. No family members, it seemed, came with them. The defense subpoenaed three others: the sorority housemother, Ella Brown, and Donna Holloway.

Most of the rooms at the Murray, Park, and Grand hotels were filled. The eating places, including the drive in, enjoyed the best business in weeks.

By order of the court each witness was excluded from the courtroom until that person had given his or her testimony.

Those, together with their families as well as the usual court hangers on, created a throng that crowded the anteroom outside the courtroom doors each morning. Both Merrill Hodder and Merci Bruce tried to let the people they'd subpoenaed know when their testimony would be needed. At other times they were allowed to leave the courthouse.

Lillian Dodson worried about Forrest, left alone at the Dodson ranch. He'd recovered most of his health and strength before the trial and could care for himself. He could again ride horseback to tend to the cattle even though those days were shorter than they had been before his medical ordeal.

But what if something went wrong? Lillian called him each evening to report on the trial and to assure herself that her husband was doing as well as could be expected. To fill the time the women read the Livingston Enterprise newspaper, the Billings Gazette, as well as books and magazines. When the wind wasn't howling, they window shopped to pass the time. They frequented a coffee shop that served pastry. At mid-morning, the place filled with locals. The conversation that the Dodson women overheard among the regulars focused on the trial. No one, it seemed, was in doubt about the outcome—Cass Bruce would be convicted unless the out of town lawyers outsmarted the hometown county attorney.

One morning an elderly woman with a cane hobbled across the room to approach their table. "Pardon me. But I believe you're the mother of the young man whose trial is taking place at the courthouse."

Lillian looked up. "I'm not his mother. We're friends."

"My husband's a rancher, and he met T. C. Bruce once at a Stockgrowers Association meeting. He really liked him

Jim Moore

and says that the grandson of that man cannot be a killer. We hope the jury finds him not guilty."

Lillian smiled. "That's nice to hear."

The old woman returned the smile. "Well, just wanted you to know."

While Hannah shared her mother's concern for her father's condition, she also worried about Cass Bruce. She'd seen the burden of the trial wear on his spirits, so much so that it had begun to affect his physical appearance. She tried to touch him as he entered the courtroom at noon on the first day, just to let him know she cared. Merci stopped her, whispering, "Not a good idea." Hannah's worries remained, but she kept them to herself.

CHAPTER FIFTY-NINE

O n the morning of the fourth day of the trial, Geoff led the way into the courtroom with Cass and Merci close behind. The rest of the Bruce group followed. Cass and the lawyers took their places at the counsel table. A single reporter for the local newspaper occupied one spot among the crowded courtroom. A murder trial in Park County, Montana, was news, at least locally.

The judge mounted the bench. Merrill Hodder called Lyndon Welch as his next witness. Welch's testimony nearly duplicated that of Greg Lovell. Again, there was no cross-examination.

Next was Harry Croswell. He gave Cass a small wave of his hand that he held down by his thigh as he strode by on the way to take the oath. Croswell's response to Hodder's questions differed not at all from that of Lovell and Welch. However, as the county attorney finished telling the judge there were no more questions, Croswell leaned to the side of the witness chair to speak directly to the jury. In a firm voice, he said, "I know Cass Bruce. He didn't kill anybody."

Hodder, whose back was by then to the judge, whirled around to bark, "Object to that remark. It's gratuitous and it's not based upon any fact before the court." His anger was evident. "That man should be punished."

There was a deep frown on Judge McNair's face as he leaned across the bench in the direction of the witness. "Mr. Hodder's right, young man." He poked the handle of the gavel at Harry. "This court deals in facts. You have no business expressing your opinions here."

Croswell glanced up at the judge before dropping his eyes, then he looked directly again at the judge. For a moment it appeared he would respond.

The judge didn't give him that chance. He swiveled toward the jury. "You are to completely disregard the last statements of this witness. It is not testimony. It has no probative value." He paused for a long moment. "Do you all understand?" Each responded with a nod.

Cass remained poker faced but said silently, "Thanks, Harry."

Judge McNair said to Geoff, "Mr. Myklebust, do you have any questions for this witness?"

"No, sir. I do not."

The judge shifted in his chair to speak once again to Croswell. "You're excused, sir." As Harry stepped away from the witness stand, the judge added, "And if you're ever a witness in court again, young man, remember the rules."

"Yes, sir, I will."

The judge looked at Hodder. "Your next witness, sir."

"The state calls Ezekiel Howard."

8 Seconds

The college cowboy they all knew as Zeke seated himself squarely in the witness chair, placed his hands on his knees and looked at the county attorney. When asked, he said, "My name is Ezekiel Howard. I live in Lodge Grass, Montana."

"Are you one of the Montana State rodeo cowboys?"

"Yes, I go to the college, and I like to rodeo."

Hodder, standing at his usual place before the witness stand, led the young man through the same litany of events that led up to the death of Summer Hetherington. Zeke's testimony differed not a whit from the others until Hodder asked, "Whose idea was it to go to the hot springs?"

Zeke jerked his chin at Cass. "Cass Bruce. It was his idea."

"When you got there, who paid your way in?'

"Cass Bruce. He did it without asking the rest of us."

"Mr. Howard, who decided when to leave the pool?"

He looked in Cass's direction. "Cass. It's always Cass. He doesn't pay any attention to the ideas of the rest of us. I guess he thinks he's smarter than anyone else."

"And you didn't approve?'

"No, I sure didn't."

Hodder stepped closer before asking, "What kind of relationship did Cass Bruce have with Summer Hetherington?"

Geoff spoke without standing. "Objection. This witness can only speculate as to that relationship—if there was one."

The judge nodded his head. "Sustained. Please restate your question, sir."

Hodder nodded. "Mr. Howard, what did you observe with regard to the relationship of Cassius Bruce and Summer Hetherington?"

"He spent as much time around her as possible. He reset a shoe on her horse, always hurrying to help her any way he could—feed her horse, throw her saddle on the horse's back."

"What about times away from the horses? What other times were they together?"

"He bragged about taking her to a movie." Zeke stopped, looked at Cass for a short second, before blurting, "Look, it was obvious that he wanted to get to her. I just never thought she was much interested in him. But he's used to having things his way. Who knows? Maybe he raped her and then had to get rid of her when she told him she was pregnant."

Geoff was on his feet and his voice carried a sharpness not heard before. "Objection! Move to strike. This man's speculation is not evidence. His beliefs are not something to which the jury may give even slight consideration."

Hodder didn't give up easily. "Not so, Your Honor. They're statements based upon this witness's personal observations. In that sense they're not speculative."

The judge, who had been scowling at Zeke Howard, jerked his head around to face the county attorney. His voice was a growl. "Mr. Hodder, you know better than that." Looking again at the witness he snapped, "You, sir, are here to give testimony about matters of which you have personal knowledge. You are not here to tell the jury what you think." He waited while staring at Zeke. "Do you understand?"

Zeke's eyes were wide. "Yes, sir. I'm sorry."

The judge's scowl didn't relax. "Sorry doesn't change what you did." Then he looked to the jury. "Mr. Howard's last statement is not based on fact. You may not consider it as evidence. You may not consider it at all." He turned back to the county attorney. "More questions for this witness?" The tone of his voice almost dared Hodder to ask more.

"No, Your Honor."

"Mr. Myklebust?"

Geoff glanced at Merci who was moving her head from side to side. He looked to the judge to say. "No questions."

McNair mumbled, "Recess. Fifteen minutes."

In the small courthouse conference room, Merci shook her head. "In my interview, Zeke seemed a little jealous of Cass, but I didn't expect the vitriol he spouted today."

Geoff waved his hand at the chairs and took one for himself. "It doesn't matter much." He put a reassuring hand on Cass's shoulder. "What he said about you being responsible for her pregnancy had to be on the minds of the jurors already." He turned to Merci. "We have yet to hear from April Menard. The manner in which she testifies will be critical."

CHAPTER SIXTY

When Court convened, Justin Madden was on the witness stand. Once again, the jurors heard a recitation of the events at Hunter's Hot Springs the night of the death of Summer Hetherington. Finally, the county attorney asked, "At the time when you were all leaving the pool for the autos, did anything unusual happen?"

Madden's eyebrows lifted. "You mean Cass Bruce going back to the pool?"

"Yes."

Justin shifted in the chair. "That didn't register with me at the time. I only remembered after April mentioned it."

"But you do now remember that it happened?"

"Yes. After April reminded me, I thought back on the way things occurred. A picture of Cass hurrying back through the main door to hot springs came to mind." He shrugged, "I think that Cass has already told the sheriff that he was the last one away from the pool."

"Indeed, he has." Hodder said to the judge. "No more questions for Mr. Madden."

"Mr. Myklebust?"

"No questions, Your Honor."

The judge turned to Hodder. "Next witness sir?"

"The state calls April Menard."

April, her athletic figure accented by a royal blue dress of perfect fit, walked with assurance along the aisle to take the oath. She moved to the witness stand as though for her it was a common occurrence. Not once did she look at Cass.

Hodder was back in his usual place and in his usual stance. "Please state your name and place of residence."

"My name is April Menard, and I live in Lewistown, Montana."

"Do you attend Montana State College?"

"Yes, I'm a senior this year."

"Are you also a member of the college rodeo team?"

April shook her head. "No. I don't rodeo." She brightened. "But my boyfriend does."

"Who might that be?"

"Justin Madden. I believe he was in here to testify right before you called for me."

"Indeed, he was." Hodder was silent for a second. "Mr. Madden told the jury about the trip to Hunter's Hot Springs. Were you among those who went there on the evening of May thirteenth of this year? After the college rodeo?"

April leaned forward as she spoke. "I was one of nine. Three of us were girls."

The county attorney shifted a step to his left. "The jury has heard that there came a time when you decided to leave.

How did that come about?"

She leaned even farther forward in the chair, giving impression that she was anxious to tell her story. "Someone hollered that it was late and we might miss the curfew. So we scrambled out of the pool and into the dressing rooms."

"Then what happened?"

"We hurried to get out of the swim suits and into the cars."

"When you were getting in the cars did anything occur that kept you all from just driving away?"

April sat on the very front edge of the chair. "Yes, it did."

"And what was that?"

For the first time April Menard looked directly at Cass. He held her gaze for only an instant before she turned away. "Cass Bruce had reached his car and opened the driver's door when he hollered that he'd left his wallet and took off on the run to get it."

"At the time this happened were the rest of you in the autos?"

April sank back into the chair. "When Cass got back with his wallet all of us except Summer Hetherington were loaded and ready to go." Before the county attorney could ask the next question, she hurried to add, "But none of us realized that Summer wasn't with us. Those of us in one car thought she was in the other car and vise versa."

"So, Miss Hetherington never came out of the pool?"

"No." April swallowed and looked down at her feet. "I guess we just left her there."

Hodder gave her a second before asking, "Who was the last one to come out of the pool room before you all loaded up and drove away."

April looked toward Cass. "He was. Cass Bruce was the last one in that place with Summer Hetherington." Then she dropped her eyes to her hands that were twisting on her lap. A single tear crept out of the corner of her eye and trickled slowly down her cheek.

The county attorney wanted the jurors to contemplate the words and the picture as long as possible before he finally said. "No more questions of this witness, Your Honor."

The judge, like the jurors, was aware of April's emotions. "It's somewhat early for lunch, but we'll be in recess until one thirty."

In their workroom at the hotel Geoff and Cass settled into chairs. Merci said, "Well, Mr. Hodder and that young woman orchestrated her testimony perfectly."

Cass shook his head. "Perhaps so. But April told the truth." He heaved a sigh. "I didn't expect her to tell it in such a dramatic way. The jurors have to think I went back into the swimming pool with one purpose—to kill Summer."

Geoff's voice was soft but firm. "She isn't finished. We can still cross examine her when court convenes after lunch—but we won't." Cass just stared at him without comprehension. "We'll call her back to the stand during our case in chief. Your aunt and I discussed the order in which we should question our witnesses. I favored a vigorous cross-examination of Miss Menard. Merci insisted her testimony would be more effective if it occurred after yours." He paused and the corners of his lips lifted into that barely discernible smile. "Let's just say we had a lively argument." He glanced at Merci. "In the end she convinced me. And that's the reason

Jim Moore

we will not question April Menard at this time."

Merci leaned with her elbows on her knees to face Cass. "When court re-convenes, Hodder will probably rest his case. "If he does, we're up."

Geoff, erect in his chair, squared himself to look directly at his client. "As we've told you several times, it's generally a bad idea for the defendant to testify. If he does, he's then subject to cross-examination. All too often, under relentless questioning and accusations from the prosecuting attorney, the witness then says things that hurt rather than help."

Cass had become anesthetized. After hearing accusations day after day his mind had become numb. But now, listening to his attorneys talk about his possible testimony, a cold fear ground itself into his gut. He mustered all his willpower to tamp it down before he answered. "You've told me all of that over and over again. I've listened. But I'm terrified now that it's actually time to convince the jury I didn't kill Summer."

"That's understandable. But Merci and I agree that in this case to keep you from telling your story would be a mistake."

Merci remained sitting with her elbows on her knees. "That hasn't been an easy decision. But you're believable when you speak. You have an ability to convey a sense of honesty."

The cold cramp remained, but Cass showed the wan smile that was now the only smile he had. "I'm glad you think so." He turned to Geoff. "When will you call me as a witness?"

"That's the decision we have to make right now." He looked from Cass to Merci and back. "Our other witnesses are Summer's roommates, the sorority housemother, Doris

Hamilton and Wayne Foley. We have to assume that some of them might change their stories since Merci's last interviews. If so, Merci and I will do our best to clean up any problems the changed story might create. That said, I believe we agree that the jury should hear from you first off. If you make the proper impression—and I believe you will—they'll be more inclined listen to the others with some sympathy for you."

Merci was now erect in her chair. "In other words, Cass, you're first up, right after we return to court." Her concern was evident in the tone of her voice. "Are you up to it?"

Cass stood, squaring his shoulders. "I'm ready."

CHAPTER SIXTY-ONE

Hannah and Lillian took their lunch in the dining room of the hotel. While eating, a big bellied man, dressed in worn country clothing approached their table. He seemed hesitant to take the last steps to stand near at hand. When he did so, he turned the brim of a soiled western hat around and around in his hands. Both of the women glanced at him and immediately looked back to the food. The man spoke in a tentative voice. "Aren't you the family of the guy they're calling a murderer?"

Lillian looked up with a frown. "He's a friend."

"Excuse me for bothering you, ma'am, but I know something I think your friend's lawyers should know."

Hannah was quick to ask, "What's that?"

"Well, I have a place out north of Springdale. I run a few cows. It ain't much, but I like it. To get in and out of there I drive by Hunter's Hot Springs. One evening last spring I drove into town for a beer with some friends. As I went by the Springs, I saw a big Buick parked behind a shed out back. I wouldn't have thought much about it, but we don't see many cars that fancy out where I live. The thing was long and black and had four holes in the front fenders, a Buick. I believe those big ones are called Roadmasters."

When he paused Hannah prompted, "What about it?"

"Well, as I was driving home later in the evening I met that same car going toward Springdale."

Hannah stared at the man and waited.

"As I said, we don't very often see a car like that around here. So that one, parked by the shed and then driving past me in the evening, stuck in my mind." The man shifted from foot to foot. "We've all heard about the killing of the girl at the Springs. I guess there's a question if the kid they've accused of doing the killing was the only one out there that night." He paused. "I can tell his lawyers that there might have been at least one other person—the one driving that Buick."

Hannah was on her feet. "What's your name sir?"

"I'm Hugo Gee, ma'am."

"Will you tell all of this to Cass Bruce's lawyers?"

"Cass Bruce? Is he the kid they've charged?"

"He is."

Hugo Gee grinned. "Sure. I'll tell them." He stopped turning his hat. "I bothered you because I thought it might be important."

"I think it will be." Hannah smiled. "How can they get in touch with you?"

"Ask at the post office in Springdale. The postmistress will tell you the way." The corpulent rancher touched her hand and then turned to waddle away.

Hannah stared at her mother. "They won't let me talk to Cass." She ran a finger along her cheek. "I know. I'll tell Cass's dad. He'll tell Merci what this guy said. This sounds important."

Hannah found Spencer in the entryway to the courtroom and told him Hugo Gee's story. Spencer caught Merci and Geoff at the door to the courtroom. Geoff listened and didn't hesitate. He put a hand on Spencer's shoulder. "Find that guy as fast as you can and get him here so we can question him. It may make the difference in the verdict."

CHAPTER SIXTY-TWO

Geoff, as usual, led the way. They pushed through the swinging gate and on to their counsel table. Cass held the chair for Merci, then glanced around the room before slumping into his own. In the beginning it had seemed rather spacious. Now it felt more like a gloomy, cramped room in a grotto populated only by those wishing to do him harm. It took will power to brush that thought from his mind.

Merrill Hodder paraded up the aisle, April Menard in tow. He directed her to return to the witness stand. Once there, she tucked her skirt around her legs and seemed to take special care to avoid looking at Cass.

In short order, Judge McNair assumed the bench to bark, "Court's is session." He turned first to April. "Thank you for returning to that chair." He turned to Geoff. "Questions for Miss Menard, Mr. Myklebust?"

Jim Moore

Merci answered. "Not at this time, Your Honor. However, we have Miss Menard under subpoena and may wish to ask questions of her later."

"Very well." The judge addressed April. "You're finished for now. Since you may be called to the stand again, don't leave town. And don't remain in the courtroom to listen to the testimony yet to come." April hurried from the room and the judge looked at the county attorney. "Your next witness, sir?"

Hodder pushed himself up from his chair and straightened his suit coat. With solemnity he announced, "The state rests."

Judge McNair turned to the defense table. "Are you ready to present your first witness, Mr. Myklebust?"

Geoffrey stood. "We are, Your Honor." He turned to Cass who was slowly rising to his feet. "We call Cassius Bruce." There was a small stir in the room. This was what the spectators had waited for.

Cass pushed his chair away from the counsel table. He stood a moment, took a small breath and glanced at Merci. Fortified, he strode around the end of the table to stand before the judge's bench in the well of the courtroom. When asked whether he swore to tell the truth, he responded in a firm voice, "I do." He stepped to the witness chair where he settled himself squarely. He turned to look from one juror to another. Each returned his gaze with the same sober expression.

Cass returned his attention to Geoffrey who said, "Please state your name and address for the court record."

He and Geoffrey had gone over and over the questions.

Cass felt fully ready to answer them. Merci had spent time with him differently. She'd described the things that witnesses do under questioning—the quick shifting of eyes, the nervous movements in the chair, the rubbing of the hands, the wiggling of the feet, the scrunching together of the shoulders. Such body movements often demonstrated a lack of candor, indicating an attempt to avoid telling the truth. She called them giveaways. The jurors would notice the giveaways, perhaps without even realizing that they had done so, and then discount the testimony of the witness. As each of the other witnesses testified, Cass had watched. The way they behaved was equally as important as the words they spoke. Now he'd have to apply that knowledge.

"My name is Cassius Bruce. My home is in Harlowton, Montana."

Geoff stood, arms relaxed at his sides. It seemed he stood that way forever before he asked, "Mr. Bruce, did you kill Summer Hetherington?"

"No sir. I did not." Cass looked directly at Geoff as he said it. He waited an eye blink, turned his upper body to the jury and leaned slightly in their direction. "I want you to know. I did not kill Summer Hetherington." He held that position for a moment, eyes running from one to another of the jurors. Some blinked, others turned away. None held his gaze. Cass returned his attention back to Geoffrey.

"You've heard the testimony of the others who've been on that witness stand. They've told of the trip to Hunter's Hot Springs. Have their stories been consistent with your remembrances?"

"In general, they have."

Jim Moore

Geoff waited again before saying, "In general, you say. Were there things said with which you disagree?"

"Not any statements. Just inferences." He turned to face the jury. "For instance, Zeke Howard talked as though I was somehow in charge that night, like neither he nor the others had any say in what we did." He turned back to Geoff. "Our decision to go to the hot springs was spontaneous. After the rodeo, one of the girls said she needed a bath. Lyndon said it would take a swim to get him clean. That's when Hunter's Hot Springs came up. A swim seemed like a good idea. No one was forced to go who didn't want to. In fact, Wayne Foley and Doris Hamilton were there when we discussed it, but they went off to do something else."

"Mr. Howard seemed upset because you paid for the swim and all of the swimsuits."

"I didn't keep him from paying for his own. I just offered to handle it for all of us. That way Mrs. Stensrud only had to deal with one person. It let us all get into the pool sooner."

Geoff took one step forward, and the seriousness of the next question was evidenced by his facial appearance. "What about the implication that you were responsible for Summer's pregnancy?"

Cass turned again to the jury. "I didn't get Summer pregnant." Back to face Geoff, he said, "She and I were friends. We were good friends, but nothing more."

"Good friends? Didn't you take her to a movie?"

A quick smile appeared on Cass face. "One afternoon we were sitting around when Summer mentioned she'd like to go to an old movie at the Rialto theatre. My watch said it was one thirty, early enough to get there for the matinee. So, I just

said, 'Lets' go.' And we did. It wasn't a date or anything."
The smile was gone when he turned to the jury. "I took her
for an airplane ride once too. She'd heard that I belonged to
the flying co-op and asked about it. The next day was Sunday,
and the morning was bright and still, a perfect day to fly, so I
called her and asked if she'd like to go. She said she thought
it would be fun. We took the co-op Cessna airplane and spent
a half hour flying around the valley. That's all there was to
it."

"Did you do other things alone with her?"

"No. Those were the only times we were alone together."

Geoff waited again before asking, "Did any of the other
witnesses say things with which you disagree?"

"There seemed to be a belief that I killed Summer when I
went back to the pool area to get my wallet. If Mrs. Stensrud
and the others had given it any thought, they would have
known I couldn't have done it. I was in and out of there in
less than a minute. There wasn't time for me to grab her, pull
her head back, stab that icepick up into her chin, drag her to
the pool, and drop her in the water." He looked at the jury.
"I just dashed into the men's dressing room, grabbed my
wallet, and ran back to the car."

Geoff made a quarter turn toward the jury. "If you didn't
commit this crime, the jury must wonder who did. Do you
know who that person might be?"

Cass seemed to slump downward in the witness chair.
"No, Mr. Myklebust, I don't. I wish I did."

"You cannot accuse anyone else, is that what you're
saying?"

Cass shook his head. "I don't know who killed her."

Jim Moore

Geoff waited an instant before saying in his soft voice, "But it wasn't you."

"No, sir. It wasn't me." He turned again to the jury. "I'll say it again. I didn't kill her."

Geoff nodded once to his client and waited a second before looking at the judge. "No more questions of Mr. Bruce, Your Honor."

Judge McNair straightened his back and looked at the clock. "We'll be in recess for fifteen minutes." He turned to the jury. "My admonition remains in place. Don't discuss matters relating to this trial until I tell you that you may. You will be tempted to do so, but don't." He banged the gavel once before heading out the door to his chambers.

Cass stepped down from the witness chair to join Geoff and Merci as they waited for the jury to clear the room. When most of the spectators straggled out the doors, Merci grasped Cass's upper arms and looked up into his face. "You handled that as well as you possibly could." She gave his arms a little shake before releasing them. "I'm proud of you."

Her nephew favored her with a wan smile. "I'm just relieved to have that much over with." He turned to Geoff. "Thank you. You made it as easy for me as you could."

Geoff nodded. "I agree with Merci. Your testimony was believable. But that was the easy part. The next will be difficult."

Merci had focused her attention only on Cass throughout his testimony. He'd remembered all of her instructions and admonitions while responding to questions from Geoff. Could he do as well when questioned by Hodder?

His grandfather, T. C. Bruce, knowing that the ones who

must be impressed were the jurors, watched only them. They'd all been attentive and gave no indication that they found Cass's words as anything but truthful. The real test was about to come. Would they still believe him after the county attorney tried to tear him apart? He said a silent prayer.

CHAPTER SIXTY-THREE

In the instant before the judge burst back into the room, Cass's stomach turned. He thought, for that instant, that he would upchuck right there in the courtroom. It was akin to the wrenching sensation he'd sometimes experienced as he settled down onto a bareback horse at a rodeo.

Judge McNair looked toward the defendant standing by the counsel table. "Mr. Bruce, please re-take the witness stand. You're still under oath." At the sound of those words, the awful squeamish feeling in Cass's innards disappeared. He settled into the chair with quiet self-assurance. Merci's last words were in his mind. "Just answer each of his questions in the shortest way possible. 'Yes' and 'No' are best."

Hodder stood, hands clasped behind his back, and stared at Cass, without speaking. At last he began. "So, Mr. Bruce, you had no relationship with Summer Hetherington other than an afternoon movie and an airplane ride. Is that what you want the jury to believe?"

"No, sir."

"That's what you told the jury, isn't it?"

"No, sir."

"It's true, isn't it, that you connived to spend as much time around her as you could?'

"No sir. We spent time together doing rodeo things but not much else."

"You followed her around. You sought chances to spend time in her presence. Isn't that correct, sir?"

"No, sir. It is not."

"You said that the movie you attended with Summer was at the Rialto Theatre. That isn't true, is it, Mr. Bruce. That date was at the Starlite Drive-In Theatre wasn't it?"

"No, Mr. Hodder. Summer and I never went together to the Starlite. We went to the Rialto. And it wasn't a date. We both wanted to see the movie, so we just went together."

"You paid her way in, didn't you?"

"Yes, sir, I did. My mother taught me to do things the gentlemanly way."

"Ah yes. Always the gentleman." It was spoken with a negative head jerk and loaded with sarcasm. "When you were at the drive-in theatre with Summer, you did a little necking didn't you?"

"No, sir. Since we were never there together, we couldn't have done that."

"And that necking ultimately led to something more, didn't it? Then Summer became pregnant. That's what happened isn't it, Mr. Bruce?"

Despite his aunt's caution about the giveaways, Cass irritation became evident. He shifted in the chair while giving his head two vigorous shakes. His voice had a bite when he said, "No, sir. What you just said is not true."

Hodder plowed ahead. "When she told you she was pregnant, you decided you had to do something about it, didn't you?"

"She didn't tell me she was pregnant. I knew nothing about it until after she was gone."

"The opportunity to do something about it came that night at Hunter's Hot Springs, didn't it, Mr. Bruce?"

Geoff was on his feet and speaking in his soft but commanding voice. "Objection. Mr. Hodder's questions have been asked and answered. May I suggest that he either move on to something more informative or pass the witness."

Judge McNair's head was nodding before Geoff stopped speaking. He eyed the county attorney to say, "Mr. Myklebust is correct, sir. Please move along."

The county attorney faced Cass again. "Who, Mr. Bruce, beside you, had the means, the motive and the opportunity to murder Summer Hetherington?"

This time Cass cocked his head to stare at his questioner. His disgust at the question was evident. "Mr. Hodder, if I knew who did that to Summer, I would have told you a long time ago." He sat forward as he added, "And I didn't have any of those things you just said: means, motive and opportunity."

"You had the means, didn't you? The icepick?"

"It was there, available to any one of us. If that's what you consider means, it wasn't exclusive to me."

"And you had the opportunity. You were the last one alone in that pool with Miss Hetherington, weren't you?"

"I was the last one of our rodeo group to leave the pool area that night. But I don't know what might have happened when I wasn't in there." He paused. "And there may have been someone there that I don't know about."

"Ah yes, the phantom murderer. Some other guy must have done it. When all else fails, point at someone else, even when there's no one to point to." Hodder leaned forward and spoke with force unheard before. "You listened to Mrs. Stensrud's testimony. Now you're accusing her of lying when she said there was no one else at the hot springs that night."

Geoff was on his feet again. His voice now had a bite. "Objection. Mr. Hodder's comment was inappropriate and intended only to improperly influence the jury. He's to ask questions, not try to put words in the witness's mouth."

Merrill Hodder's emotions shown in the quick way he turned to Geoff and barked, "Everything I said is based on the record. The only defense you have is to try to convince the jury there's a phantom killer—anyone other than the defendant"

"That's enough!" The bang of the gavel and Judge McNair's bark startled most of those in the courtroom, including Cass. He jerked to the side of the chair to look at the judge. McNair continued in a harsh voice. "Enough, Mr. Hodder." He took a breath, held it for a moment, before saying in a more moderate tone of voice, "You will only address the court, not the opposing attorney. You know that, sir." Hodder now had his arms crossed in a defiant pose. The judge scowled. "Mr. Myklebust is correct. Your last comment was totally inappropriate." The judge sat for a moment just looking at the county attorney. "I'm disappointed, sir. Never before in all your years in my court have you behaved in such a manner. Don't let it happen again." He turned to the jury. "In a moment of passion, the county attorney said things that he should not have said. They are not to be taken by you as evidence." He returned his attention to Hodder. "Now continue with your examination of this witness."

Merrill Hodder remained quiet for a second, peering at the floor. Resuming his accustomed stance, hands clasped behind his back, he said. "Mr. Bruce, let's review the evidence. You and the dead girl had more than a passing relationship. You and you alone arranged to have the murder weapon, the icepick, readily available for the time when you needed it. You were the last one to leave the place where Summer Hetherington's body was later found. These facts apply to no person other than you. All of that is correct, is it not, sir?"

Cass took a moment to consider his answer. Before he could speak, Hodder said, "The question only requires a yes of a no. Which is it?""

Cass stared at the county attorney. Finally, he said, "I can't respond to three statements with a single yes or no." He turned to the jury. "No. Summer and I were friends, nothing more. Yes. I was the one who asked Mrs. Stensrud for the ice and was given the icepick. Yes. It seems that I was the last of *our group* to leave the pool that night." He ran his eyes along the line of jurors. "However, I must not have been the last one to leave the pool. There had to be another person out there on the night that Summer died. There just had to be, because I didn't kill her." He swiveled to face Hodder again. "I can tell you and the jury nothing more than that, sir."

T. C., his eyes on the jury, almost smiled as one juror all

but imperceptibly dropped his chin in acceptance.

Merci thought the county attorney must have practiced his next moves. As he looked at the jury, an appearance of sadness swept over his face, as though he bemoaned the fact that a witness would lie in a court of law. He shook his head and walked ever so slowly back to his place behind his counsel table. Once there, he stood for a long instant before saying with solemnity, "No more questions."

Judge McNair asked, "Redirect, Mr. Myklebust?"

"No, sir."

"Good." He glanced at the clock "It's the end of the day. We'll be in recess until nine in the morning." He hustled from the bench to disappear through the door to his chambers.

Cass felt a sudden sense of release. The constant foreboding that had haunted him from the day of his arrest was gone. He blew out an enormous sigh before rising slowly from the witness chair. Merci was there to grab his shirt sleeve when he stepped down from the platform. In a soft voice, so that it reached only Cass's ears, she said, "Perfect! Your last statement was perfect."

Cass rubbed his hands together. "It's over. That's all I can think of. I hope it was good enough, but at least my testimony's over."

Geoff, standing a few feet away, spoke softly. "Correct. The hardest part of your defense is over. Let's hope our other witnesses are as convincing and helpful."

Cass nodded his thanks and then hurried through the gate in the barricade to his parents. His mother threw her arms around him with her head pressed against his chest and kept muttering, "Thank God that's over."

Chapter Sixty-four

The morning of the fifth day of the trial arrived. Judge McNair faced the defense table to ask, "Call your next witness, Mr. Myklebust. "

A barely audible murmur ran through the room and the judge raised his eyebrows when Merci rose to her feet. "We call April Menard, Your Honor."

"You will be asking the questions, Miss Bruce?"

"I will, Your Honor." There was a twinkle in her eye when she added, "With your permission, of course."

McNair leaned abruptly back in his chair. "You're a licensed attorney. You don't need permission to practice in this court."

April Menard went again to the witness stand. The judge reminded her she was still under oath. The young woman seemed more nervous than when she sat in the chair the first time. It showed in the white knuckled way she grasped the arms of the chair.

Merci moved around the counsel table to stand directly before the witness. "Miss Menard, let's review the sequence of events that you described when you last testified. I want to be sure I have it right. But this time let's only concern ourselves with the actions of the women. This is the way I understand it. Tell me if I'm wrong. When the call came to get out of the water, you, Summer Hetherington, and Hannah Dodson went to the women's dressing room. Is that correct?"

April, relaxing her grasp on the chair arm, straightened and answered quickly. "Yes, that's what happened."

"Once in the dressing room you all hurried to change out of your swim suits and put on the clothing you wore on the trip to Hunters. Is that right?"

April nodded her head. "Yes. I stripped off the swim suit, dropped it on the floor and dried myself with one of the towels that was on a bench. After that I pulled on my underwear, my shirt and my Levis."

"Which one of you finished dressing first?"

"Hannah. She was fast, and she rushed out of there."

Merci cocked her head. "So then it was just you and Summer Hetherington in the women's dressing room. Correct?"

April didn't answer as she peered into the distance. Finally she looked again at Merci. "That's correct. As I said, I just dried off and dressed. But Summer turned on the shower to rinse off. I put on my socks and boots and left."

Merci crossed he arms. "So from the time Hannah Dodson left to go to the automobiles, you and Miss Hetherington were alone together in the dressing room. Right?"

The implication of the question suddenly registered with

April. Her eyes widened. "Yes. We were alone in there." Her grip on the arms of the chair tightened, and anger tinged her voice. "But you're implying that I had time to kill Summer. That's not true."

Merci waited an instant to give the jury time to absorb the testimony. "In answer to a question from the county attorney, you implied that Cass Bruce killed Summer. It's true, isn't it, that there's no more evidence that he killed Summer Hetherington than there is evidence that you killed her? That he had no more time alone with her than you did?"

"It's ridiculous to say I'd hurt Summer, much less kill her." There was now a tremble in her voice. "You're trying to imply that I'd do something that I'd never do."

"It's just as ridiculous to imply Cassius Bruce did it. She was his friend, too."

Hodder barked, "Objection. That's not a question. Miss Bruce is trying to testify."

Judge McNair was quick to rule. "Sustained!" A deep frown crinkled his brow. "Questions only, Miss Bruce. No more gratuitous remarks."

"Sorry, Your Honor," she said with the slightest nod of contrition. Merci glanced at the young woman on the stand, whose eyes brimmed with tears. To the judge she said, "I have no more questions for Miss Menard."

"Cross, Mr. Hodder?"

"None, Your Honor."

"It's time for a break. Fifteen minutes." The judge rushed from the room.

As the family stood to leave, T. C. pulled Merci aside. "You handled that perfectly. Made me proud."

She reached an arm around his waist. "Thanks for the compliment, Dad. But it doesn't change much."

Back in the little conference room in the courthouse Cass blew out a long puff of air. "Boy, Auntie. You sure turned her testimony around."

Geoff, always the realist, dampened the moment. "We can't show that April Menard had a reason to kill the girl. Without that, the rest is just raw speculation. Merrill Hodder will emphasize the lack of reason, and the jury will buy it."

Cass turned on him. "Hodder can't show a reason for me to kill her either."

"No, but she was pregnant. He'll infer you're the responsible one. That's something the jury can latch onto."

Cass pondered that for a moment. Then he asked, "Who will you call as the next witness?"

As they planned their trial strategy, Geoff and Merci spent much time considering the way to handle Wayne Foley. Should Summer's roommates be called to tell the jury of the times Summer hurried from the sorority house to scramble into his big Buick automobile—despite the fact that he was engaged to marry another woman? Or, would it be more effective to put him on the witness stand and confront him with their knowledge of the relationship between the two and catch him off guard? In the end they agreed to the former. So, to answer Cass's question Geoff just said, "Donna Drummond will be next up."

CHAPTER SIXTY-FIVE

Spencer followed a narrow dusty track north from Springdale, past Hunter's Hot Springs and into the hills beyond. Hugo Gee's ranch wasn't hard to find. Its ramshackle buildings rested under tall cottonwood trees next to a small stream. The owner, carrying a bucket, was slowly making his way up a slope from a barn toward the back of the house. When Spencer pulled his car to a stop next to an old pickup, the man changed direction. By the time Spencer got out of the automobile, Hugo Gee was only a few steps away.

Spencer moved forward to put out a hand. "My name is Spencer Bruce. It's my son, Cassius, who's on trial for the killing of the college co-ed." He waited for Gee to respond. The older rancher just nodded his head. Spencer dropped the hand. "You told Hannah Dodson that you saw an automobile at Hunter's Hot Springs the night the girl was killed. Is that right?" Gee nodded again. "Yup. That's what I told that girl at the cafe the other day. I don't know her name."

"As I said, her name is Hannah. What more can you tell me about that automobile?"

Gee cocked his head to peer at Spencer. "You're that kid's father? The one they say killed her?"

"Yes. But I'm certain he didn't do it. That's why I'm interested in anything that might help find the real killer."

Gee waved a hand toward the porch. "Come on over where I can rest." He led the way to a couple of sagging recliners, put the bucket on the floor, dropped into one chair and pointed for Spencer to take the other and said, "As I told the girl, when I drove by Hunter's on my way into town that evening I saw a great big Buick automobile parked behind a shed. It was really out of place, so I slowed down to look it over. The thing was shining clean, just like new. But what really struck me was the trailer hitch on its back end. Why would anyone use a car that expensive to pull a trailer? Most of us around here use an old pickup."

"Anyone around the car?"

"Nope. Not that I seen. But I didn't hang around. I just drove on by."

Spencer leaned toward the man with his arm resting on the arm of the chair. "Hannah said you saw that car at a later time. What about that?"

"I had a couple of beers and then drove back out here. Just north of town I met that big Buick coming toward me from Hunters."

Spencer straightened. "Could you see who was driving?"

Gee shook his head. "No. It was pretty dark by then."

305

Jim Moore

Before Spencer could ask another question, he continued. "I've thought a lot about it. First of all, the reason I remember the day is because it was at the same time we heard about the murder. And then when the local gossip about the trial told me the times when those rodeo people were at the pool, I wondered if there might be some connection—strange car, unusual doings." He looked right at Spencer. "That's when I decided to tell someone."

"Can you come to Livingston right now to tell all of this to my son's lawyers? And to a jury?"

"I suppose I can. Ain't got much else to do right now."

CHAPTER SIXTY-SIX

C ourt in session, Merci stood to say, "The defense calls Donna Drummond."

The young lady glanced from side to side as she walked the aisle toward the front of the courtroom. Once seated in the witness chair, she pulled at her skirt to cover her knees. At last she faced Merci, displaying a worried look.

Merci stood a distance from the witness stand to ask, "What is your full name, and where to you live?"

The young woman relaxed a little and said, "My name is Donna Marie Drummond. I live in Townsend, Montana."

"You and I have met before, haven't we?"

"In Townsend last summer. You asked me about Summer Hetherington."

"Miss Drummond, how were you acquainted with Miss Hetherington?"

"We were sorority sisters at Montana State College."

Merci asked, "What can you tell us about her?"

Donna dropped her eyes to her lap for a moment before speaking directly to her questioner. "As I said when you and I talked last summer, Summer was one of the nicest persons I've ever known. She was also one of the most intelligent. On top of all of that, she was flat out beautiful." Donna shook her head. "And now someone's killed her." A tear appeared at the corner of her eye. She brushed it away the back of her hand.

Merci stood silent to allow the Miss Drummond to collect herself. After that moment she said, "We know that Summer had a horse and was a barrel racer at rodeos. What other interests did she have?

"The horse was the big interest."

Merci nodded. "What else? What about Summer and the guys?"

A gentle smile spread over Donna's face. "She may have been the best-looking woman at Montana State College. With the veterans back from the war there are two men for every girl on the campus. It's easy to get a date, and Summer could have any man she wanted."

Merci waited once more before saying, "Lots of men wanted to date her. Is that what you're saying?"

"Oh yes." Donna glanced at Cass. "But the only man she spent much time with was Cass Bruce." She turned to speak to the jury. "But it didn't seem like they were dating or carrying on a romance. He'd show up and they'd go off and do things together."

"What kind of things?"

"I guess he helped her with her horse a lot." Donna paused to think. "They went to a movie once that I know of.

They just seemed to enjoy the company of one another."

"Did any other man interest Summer? Someone she seemed to think of in a more romantic way?"

Donna dropped her eyes to her lap. For a half second, she sat silently and twisted her hands together. When she raised her head, she wore a frown. "The last two or three months she'd been seeing a guy named Wayne Foley. He's really, really good looking and supposedly has lots of money."

"How did they get acquainted?"

"He's a rodeo guy too. I guess that's where they met."

"Did he help her with her horse like Cass Bruce did? Was that what brought them together?"

Donna shook her head vigorously. "Oh no! The first time he came to the sorority house to get her, she was all dressed up and waiting for him. He parked his big car at the curb and knocked on the door. Mrs. Newman, our housemother, let him in. I guess he was polite enough with her, but he seemed rather impatient and anxious to get going. No small talk."

"Did Summer tell you where they went and what they did?"

"No, she didn't. That was different. She would often share funny things that happened on dates." Her face softened. "I did the same things with her." She pinched her lips for a moment. "With Wayne Foley, it was different, like I said. She didn't seem to want to talk about the things they did together." Donna paused. "Well, one time she said they went for an airplane ride. But that's all she said about it."

"I take it you didn't approve."

"Of Summer's dates with Wayne? They were none of my business."

Jim Moore

Merci persisted. "Still, it sounds like you had some concern. Was there something about Mr. Foley that bothered you?"

"For one thing, he was supposed to be engaged to be married."

Merci raised her eyebrows. "Did Summer know that?"

Donna shook her head. "I don't know for sure. But she must have. It was common knowledge."

"Did you talk to her about it?"

She shook her head. "Just once. She told me to mind my own business." Donna looked directly at Merci. "I don't know what it was that she found so attractive in that man. Maybe it was good looks or the big Buick car or the large ranch his family is supposed to have. I just don't know."

"Did Cass Bruce know of all of this?"

"If he did, it didn't seem to bother him. He'd help Summer with her horse, and they still did some other things together. But not in the evenings. Those were saved for Foley. He'd pull up to the curb in front of the sorority house, and she'd hurry out to jump in the car without a word to anyone."

Merci stepped back. "Thank you, Miss Drummond." She turned to the judge. "No more questions, Your Honor."

"Cross Mr. Hodder?"

"None, Your Honor."

McNair nodded and looked up at the clock before saying, "Time to eat. Court will be in recess till one thirty." To the jury he said, "Remember my admonition. Don't discuss this trial with anyone."

310

Chapter Sixty-seven

In their workroom at the Murray Hotel, Cass, Geoff, and Merci undertook a review of the evidence they'd presented. Geoff began with the obvious. "The jurors heard your testimony, Cass. I believe they found it to be truthful. But our evidentiary problem remains—who else could be the killer? The jurors must still wonder who else that person could be."

Merci leaned forward. "But the jury also heard evidence that April Menard as well as Mrs. Stensrud had the opportunity to commit the crime. Even though there's no apparent reason for either of them to want Summer dead, they can't discount that opportunity entirely. They may use it as a reason to question the notion that there was no one else around."

Geoff again. "Of course. It's bound to be on their minds while they deliberate.

Cass had remained quiet. Now he asked, "It seems to me

that Donna Drummond's tale of Wayne Foley's relationship with Summer Hetherington provides another person for them to consider—someone beside me."

"It surely does. And we still have Mrs. Newman, the sorority housemother, as well as Ella Brown, another of Summer Hetherington's sorority sisters, both of whom can buttress that testimony." Merci shifted her eyes to Geoff. "Should we put them on the stand or will that just be a time-wasting duplication? Your thoughts, Mr. Myklebust?"

"I've given it thought. I believe we should let the jurors hear what they have to say. Hearing over and over again of Foley's attention to Summer when he's engaged to another woman is almost certain to turn their thoughts against him." He turned to Cass. "They're more likely to see him as someone besides you who could be the murderer, Cass."

Cass nodded his agreement. "That possibility sounds good to me."

"We may still want to call Doris Hamilton. But who knows what she might say?" Merci stood.

Geoff and Cass followed her movement. Before they left the room, Geoff added, "Our final witness has to be Wayne Foley. And the jury will be anxious to listen to him."

Spencer Bruce, returning from his visit with Hugo Gee, rushed along the hallway just as Cass and the attorneys were about to enter the courtroom. He stopped them at the doorway. "I found the fellow that Hannah told us about. After you listen to what he has to say I'm sure you'll want him to testify." He took a breath. "He's waiting outside. I think he likes the idea of telling his story."

CHAPTER SIXTY-EIGHT

A strange face had appeared among those waiting for Court to convene, so an air of expectation pervaded the room. The spectators seemed to sense that there might be interesting testimony in the offing.

"Mr. Myklebust, please call your next witness."

Geoff half turned to look ever his shoulder at the entry door. "We call Hugo Gee."

The rancher had put on a clean shirt and denim trousers. The western hat he held in his hand, however, showed all the grime of years of wear in the out of doors. There was manure on his boots. He marched with purpose to the barrier rail and on through the gate to stand before the judge's bench. He turned to the clerk, raised his hand for the oath and said, "I do." He tossed the old hat onto the top of the defense counsel table. Grasping the arm of the witness chair, he pulled himself up onto the platform. Once seated, he looked around the

Jim Moore

room and spied a friend in the gallery to whom he offered a small wave and smile. Then he focused his attention on Geoffrey.

"Please state your name and address, sir."

"I'm Hugo Gee. I live on a ranch north of the town of Springdale. Springdale's a few miles east of here."

"Is your home near Hunter's Hot Springs?"

Gee's head bobbed up and down. "Yes, sir, it is. I drive by it every time I go to town."

Merci watched as Merrill Hodder and Josh Waddell engaged in vigorous whispering. She could guess that Hodder was asking what this witness might have to say. Waddell finally just shrugged his shoulders and looked away.

Geoff asked the man on the witness stand. "Did you pass by Hunter's on the evening of May thirteenth of this year?"

"I did. I remember the date because the next day we heard about the young woman being killed in the Springs."

"What, if anything, that you observed at Hunter's Hot Springs, that evening, is of importance to these proceedings?"

Merrill Hodder was on his feet. "I object." His voice was loud. "Counsel's questions and the answers, whatever they might be, have nothing to do with the issue before the court. They're time consuming and wasteful."

Geoff stood quietly as the county attorney spoke. His reply was in the usual measured tones. "Not so, Your Honor. If you'll allow me to ask a few more questions of Mr. Gee, you'll find they're very relevant."

"All right, sir. A few more questions. Objection overruled."

Geoff asked, "Should I repeat the question?"

"Ain't necessary." Hugo Gee shifted in the chair. "I was on my way into town when I saw a big automobile parked out back of the main building at the Springs. It was so out of place that I slowed down to give it a good look."

"What did you observe?"

"Well, it was a Buick, one of those big ones with the four holes in the front fenders, lots of chrome. I think they're called Roadmasters. It was shiny clean, not like most cars we see around here that are all dusty and dirty. It looked like it had just been washed"

"Did you observe anything else unusual about the car?"

"It had a trailer hitch on the back." Gee paused, then asked, "Who ever heard of pulling a trailer with a car like that? Most trailers 'round here are pulled by a pickup— almost always a dirty one."

"About what time did this happen?"

Gee looked off at the corner of the room. "I believe it would have been about seven in the evening."

"Mr. Gee, did you see that Buick again?"

The rancher rubbed the back of his hand along the side of his jaw. "I sure did. Later that night as I was driving back to the ranch it went by me headed south toward Springdale."

"And what time was that, sir?"

Gee gave it a moment of thought before answering. "I'd visited with friends and had a couple of beers. I think it was maybe nine thirty, ten o'clock."

"Did you see who was driving the car?"

Gee shook his head. "It was pretty dark by then. So no, I didn't see the driver."

Jim Moore

Geoff paused. He wished he could look over his shoulder at Spencer to see if he'd missed anything. Instead he smiled at the witness. "Thank you, Mr. Gee."

As Geoff moved toward his chair, Hugo Gee stopped him. "I can tell you another thing. I saw that car parked in front of the Park Hotel this morning. Same car, same trailer hitch. It had a number ten license plate. That's Carbon County. Red Lodge is the county seat."

Its significance registered with Geoff almost instantly. The Foley ranch was near Roscoe in Carbon County. Car to pull a horse trailer. Rodeo. The auto must belong to calf roper Wayne Foley. He smiled ever so slightly as he turned back to Hugo Gee. "That is helpful, sir. Thank you again." He lifted his eyes to the judge. "No more questions of this witness, Your Honor."

Judge McNair didn't hesitate. "Court's in recess. Fifteen minutes." The room erupted in loud chatter.

CHAPTER SIXTY-NINE

Court was back in session. Judge McNair looked down at Hugo Gee, resting at ease in the witness chair. "You're still under oath, sir." He turned to the prosecution table. "Cross-examination, Mr. Hodder?"

The county attorney understood the implication of Gee's testimony as well as Geoff. He was on his feet, around the corner of the counsel table and standing before the witness in an instant. There were not a lot of people in Park County and Merrill Hodder knew many of them personally. Hugo Gee was among these that he knew quite well. Anger was in his voice when he barked, "Hugo, why didn't you tell me about all of this before now?"

The rancher's face fell. "Gee, Merrill. I just didn't think to do it."

"Well, you should have told me, so the sheriff and I could conduct a proper investigation—find out whose car that was and find out what it was doing at the Springs the night you say you saw it."

Gee shrugged. "It don't make no difference. I just told the jury everything I know. There ain't more to it."

Judge McNair faced the county attorney. "Mr. Hodder, ask a question if you have one."

Evidently Hodder concluded anything he asked of Hugo Gee would only confirm what had already been said. He clenched his teeth until the muscles in his jaw stood out. When he spoke his voice was directed to the floor. "No more questions." Back in his chair he glared at the sheriff who sat with his arms crossed and ignored him.

"Redirect Mr. Myklebust?"

"No, sir. None."

McNair nodded to Gee. "You're finished, sir. You may step down." The judge remained quietly in his chair for a moment, staring at the top of the bench. Then he shook his shoulders once and called for a break.

Cass caught Hugo Gee as he stepped down from the platform on which the witness chair rested. He handed the hat back to the rancher and put out a hand. "Thank you, sir, for coming forward with the information about the auto."

Gee shook the hand once before dropping it. "Just trying to do the right thing." That said, he hustled out of the courtroom.

As they walked the aisle to the back of the courtroom, Geoff muttered just loud enough for Cass and Merci to hear. "Now we get Mr. Foley on the witness stand."

CHAPTER SEVENTY

Wayne Foley's and Doris Hamilton's subpoena by the defense caused some consternation within the Foley family. Could—or would—either of them say anything that could prove to be detrimental to the Foley business. Grandma Imogene, in the east, was also concerned about her carefully cultivated relationship between her grandson and the young woman she thought could give him the strength she believed he lacked. She considered a return to Montana just to accompany them to court. In the end Wayne, with Doris's help, convinced her not to do so.

The young couple stayed in separate rooms at the Park Hotel and, like all of the other potential witnesses, reported to the courthouse each morning. Each morning they were told that their testimony wouldn't be needed. Since they weren't allowed in the courtroom to hear the testimony of the witnesses who went before them, they passed the time

Jim Moore

visiting with others caught in the same frustrating situation, driving south to view Mammoth Hot Springs at Yellowstone Park, touring Livingston's huge railroad repair shops and catching a movie. All the while they speculated on the questions each would be asked. Today they would find out.

Geoff stood to say, "The defense calls Wayne Foley."

That young man was dressed in a dark gray, carefully tailored business suit, a starched, gleaming white shirt and a patterned maroon tie. He wore flat heeled western boots, shined till they reflected the overhead lights of the room.

He appeared unsure what to do after he entered the courtroom. Wayne glanced toward the people in the jury box and at the spectators filling the benches. Then he focused on the judge, seated high on the bench at the far end of the room. McNair, seeing his confusion, waved a hand for him to come forward. When he reached the gate in the barrier to the well of the courtroom he stopped. The judge smiled and said, "Come on through, Mr. Foley. It's safe." With the witness standing almost rigid before the bench, the judge added, "Stand over there, raise your hand and take the oath." The clerk droned the oath. Foley responded by saying the required "I do," The judge pointed to the witness stand. "Now take that chair. Mr. Myklebust will ask questions of you."

Foley eased carefully into the chair and ran his eyes about the room. In the end he focused on the members of the jury and offered them a tentative smile.

Geoff stood a few feet in front of the witness. "Please state your name and place of address, sir."

The young man relaxed at the simplicity of the question.

"My name is Wayne Foley. I live part time in the east but most of the time I'm at our family ranch near Roscoe, Montana."

"Your occupation, sir?'

"I've been attending Montana State College but graduated this past spring. I plan to go to work in the family business."

"You were a member of the Montana State College rodeo team, were you not?"

"I was. Calf roping has been my event."

Geoff's said in a kindly way. "With considerable success, I understand."

Foley smiled. "I generally got my share of the money."

The lawyer waved a hand in Cass's direction. "I'm sure you know Mr. Bruce."

The smile faded as Foley looked, for the first time, across the empty space to the table where Cass was sitting. Cass held his gaze until Wayne pulled his eyes away to face Geoffrey. "Of course, I know Cass. We attended the same college. We've rodeoed together."

"Did you know Summer Hetherington?"

Wayne Foley didn't respond for a second. His eyes dropped to the floor, and he reached with his right hand to rub briefly at his left shoulder. His face bore a deep frown when he looked up to respond. "Yes. I knew Summer. She was another one of the college rodeo participants."

Geoff paused in his questioning for a moment and stared at the witness. The look seemed to unsettle Foley. He tilted his head to the side and narrowed his eyes as he waited for the next question. That question came in the same soft voice. "After the college rodeo on a Saturday night, about four months ago, a trip to Hunter's Hot Springs was discussed by the rodeo participants. Is that correct?"

Foley nodded. "Yes, sir."

"You and Doris Hamilton were among those who considered the idea, weren't you?"

Merrill Hodder was on his feet. "Objection. Mr. Myklebust is asking leading questions of the witness."

Geoff didn't wait for the judge to rule. He turned to Hodder and nodded his head. "You're correct, sir. Let me re-phrase." Turning back to face Foley, he asked, "Were you and Miss Hamilton among those who talked of going for a swim at Hunter's Hot Springs the night that Summer Hetherington lost her life?"

"Yes. Both Doris and I were there when it was discussed."

"Is Miss Hamilton your fiancée?"

"Yes. We plan to be married soon."

"We understand that you and Miss Hamilton didn't go with the others to the hot springs. Why was that, sir?"

"Doris had a final exam the next week that she was concerned about. She said she just wanted to study and rest."

"What did you do that evening?"

"After I dropped Doris off at her room, I went back to my place—a house just off campus that I rented during the school year. I put the car in the garage, fixed me a bite to eat, and did some household chores. Then I went to bed."

"You went nowhere else that night?"

Foley's frown indicated some annoyance at the question. "No, sir. I did not."

Geoff's face remained impassive as he asked in a kindly voice. "If someone were to say he saw your auto parked near the hot springs that night, would he be lying?"

Foley appeared to be startled by the question. "He sure would. As I already told you, my car was parked in my garage all that night."

Geoff stepped closer. "Mr. Foley, how well did you know Summer Hetherington?"

Foley's eyes flitted to his right and then back to his left. He uncrossed his legs and shifted his position in the chair. Finally, he focused again on Geoff. "I knew Summer like I knew the others who rodeoed. We all spent time together, caring for our horses at the fairground, sometimes just socializing at the Student Union where we talked about our sport. Many of us attended the same rodeos during the summer season." He stopped and dropped his eyes to speak toward his hands, now folded in his lap. "She was really a wonderful person. What happened to her is sad."

Geoff waited a second before asking, "Didn't you spend time alone with her?"

A frown formed as he looked at directly at Geoff. "What do you mean?"

"Well, we've been told that you took her for an airplane ride."

Wayne relaxed a bit. "Oh that! She knew I could fly. One day she asked me about it. It just seemed like a good idea to show her what it was like to ride around in airplane rather than try to describe it. One nice calm day we flew to Roundup in the college co-op airplane so she could see her parents' farm from the air." He turned to the jury. "There was nothing more to it than that."

"It's important that the jury understands your relationship

with Summer Hetherington. Is it your testimony that you never picked her up at the sorority house for a date?"

Foley began to speak, paused and pondered. Finally, he said, "I may have." He seemed to realize how ridiculous that must sound. At last, with a decision made, Foley turned to the jury. "Yes. I did pick her up once. But it wasn't a date. We just drove around for a while."

Geoff's placid demeanor was disarming. "Only once, and it wasn't a date? That's all?"

"Yes, sir. That's all."

Geoff turned an inquiring look at Merci who signaled he should stop. He turned to Foley to say, "Thank you, sir." Then to the judge, "No more questions of Mr. Foley."

Judge McNair asked. "Cross-examination, Mr. Hodder?"

Hodder looked once at Josh Waddell, frowned, and pondered for a moment before saying, "No, Your Honor. No questions."

The judge seemed in a hurry as he spoke to the room in general. "Tomorrow is Saturday. Ordinarily I would adjourn court for the weekend. Unfortunately, I have a domestic matter scheduled for Monday. Such matters must be heard promptly; they can't be put off. For that reason, we'll be in session tomorrow at the usual hour." He directed his final remarks to the jurors "This change may cause hardship for some of you. For that I apologize and beg your indulgence." He banged the gavel and muttered, "Courts in recess until nine o'clock in the morning." Then McNair rushed from the room. Merci chuckled quietly, "That man needed to get to the rest room."

Cass stood respectfully beside his lawyers while the jury

cleared the room. For the first time since he found himself charged with the crime of murder, he felt there might be a positive end to his torment. He turned to Geoffrey. "The jury must realize he's lying."

"Some may conclude that Mr. Foley didn't dare be truthful. By doing so, he'd invite an accusation that he killed Summer Hetherington."

"Could they decide that he really was the killer?"

"They could." Geoff seeing, for the first time, a glimmer of hope in his client's eyes, he added, "Unfortunately the principal question remains, how did he get into the pool area? Mrs. Stensrud's testimony was believable when she swore the place was locked up tight. It would be best not to become too optimistic." When the look of hope disappeared, he added, "But from our perspective, if they decide that he might possibly be the killer, it could be enough for a not guilty verdict."

"What happens now?"

Geoff picked up a file that was lying on the table top and then looked directly at his client. "When court next convenes, we rest our case—and then let the jury do its duty."

CHAPTER SEVENTY-ONE

Wayne Foley met his fiancée as he came out the door to the courtroom. He grabbed Doris's arm and dragged her out onto the street. "What the hell did you do? Did you take my car and go to Hunter's the night Summer was killed?"

Doris shrugged. "So? What if I did?"

Wayne Foley was tired. Most of all he was tired of answering questions.

"What did they say in there?" Doris demanded to know.

That lawyer wanted to know why we didn't go to Hunter's Hot Springs with the others that night."

"What else?"

Wayne looked Doris directly in the eye. "He asked how well I knew Summer."

She didn't blink. "What did you tell him?"

Now real anger crept into Foleys' voice. "What do you think I told him? I said I knew her through the rodeo club."

"Was that all he wanted to know?"

"I *wish* that was all he wanted to know." He grabbed her arm to pull her toward his auto, parked down the street. "I've got to get away from here. You and I have a lot to talk about."

He drove the highway south from town to a place where a gravel road led to a bridge across the Yellowstone River. Not far beyond the bridge he came upon a flat graveled turnout adjacent to a tall craggy, rough surfaced slab of fallen rock. Empty bottles and trash gave evidence of many previous beer parties. Wayne pulled to a stop next to the rock slab and shut down the motor. Then he just sat and stared out the window at nothingness for a long time. All the while Doris leaned against the passenger door, silent and unmoving. At last he turned to face her. "All right, tell me."

Doris held his gaze for an instant before shifting her own gaze to the river. "It began when you told me she was pregnant and claimed you were the father. You began to make noises about telling Grandma Imogene what you'd done and maybe 'doing the right thing.'" She looked over at him once and then returned her eyes to the distance. "Surely you know what her reaction would be. It would be the end of all we've planned. Your grandmother chose me to be your wife for a reason. She knows I have the toughness that's missing in you. If you are to be the head of Foley Industries, you'll need me to stiffen your spine—to be with you when difficult and unpleasant decisions must be made."

Wayne didn't move. He listened without changing expression.

"If Grandma Imogene learned what happened, it would

be the end of our plans for a nice, comfortable, loving life together. She'd send me down the road and insist you marry Summer." Doris swiveled in the seat to look directly at him. "Not only that, Wayne. You would never be head of the Foley family and its fortune. You'd never be anything but a do-nothing, money-wasting burden on whoever ends up in that position."

Wayne straightened and snarled, "I don't need any part of the family business. I can be the world champion calf roper. That's what I really want to do."

She shook her head. "You do great at the college rodeos and the shows here in Montana. But you aren't tough enough to compete with those who do it day after day—always on the road, never any rest." She moved close to him and placed her hand on the back of his neck. "Wayne, you're a nice man and I'm very fond of you. But you just aren't tough, you're not ruthless. You don't have the unforgiving resolve required to run a major business organization. Grandma Imogene knows that I have that toughness."

He stared at Doris as though he didn't comprehend her meaning. His mind was back on the fact that his auto was at the hot springs the night of the killing. "So, you used the key I gave you, took my car and drove to the hot springs that night. Is that the way it was?"

"Yes." Doris leaned against the seat with her arm stretched out along its top. "You may as well know the rest now as later. I did it, Wayne. I killed her." The expression on her face didn't change. No show of regret. No emotion. "But I did it so your quickie with Summer in the back seat of this car wouldn't ruin both of our lives."

His eyes never moved from hers. His breathing became shallow. He couldn't speak.

"Listen Wayne, I couldn't let her steal the future you promised me. I decided she had to go the minute you began that talk of 'doing the right thing.' I kept a watch on Summer, waiting for an opportunity. When the rodeo bunch decided to go to Hunters, I made a run for it to get there before they did, hoping it might offer a chance to find her alone. I parked the car where it was hidden and out of the way. And I found an unlocked door in the back of the building that led directly to the pool. Inside there was a huge closet filled with cleaning supplies next to the dressing rooms. I hid in the back of it." Doris's expression didn't change. "Lucky me. Not more than a minute later, I heard Mrs. Stensrud making the rounds, locking the doors. But I was already in."

Wayne's mind was awhirl. Could this be the same woman he'd spent so much time with—had agreed to marry? She'd committed murder and seemed unmoved by it. She showed not the slightest sign of remorse. The information overwhelmed him. It was too much to comprehend.

Doris continued her monologue. "I listened at the door of the closet as the rodeo bunch came in and splashed into the water. And I waited. Finally, I heard someone yell that it was time to leave, so I cracked the door just enough to watch them leave the pool, one after another." She looked at Wayne. "I watched the men leave their dressing room. I saw Hannah run out of the women's room, and soon April ran after her. That left Summer alone after all the others were out of there. I stepped from the closet, grabbed the icepick and waited." She closed her eyes. "I was so lucky, the way it worked out.

Jim Moore

I had thought I'd have to strangle her, and I didn't know if I could. But the icepick made it easy. When she came out of the dressing room, I just grabbed her hair, jerked her head back and jammed the pick up under her chin." Doris looked up. "She collapsed like a sack of flour. I dragged her to the pool and let her slide in." She sat still for a moment. "And then I got out of there as fast as I could."

Wayne was speechless. He reached for the key to start the car but pulled his hand back. He grasped the steering wheel with both hands, head hanging down. At last he muttered, "I've got to get some air." He opened the door, scrambled out and stood facing the towering rock, one hand propped against it. When Doris followed him from the car, he turned to face her. "Why are you telling me this now?"

"To make certain that you don't do anything foolish."

"Anything foolish?" His voice raised to a higher pitch in disbelief. "Anything foolish?"

"Like tell someone you are the father of Summer's child."

Wayne's stunned disbelief turned to anger. "Do you realize what you've done? If that jury finds Cass Bruce innocent, I'll be the next person the sheriff thinks is the murderer. He knows the car was out there. He'll soon know that I'd been seeing Summer, if he doesn't already. He and the others will feel certain they've finally found Summer's killer and I'll be the next one on trial." He was quiet for a second. "I can't wait for that. I have to do something."

Doris moved to put an arm gently around his waist. "That's exactly the reason I had to act. Before you could do something foolish." She faced him squarely. "Stay calm. The jury will convict Cass Bruce, and that will be the end of

330

it. And you and I can go on with our lives the way we've planned."

Fury such as he'd never known boiled up in Wayne Foley. He shoved her away. "End of it? Lives we've planned?" He grabbed the front of her shirt with both hands and gave her a forceful shake, his voice now a snarl. "Don't you understand? There'll never be an end to it." Using all of the strength and agility that allowed him to easily throw a calf to the ground, he whirled her body around and slammed it against the rough stone precipice. The side of her head smacked one of the sharp outcroppings with a force that shattered the side of her skull and drove the protrusion into her temple. Doris Hamilton's lifeless body crumpled limply to the ground.

For a minute. Wayne's mind didn't comprehend what had happened. He stepped away to stare down at his now lifeless fiancée. The anger bled away and the consequence of his action flooded his mind. He'd just committed murder.

Years of habit brought Grandma Imogene into his thoughts. What he'd done could never be hidden from her. She'd disown him in an instant. Worse, she'd wreak vengeance by seeking the most severe punishment for him. What could he do? He was breathing hard as he muttered to himself. "I've got to think."

His immediate idea was to hide the body and go on as though nothing had happened. Wouldn't work. As soon as Doris came up missing, they'd all look to him for answers. What then? Sooner or later they were bound to find out what had happened out here by this rock. When they did, he'd be charged with murder. Then he'd be the one headed for the penitentiary—or worse. What to do?

Jim Moore

First, he had to get the body into the trunk of the car. Wayne soon found that a dead human body is not as easy to manhandle as a live rodeo calf. He dragged Doris's limber remains to the back of the auto and opened the trunk. Weak with fear, he shoved her limp body over the rim of the trunk and jammed it into the cramped space. Wayne looked one final time at what remained of Doris Hamilton before closing the lid to the trunk. As he did so, he muttered, "Good God! Forgive me."

Back in the driver's seat, he closed his eyes and laid his forehead on the steering wheel. The consequences of that moment of uncontrollable anger filled his mind. Life, as he had always known it, was at an end. Doris was right, he wasn't tough. He could never survive time in the penitentiary. Even if he wasn't sent to prison, he couldn't cope with a life other than one he'd always lived. After a long while he lifted his head, turned the key to start the car and turned back along the road toward Livingston. From there he took the road that led eastward toward Roscoe.

About a half a mile west of the turnoff to Springdale, the highway curves to the left and tracks around the base of a tall, sheer sandstone cliff. Wayne, holding the auto at a constant sixty miles an hour, rounded a corner a mile farther west and caught sight of the cliff. He slowly increased the pressure on the gas pedal to accelerate the speed. Before he reached the beginnings of the curve around the cliff, his body began to shake.

At the point where the roadway began its turn to the left, Wayne gripped the steering wheel firmly with both hands and whispered, "There's nothing left." He pressed harder on the accelerator and turned the steering wheel slightly to the right. The auto, now traveling at ninety-five miles an hour, tore through a barbwire fence, across a small ditch and smashed, head on, into the rock face of the cliff.

Wayne Foley died as quickly as had both Summer Hetherington and Doris Hamilton—in less than eight seconds.

CHAPTER SEVENTY-TWO

The courtroom buzzed with the conversation of the spectators. The defendant and his lawyers sat quietly at their counsel table. So, too, the county attorney with the sheriff at his side. Judge Nathanial McNair was late in making his appearance. At last he bustled through the door, robe flying behind him, and up to the bench. "Court's in session." He straightened the robe around his knees before turning to Geoffrey. "Your next witness, sir?'

Geoff stood. "The defense rests."

The judge addressed the county attorney. "Rebuttal evidence, Mr. Hodder?"

"None, Your Honor."

Judge McNair relaxed and sat quietly for a moment before pushing his chair back an inch or two from the bench. He swiveled to face the jury. "I have business with the attorneys that will take a couple of hours. During that time you're free to roam but be back here at eleven o'clock." He paused. "At that time, the attorneys will give their final arguments. When they're finished, I'll instruct you as to the law of the case. After that you will go to the jury room to begin your deliberations." He leaned forward to add, "Don't discuss anything about this case among yourselves until I've told you that you may do so. Understood?" The heads of the members of the jury bobbed in unison. The gavel hit the bench and court was again in recess.

While the judge and the attorneys argued and settled the jury instructions, the others affected by the trial were left in a kind of limbo. They couldn't leave but had nothing to occupy their time as they waited. After some discussion, the Bruce family, Cass included, drove back through the main part of town to the Murray Hotel. Some morning refreshments would help pass the time. Hannah and Lillian Dodson had arrived ahead of them and were seated by a window. Eunice Bruce hurried to greet them and invite them to share a large table.

Cass, following along, reached the table just in time for Hannah to rise from her chair. For a moment they stood, almost touching, each with eyes on the eyes of the other. The sight of Hannah brought a surge of feelings to Cass that he hadn't known existed. The urge to reach out and gather her into his arms almost overwhelmed him. While he'd grown completely comfortable in her company during their time together at the Dodson ranch, he'd never realized how compelling the need for her presence had become. Before he could act upon the urge, however, he understood she might not have the same feelings. Cass stepped back in a movement that was both instantaneous and awkward. But the look that had blossomed across his face at the first sight of her remained. "It's nice to be with you again, Hannah Dodson."

The smile she shined on him was as radiant as always. Her voice was soft. "And I've missed you, Cass Bruce."

Cass held a chair for Hannah and pulled the one next to it for himself. She sat facing him. "I believe Wayne Foley has to be the one who killed Summer."

Cass, hands clasped together on the table top, didn't answer for a couple of seconds, eyes on his hands. "That seems most likely." He looked up to ask, "But how did he get into the pool area? Mrs. Stensrud was adamant that all the doors were locked."

"I can't answer that question. But I'm certain he's the one."

Spencer, sitting across the table, interrupted. "Miss Dodson, we all owe you. You found that fellow who told the jury about Wayne Foley's car being at the hot springs on the night it happened." Hannah inhaled to speak, but Spencer held up his hand. "Without that evidence, there was no one other than our son on whom the jury could focus. Now they have at least two other possible culprits." He smiled his warmest smile. "So we owe you a great deal."

"Thank you, Mr. Bruce, but Mr. Gee would have told his story to somebody else had he not happened to give it to me."

"Perhaps. But you brought it all to the attention of Geoff and Merci. And please call me Spencer. You are much more to us than a mere acquaintance. You made life tolerable for our son at a time when he needed that help."

8 Seconds

Cass watched and listened. How nice to discover a pleasant and comfortable relationship between his father and the girl seated at his side.

Chapter Seventy-three

J udge McNair gaveled court into session promptly at eleven o'clock. The lawyers would make their final arguments. Cass expected their attempts to persuade the jury would demand and hold his attention. Not so. Merrill Hodder's mechanical recitation of the events at the hot springs quickly benumbed his mind. Only when Hodder pounded with his fist on the table to argue that only the defendant could have committed the crime did any of it register with him. As that noise faded away, he was again plagued by the terrifying prospect of conviction and prison.

Geoff's response was given in the same quiet, attention-demanding voice that all had come to expect. Cass tried to concentrate as the lawyer recited both the legal reasons and the factual reasons why the jury should return a not-guilty verdict. But the specter of a prison cell surrounded by hardened criminals filled his mind and refused to go away.

8 Seconds

When Geoff at last finished with his final argument and returned to his chair, Cass felt nothing as much as relief. The end of his torment must at last be near. But then the judge lifted pages of paper from the bench top and began to read instructions to the jury. As he droned on, Cass was overcome with weariness of body as well as mind. The agony seemed unending. He slumped downward in his chair.

Finally, Judge McNair read the last instruction and handed the papers to the clerk who, in turn, handed them to the nearest juror. McNair glanced at the clock. Looking again at the jurors he spoke with solemnity, "It's noontime. Go to the jury room. Lunch will be delivered to you. The bailiff will take your orders for the food each of you prefer. The county is paying for your meal." He paused. "You must first elect a foreman, so consider that as you wait for the food. Then you should begin your deliberations. If you have questions about the law, review the instructions you've just heard." He leaned toward them. "Now go and do your duty." He banged the gavel, rose from his chair, and walked to his chambers.

Cass watched the twelve who would decide his fate trail out another door. Despite the fact that he had little religious inclination, he found himself muttering a silent, "Dear God, let them find me innocent."

As the others were finding their way out of the room, Geoff said to Cass. "Now we wait."

"How long will the jury take to decide?"

"That's always the great unknown at this point in a jury trial." Geoff tamped some papers together and inserted them into a file folder. "We must be available when they send word to the judge that they've reached a verdict. The jurors will probably eat lunch before they begin serious deliberations. It's unlikely they'll reach a verdict for a couple of hours. But it could take a day or even several days to agree. Stay close and check in here from time to time."

Cass persisted. "You've been doing this for a long time. What's your best guess on the time?"

"There's nothing to be gained by guessing. We just wait. But stay close by in case they're quick."

There was a small lobby on the ground floor of the courthouse. Cass found his family gathered together. Lillian and Hannah Dodson were with them, discussing how to pass the time as they waited for the jury to act. He edged up to Hannah, clasped her upper arm gently and whispered in her ear, "Come with me." She followed him out the door and down the long front steps to the sidewalk. It was an uncommon late summer day, brisk but sunny, without the usual wind. Hannah ran her arm through his as they began a slow stroll eastward toward the river. Neither spoke for a long time. At last they came to a large dead tree that lay near the walkway. Cass gestured to it. Hannah found a place where the bark had worn away leaving a smooth spot to sit.

Cass sat beside her and put his arm around her waist to pull her close. Hannah responded by moving even closer. Finally, Cass spoke while staring into the distance. "If I get out of this thing, I'll get my stuff out of the bunkhouse at your place. You don't need me any longer, and you've put up with me long enough."

Hannah's eyes remained on the distant river. "Dad sold

340

the yearlings a couple of weeks ago. They're set for delivery on October fifth. He hopes you'll be there to help."

"You folks don't need me to deliver the steers. You've been doing it for years."

Hannah turned her head to look up at him. "He wants you there, Cass. Please say you'll do it."

Cass, eyes still on the far mountains, remained still. At last he shook his head. "How can we even be having this conversation? By tonight I may be locked in a jail cell."

"I've said lots of prayers, Cass. And I've finally decided that it's not going to happen. A just God won't let that jury send an innocent person to prison."

Cass looked down at her face. "Believe it or not, I've said some prayers, too. But I'm not sure God is paying much attention to the prayers of any one of us. There are too many people of the world begging for something. Our problems must seem small to Him."

A touch of a breeze tugged at Hannah's clothing. She withdrew her arm from his and tucked her skirt around her legs. With her hands resting on her knees, she murmured, "I'll just continue to believe."

Cass pushed himself to his feet and offered a hand to her. "We need to get ourselves back to the courthouse." Without thought he wrapped both arms about her waist. Hannah snuggled close, her cheek against his chest.

He spoke to the top of her head. "Thank you, Hannah Dodson, for your faith in me. I don't know how I'd have survived without you."

While Geoff stopped at the lavatory, Merci slumped into

Jim Moore

a comfortable chair in their workroom. She kicked off her shoes, leaned back and blew out a huge sigh. The fate of her nephew was in the hands of the jury. She'd done all she knew how to do to protect him. She was exhausted. All that was left was to wait—and maybe offer a prayer. She rested her head against the back of the chair and closed her eyes. In less than a minute she was sound asleep.

That's how Geoff found her—eyes closed, breathing deeply, clothing slightly askew. He stood absolutely still. It was the first time he'd really seen his fellow lawyer as a woman who was not only attractive but apparently vulnerable. Until that moment, vulnerable was a word he never would have used to describe her. Now, seeing her completely relaxed, her features softened, her femininity so evident, Geoff suddenly felt the desire to protect her, to care for her. That feeling was instantly replaced by the realization that she'd spent her life making her own way. Surely, she would feel no need for him to offer her protection. Despite that thought, his feelings remained.

CHAPTER SEVENTY-FOUR

A t ten minutes after two o'clock Geoff dropped the phone onto its cradle. "They jury has a verdict."

Too quick. The verdict was too quick. That was Merci's thought as they hurried to the courthouse from the Murray Hotel. *They must have found him guilty.*

Cass and the entire Bruce contingent were waiting near the courtroom entryway. Geoff led the way into the room and on to the counsel table. Cass followed with Merci close behind. The others sought their regular slots on the benches. Merrill Hodder, with Josh Waddell at his side, was already seated at his usual place. Ephram and Sue Hetherington sat side by side, stoically waiting for court to resume. The tension was palpable.

Cass, sitting as usual between Geoff and Merci, found it difficult to breath. This was the time he'd longed for and dreaded, the time when he would learn his fate, the time when his world would end or he'd be delivered from the hell

343

he'd suffered for months. Once again, a prayer crept silently into his mind. "Dear God, let me have my life back."

Judge McNair, solemn faced, walked slowly through the door from his chambers and mounted the bench. Once seated, he looked to the bailiff. "Bring in the jury." Every eye in the room followed the twelve as they paraded through the door and took their places in the jury box. The judge gave them a moment to settle in while he looked to the county attorney. Satisfied that the prosecution was present, he turned to the defense table. Noting that Cass and his lawyers were seated where they were supposed to be, he turned to speak to the room in general. "Court's in session."

For a second there was complete silence in the room. Then McNair turned to the juror seated in the chair closest to him. "Are you're the foreman, sir?"

'I am."

"Have you reached a verdict?"

The man stood. "We have, Your Honor." He held up the verdict form.

"Please give it to the clerk." The juror did so. The clerk, in turn, handed the form to the judge. His face showed no emotion as he took time to scan the short document. At last he gave it back to the clerk who handed it to the juror.

Now the judge turned his eyes to the defense table. "Will the defendant please rise?"

Cass rose to his feet and assumed a military-like posture, back straight and arms at his side. His eyes focused not on the judge or the jury but fixedly on the back wall of the courtroom. Geoffrey and Merci stood at his side.

The judge directed the request to the juror holding that

344

crucial piece of paper. "Mr. Foreman, please read the verdict."

The juror held the verdict form in one hand and shook it once as though to eliminate wrinkles. He held it up to eye level, paused a moment, and then intoned "We, the jury, duly empaneled, find the defendant not guilty of the crime of murder in the first degree."

Babble erupted in the courtroom.

Cass heard none of it. His body seemed to weaken, and he thought he might collapse. He dropped his hands, fist clenched, arms rigid, onto the table top. Then, as though by magic, his terrible mental burden evaporated like steam disappearing in the wind. He would not go to prison. He could begin again to live the life he had lived before the death of Summer Hetherington. A smile blossomed on his face as he straightened to turn to Merci. He gathered her into a fierce hug. When he swiveled to his left, he found Geoffrey, sober faced as always, with his hand reaching out. Cass, caught up in his feelings of relief, clamped the hand in both of his. "Thank you, Mr. Myklebust. Thank you."

AFTER THAT

Merci and Geoffrey

For Merci and Geoffrey, there was much to do. Their work and sleeping rooms had to be cleared of the detritus that had accumulated during their stay. Geoff turned the key to the door to the main workroom and stepped aside so Merci could enter first. She dropped a briefcase on the floor, heaved a sigh and turned to face him. "I need to refresh and change into more comfortable clothes before I help with the packing."

"Take your time. I'll do the same."

In a few minutes, she returned to the workroom dressed in a work shirt, with the tail hanging out, a light sweater, and slacks. Because Geoff wasn't one to waste time, Merci expected he would be busy putting documents into file folders and brief cases, stuffing yellow tablets, pens and pencils, into packing boxes. Instead he stood near the window, one hand on the sill, peering off into the distance. He had changed his clothing. For the first time she saw him in something other than a carefully tailored business suit. He wore denim trousers, a light blue cotton shirt, with a sleeveless pullover sweater of a darker blue. Merci stopped at the sight.

Geoffrey turned from the window. He stood without speaking for a moment, then walked across the room to halt a short distance from her. At last, he spoke.

"When we first became acquainted, I saw you as a fellow lawyer—an excellent one and very attractive—but nonetheless, just a fellow lawyer." The look on his face was softer than the one so common when they discussed the law. It was a look she hadn't seen before. "Over the last few months I've come to know another Merci Bruce, one who is kind, patient, possessed of humor, and pleasant company."

This confession was so out of character that she was speechless for an eye blink. "Why, thank you sir. I'm not often described that way."

Geoff stepped back to the window, then faced her again. "I've lived a solitary life. For some reason it has been difficult for me to think of others in personal terms. I never wanted to find myself entangled in the life of some other person." He paused as though to gather courage. "My time in your company has affected me. When we're together I have a sense of peace. Now, when alone, I hunger for that feeling of contentment. I've satisfied it by contriving reasons why we should be together—in trial preparation if nothing else. Now That the trial is over, it will no longer provide an excuse for me to spend time with you."

Jim Moore

Merci, having experienced some of the same feelings for him, wasn't sure what to say. She took one step closer to him. "Geoffrey, early in our acquaintance, you intimidated me." She took another step and put a hand on his arm. "Over time I've learned that you are not always a fierce and determined man. You've treated me as an equal at the law. More than that, you've been sensitive to my concerns—my feelings—both legal and otherwise. As a consequence, I've developed strong feelings that have nothing to do with the law. It seems to me that must have been obvious to you for some time. I don't want to go back to our relationship as it was."

He put his hand over hers where it rested on his arm and peered down at her. "Can we spend some quiet time together now and then? Perhaps at your house or mine?"

She placed the palm of her other hand on his cheek. "We can, and we will." When he ran his arm around her waist to pull her close, she leaned her head against his chest and added, "beginning tomorrow evening." She leaned away to look at his face. "I won't be at the office tomorrow, and I hope you'll also take the day to rest." The smile she offered was filled with promise. "If you'll be at my door tomorrow evening at six o'clock, we'll share a home cooked meal, perhaps Bruce Ranch prime rib." She moved her head to look at him. "That's just one way we'll begin to share the quiet times."

Cass and Hannah

Cass spent the night with his parents in Harlowton. In bed

348

and beginning to relax, his mind turned to life ahead. What did he want to do? He hadn't been able to think of a job, a profession or much of anything but the trial. But now he had a future to think about. He could go back to his grandparents' ranch, but his brother was there, firmly entrenched. Working for some agricultural company held no appeal. Despite the circumstances under which he'd been there, he'd enjoyed his time at the Dodson ranch. Now Forrest had recovered much of his good health, so they really didn't need him. That thought and another depressed him. What if Hannah married some sport and moved away?

He held a clear picture of her in his mind—her tiny size, her curly red hair, her sunny and enthusiastic disposition. When he'd needed it most, she'd offered comfort and support. No wonder other men were interested in her. Maybe one or more had marriage in mind. He mustn't even think of that. Tomorrow he'd spend time with her again. Focus on that.

At four o'clock the following afternoon, he drove again into the Dodson barnyard. Hannah and her parents were seated together on the front step of the house, enjoying the warmth of a nice autumn day. When Hannah rose to her feet, the sight of her overcame any inhibitions he may have had. He banged the car door open to run in her direction. She took one step forward. Cass didn't wait. He gathered her tightly in his arms, lifted her into the air, and whirled her around twice. He lowered her to the ground and blurted, "Hannah Dodson, will you marry me?"

The question was spoken without prior thought. At that moment there was only one thing of which he was certain. Life with Hannah was what he truly wanted. Then her probable response struck him. She would say no. Why would she marry him when she could have some man who'd never been accused of anything as terrible as murder? He began to loosen his grasp.

Hannah placed both hands on his chest and leaned back an inch. She looked into his eyes. "Of course, I'll marry you." She stood on tiptoes, pulled his head down and kissed him full on the lips. The kiss lasted a long, hungry moment. Pulling away, she said, "I thought I might have to be the one to ask."

ABOUT THE AUTHOR

by Sanford Moore

My grandfather used to love to read me stories when I was a child. I think I loved it even more than he did. To this day, I treasure the memories of sitting on his old worn yellow couch as he would bring out his favorite children's story. As a good grandfather, he would always let my sister and I pick out which stories we wanted him to read to us. However, thinking about it now, I can see how he would artfully steer us towards the one he really wanted—*Ferdinand the Bull*. Cracking open the old worn and faded cover, he drew us in with his voice, and painted a picture that a kid would never be able to forget.

He had a remarkable voice for reading stories. It had grown a bit raspy with age, but it had a matchless melody and quiet timbre that I have never heard in anyone else. It was a voice that conveyed his love for the written word in a way that even a small child snuggled up to him could feel, and which would, as he spent time with those same children, cultivate a lifelong love of reading in them as well. I will always be grateful for that.

My Grandpa, Jim Moore, grew up on our family ranch west of the little tiny town of Two Dot in Central Montana. He attended school, and when he was seventeen, enlisted in the navy at the tail-end of the Second World War. After being discharged, he attended Montana State University where he met my Grandmother Kay while they were rodeoing. He then returned to the family ranch where he assumed management duties after his own father passed away.

Jim Moore

While living at the ranch with his family, Grandpa enrolled in a law school correspondence course and eventually passed the state bar exam. A few years later, he and Grandma moved back to her family farm South of Bozeman, where he opened his own practice.

After retiring, in addition to skiing and a couple of other hobbies, Grandpa took his love of literature one step further and began to write his own novels. One of the happiest days in his life was when Janet Hill of Raven Publishing agreed to publish his first book—*Ride the Jawbone*. Working together, they were eventually able to leave us with several enjoyable stories. These books continue to help his family keep his memories fresh in our hearts, and I hope you enjoy them as much as we do.

Sincerely,
Sanford Moore

www.ingramcontent.com/pod-product-compliance
Lightning Source LLC
Chambersburg PA
CBHW051227260626
47162CB00002B/306